HER WORK WAS EVERYTHING

HER WORK WAS EVERYTHING

ZACHARY GOLDMAN MYSTERIES #7

P.D. WORKMAN

ISBN: 9781989415238 (IS Hardcover)

ISBN: 9781989415221 (IS Paperback)

ISBN: 9781989415191 (KDP Paperback)

ISBN: 9781989415207 (Kindle)

ISBN: 9781989415214 (ePub)

pdworkman

ALSO BY P.D. WORKMAN

Zachary Goldman Mysteries
She Wore Mourning
His Hands Were Quiet
She Was Dying Anyway
He Was Walking Alone
They Thought He was Safe
He Was Not There
Her Work Was Everything
She Told a Lie (Coming soon)
He Never Forgot (Coming soon)
She Was At Risk (Coming soon)

Kenzie Kirsch Medical Thrillers
Unlawful Harvest

Auntie Clem's Bakery
Gluten-Free Murder
Dairy-Free Death
Allergen-Free Assignation
Witch-Free Halloween (Halloween Short)
Dog-Free Dinner (Christmas Short)
Stirring Up Murder
Brewing Death
Coup de Glace
Sour Cherry Turnover
Apple-achian Treasure

Vegan Baked Alaska

Muffins Masks Murder

Tai Chi and Chai Tea

Santa Shortbread

Reg Rawlins, Psychic Detective

What the Cat Knew

A Psychic with Catitude

A Catastrophic Theft

Night of Nine Tails

Telepathy of Gardens

Delusions of the Past

Fairy Blade Unmade

Web of Nightmares

A Whisker's Breadth (Coming soon)

High-Tech Crime Solvers Series

Virtually Harmless

Stand Alone Suspense Novels

Looking Over Your Shoulder

Lion Within

Pursued by the Past

In the Tick of Time

Loose the Dogs

AND MORE AT PDWORKMAN.COM

To those who know that work is not everything

Zachary had heard about the death of Lauren Barclay in the news before he was contacted by Barbara Lee. It seemed like such a tragic waste. A promising young investment banker, she had been tragically killed in a slip-and-fall accident in her home. It wasn't particularly newsworthy, except for the fact that she had been an attractive, brilliant young woman, and that played well in the press on a slow news day. There were a lot of quotes from family and friends about how awful it was and what a wonderful person she had been. There would be a lot of mourners at her funeral.

But he hadn't really given it anything more than a passing thought. He had that little twinge of regret that he got when he read about a tragic death, but since he hadn't known her and there didn't seem to be anything unusual about her death, he had just given himself a second to feel bad for her and her family, and then moved on with his day.

Barbara Lee had told him that she wanted to meet about the death of a friend, but it wasn't until they sat down together for coffee that Zachary found out the friend was Lauren Barclay.

"I just can't believe it." Barbara sniffled and wiped at the corner of her eye. "She was so brilliant, so full of life, I can't believe she's gone. It just isn't fair. She was so young!"

Zachary nodded. "I read a little bit about it… there wasn't any hint in the news that there was foul play, though. They said it was an accident. She slipped in the tub?"

"I can't believe that. You don't think that's really what happened, do you?"

He looked into her bloodshot eyes. She was probably an attractive woman when she wasn't a complete mess. Her eyes were red, her face was blotchy; it looked like her hair had been put up into a partial bun at some point, but she had wisps of hair going in every direction and she might have slept on it once or twice since she had put it up. She smelled of sweat.

"I don't know anything about it, so I wouldn't venture a guess," he said. "Why don't you tell me what you know about it? Why don't you think she slipped?"

Barbara rummaged in her handbag for a tissue and wiped her red nose. "I didn't even know she was home. She worked all hours, she was always at the office. I hadn't seen her for days. Then I got home… it was the middle of the day, and I could tell that she'd been there. I called out to her, but she didn't answer. I figured she probably came home to change and then had left again. Or maybe she'd fallen into bed and was catching a few winks before she had to go back. But she wasn't usually home during the day, so I didn't expect… to find her…"

Zachary thought he should touch her arm or make some other comforting gesture, but he wouldn't want it to be taken the wrong way. She might not think he was professional and decide not to hire him.

"I'm so sorry… you were the one who found her?"

Barbara nodded, giving another sob. A bubble of snot blew out her nose and she wiped it away. If she had been the one to find her friend's body, it was no wonder she was such a mess. He couldn't imagine what that would have been like for her.

"Take your time," he told her. "You don't need to rush into this."

"I just want… to get it all out. Everybody wants to know, but nobody wants to hear about it. They all think that they want to hear the details, but… it isn't like watching a murder mystery on TV. It's something that… it's so unreal. I didn't know what to do. It was such a shock finding her, I felt like she was a mannequin or it was a prank, I just didn't want to believe it. I couldn't touch her. I called 9-1-1. And then… the police came, and the paramedics, and they all wanted me to tell them about finding her. I had to keep repeating it over and over again."

She stopped talking to wipe and blow again. Her nose was red and raw.

"But they didn't think there was any foul play?" Zachary prompted.

"No. But they didn't ask if there was anyone who wanted her dead or if she had a boyfriend that was violent or she had just broken up with, or anything like that. Not like on a cop show or in a mystery book. They just asked about… when I'd been home last, what time I had found her, when she would have gotten home. The paramedics asked if she had a history of epilepsy or fainting spells. Just… like it was an accident."

Zachary nodded. He sipped his coffee, which was still a bit too hot, but he wanted to give her time to think and to calm down a little. He would get more out of her if she were relaxed and composed than if she got all wound up and couldn't think straight.

"So what was the timing? You said she wasn't usually home during the day?"

"No. She worked really long hours. They were supposed to be at the office before their boss got in, so like six-thirty or seven at the latest. And she would work past dark. She would come home late, sleep for a few hours, and then be back at the office before I even had breakfast. Her hours were crazy."

"How long could she keep up like that? She must have had to

take breaks on the weekend at least. Did she get a day off? Sunday?"

"She worked every day. It wasn't a rule that they had to work on weekends, but everybody did. It was so competitive. If the other interns were there on the weekend, then Lauren *had* to be there on the weekend. Otherwise, people would think that she wasn't as dedicated, and when her internship was up, they would just say goodbye and she'd have to find something else. No other investment banking firm was going to take her if she failed her internship there. She'd be… damaged goods. She'd have to find a job in something else, and she really wanted to be in finance. She really did."

"Why was it so cutthroat? Is that normal?"

"For investment banking, I guess it is. They're all like that. And Chase Gold is just a small firm, so if she couldn't make it there, there's no way that some Wall Street or Japanese company would look at her. She had to get a permanent position with Chase and work there for three years before she could go on to look for something else. No one would look at her otherwise."

Zachary shook his head. "Why would anyone want to work like that?"

Barbara pushed tendrils of hair away from her face, making a half-hearted attempt to push them back into the bun. "Lots of professions are like that, not just finance. Look at doctors and nurses. They're the same way. Long-distance trucking. Cab drivers."

"They all have rules now about not being able to work more than a certain number of hours in a row to prevent people from falling asleep at the wheel or cutting off the wrong leg."

"I guess. But this isn't that kind of place. I don't think there are any rules about not being able to work that long. She always worked for hours and hours. She slept at the office on the floor sometimes. Or didn't sleep at all for two or three days. You can't even imagine how bad it was."

Zachary thought about that. He pulled out his notepad and

jotted down a few notes to himself. Avenues to pursue. Things not to forget. Barbara's eyes tracked his pencil as he scratched out the lines.

"You look like you've never held a pen before," she commented.

Zachary's cheeks heated. He looked down at his awkward grip on his pencil. Many teachers had tried to correct it during school. He'd moved among a lot of different schools, classrooms, and institutions, and the first thing they always tried to do was correct his grip.

"I have dysgraphia," he said. "That's the only way I can write. I know it looks bad to you, but it's the only thing that feels right to me. It's the only way I can see what I'm doing and form the letters."

She shook her head and didn't make any comment on his chicken scratch. He *could* write neatly. He did when he was filling out forms or writing something down for someone else. But it took two or three times as long if he wanted to make it tidy. When he was writing for himself, he could scrawl it however he wanted to. He could still read it. Usually. Sometimes. He could normally figure out what he had meant, even if he couldn't read every word.

"Lauren had beautiful handwriting," Barbara said, tears starting to make their way down her cheeks. "She should have been a schoolteacher, it looked like something out of a handwriting textbook. But…" she sniffled, "of course, teachers don't make anything, and Lauren wanted to make a lot of money. A lot of money."

"I don't really know what an investment banker does," Zachary said, "but I know it *is* something that I associate with making a lot of money. She was pretty wealthy, then?" He was thinking about motives. If there were anything to Barbara's fears—and he had to assume for the purposes of his investigation that there was —then whoever had killed her needed a motive. And money was always a good motive.

"No, not yet," Barbara said. "She was just starting out, so she wasn't making a whole lot. We rented an apartment together, and it's a nice one, not some little rat's nest, but neither of us could have afforded it on our own. Maybe we could, but only if we didn't need to eat or pay for heating or internet."

Zachary nodded. "And if she was just starting, then she probably still had school loans to worry about too."

"Yeah. All of that stuff. She wanted to get rich, but she wasn't there yet. We are—were—both making good money for our age, but nothing like it would be if she got to be a permanent employee with a few years under her belt."

"That makes sense. What's the name of the place that she worked?"

"I have to look it up…" She pulled out her phone and fiddled with it. "We always just called it 'Chase Gold,' because it was close to that, and that's really what they were trying to do. Chase after the gold and get as much as they could. For themselves and their clients."

Zachary waited while she tapped through a few screens on her phone, searching for it in her contacts or on an internet browser. He made a couple of other short notes while he waited. Things to look into. Questions to ask. Who would want to kill a young woman who spent all of her time working and was still in debt?

"Yeah, here it is," Barbara offered. "Drake, Chase, Gould." She spelled Gould for him to make sure he got it right. "She was really devoted to her job. And I don't just mean that she liked it or put a lot of hours in. She did, but there was more to it than that. She thought they were the best company to work for, and that they were going to get her everything she wanted. She was always saying how good the management was, how well they took care of their employees, how good the other people she worked with were. She thought they were going right to the top. That they would compete with the Goldman Sachs and Wells Fargos of the world. They just started up a few years ago, and their portfolios were amazing, especially considering how short they had been in business. Or so she told me." Barbara sniffed and rolled her eyes. "Multiple times."

Zachary smiled at that. Nice to hear about someone who liked her job. "That's great."

He leaned back in his seat. The coffee shop didn't have particularly comfortable chairs. He supposed it was to encourage people to have their coffees and to move on, not to just camp there drinking lattes and using the free Wi-Fi all day long. He looked at Barbara.

"So what makes you think it wasn't an accident? Tell me about the things that made you concerned."

"You think I'm just crazy, don't you? Everybody just looks at me like I've got two heads. How could a slip in the bathtub *not* be an accident? It's like being hit by a bus, the classic accident that everyone uses as an example."

Zachary waited. He wasn't the one who was doubting her opinion or sanity. He waited for her to stop defending herself and to fill the silence with her concerns. She would, if he just waited.

"It just doesn't fit that Lauren was even home," Barbara said. "Like I said, she was never home during the day. Between ten in the evening and six in the morning, if she was lucky. That's it. No weekends. No days off. No afternoons going home to have a nap. She just shouldn't have been home."

"What was the time of death?"

Barbara looked at him. She shook her head. "I don't know."

"What time had she gotten home? You were out of the apartment from when until when?"

"I was out with a friend overnight. So I didn't get back until… ten or eleven o'clock. That's when I found her. But she was never home at that time of day."

"But if she had been running a bath at six, and hit her head then, that would make sense."

Barbara sighed. "I know. Everybody says it makes perfect sense. But it doesn't. She was young and healthy. She wouldn't just fall down and die. She wasn't drunk or doing drugs. She didn't have any diseases that would have made her pass out. To just step into the tub and fall down and die…? That doesn't make sense either."

"Sure. I understand that. No one expects something like this to happen. But she could have had the flu, or just wasn't paying attention and slipped."

"She wasn't an old lady. Maybe old ladies slip and fall like that, but Lauren never did. If she slipped, she would have caught herself. If she got hurt, she would have called someone to help her."

Zachary made a couple of notes of questions to pursue. He'd have to talk to the medical examiner's office, and he really didn't want to. He would have to psych himself up for it.

"What was the mechanism of death?"

Barbara frowned. "She… fell…?"

"Yeah. Did she drown? Or did she die from the blow to the head? Brain swelling or bleeding?"

"Drowning, I guess. She did hit her head, but then she went into the water. That's where I found her. I guess… she knocked herself out, and then she didn't know that she was drowning, couldn't do anything about it."

"The medical examiner hasn't made a finding yet?"

"I don't know. I guess that's what they're working on right now."

"Okay. We'll need a copy of their report once there is a finding. I'll put in a requisition for it."

Which meant that he would take the elevator down to the basement level at the police station. He would walk up to the desk and fill out one of the forms in his neatest printing, trying his best to avoid an intensely awkward situation with Kenzie.

He wasn't sure how she was going to react. Things had been pretty quiet since they had broken up. He felt horrible about the way everything had ended, but he hadn't called her and begged for her to come back. He hadn't given her excuses for his behavior or followed her around in his car. He had done his best to just back out of her life and forget about what they had shared together.

But going back there, onto her turf, he didn't know how she was going to treat him. Would she yell at him and call him out the way that Bridget did? Would she go all quiet or ignore him? Or just stare at him with her dark, intense eyes boring into him, hating him for the time she had wasted on him?

"Uh… Mr. Goldman?"

Zachary blinked and refocused on Barbara. It was Barbara he had to talk to and interact with. He needed to stay focused on her. "Sorry, just thinking about something. What was that?"

"If the medical examiner says that it was just an accident, that will be the end of it, won't it? The police won't investigate it as a homicide. They won't hold anyone responsible."

"No. But if I find something, we can get them to open an investigation. I've done it before. I'm assuming you already know that. That's probably why you picked me out, isn't it?"

She gave an embarrassed little shrug and nodded.

"I can't guarantee anything," Zachary said. "I don't know whether it was an accident or something else… but it sounds like it's going to be pretty hard to find evidence that it was anything else. I'll look. I'm just warning you… Don't expect miracles. Just because I've been able to prove that other deaths were homicides, that doesn't mean that I can prove any death was. Some of them are going to be just what they look like."

"I know. But… no matter what anyone else says… I want to do everything I can for Lauren. I can't just close my eyes and say 'oh, what a bizarre accident.' I need to know. I need to do everything I can to bring the responsible party to justice. If there is a responsible party."

"You said before that the police hadn't asked you anything about an ex-boyfriend or anyone who might have wanted to harm her."

"Yes. I mean no. They didn't. They didn't want to know anything like that."

"Does that mean that she *did* have an ex-boyfriend who might have wanted to harm her?"

Barbara's eyes widened. "Oh, no. I didn't mean to imply anything like that… She did have ex-boyfriends, of course, but no one who was bitter or anything. No one who ever threatened her or stalked her."

"Was there anyone who was abusive while they were together? She might not have told you that he hit her, but was there ever anyone that you suspected… that you thought might have hurt her? Even someone who was verbally or emotionally abusive. Someone you didn't feel comfortable around or were glad that she broke up with him."

"No… I don't think so… everyone that she was with was pretty casual… it isn't like she had any time for a relationship. She would take someone to a firm event, or sometimes she brought someone home from work… but she didn't really have a life outside of the office."

"She dated people from the office?"

"Yes… she went out for a meal with them, maybe brought one or two back to the apartment to…" she shrugged uncomfortably, "…to sleep it off. Just to crash somewhere before they had to go back to the office again in a few hours. There just was so little time, and she was under so much pressure… it didn't leave time for a real relationship."

"Even if it isn't what you would call a relationship… men can still decide that they want what they can't have. They might think that she should have spent more time with them, given them more attention, maybe not gone on to see someone else so soon… if they went out to eat, or he went home with her, then he might have expected more. He might have thought that it was turning into a committed relationship when it wasn't."

"I guess so. I don't know. I never saw anything like that. The guys that I met from Chase Gold always seemed pretty casual. Not like they were pining after her or acting possessive."

"Do you have the names of some of the men that she dated? Maybe an address list?"

"All of her numbers would be on her phone… I guess it's at the apartment. The police didn't take it, I don't think. They just took a quick look at her electronics, but there wasn't anything that didn't look right to them, so they said they didn't need to take anything with them."

"Who is the detective on the case?"

"I don't think there was a detective. Just… whoever comes out to have a look when someone dies suddenly. They're not really investigating it. Just filling out the forms."

"Someone would have been assigned to it. I'll look into it. See if they have any thoughts."

"They aren't going to. They are just going to think that it was an accident, like a million other accidents that happen every day."

Zachary had made sure that Barbara was able to pay his retainer and understood his fee schedule and then went to work on her case. He still had other cases to work, but they were not time-sensitive. He always had insurance cases, marital infidelities, and skip tracing and other issues to follow up on. The bread and butter that got him from day to day. The big cases were nice when they came along, but he didn't know what he would have from one month to the next, so he couldn't rely on cash flowing from big cases.

Not that Lauren's death investigation was that urgent. It looked like an accident, no matter what feelings of denial Barbara was going through. She didn't have anything concrete to suggest that it was anything other than an accident. Tragic, yes. Untimely, certainly, but there were hundreds of untimely and tragic deaths every day. Chances were, Zachary wouldn't find anything to indicate any kind of foul play. The police would have turned up something in their investigation. They were well-trained, and he was just a self-taught PI.

Still, in a death investigation, it was best to get started as soon as he could. While everything was still fresh in people's minds and the evidence—if there was any physical evidence—had not been destroyed. He'd gotten lucky in Heather's case to be able to put his hands on physical evidence thirty years after the fact, but all of what had been collected by the police had been lost in the intervening years.

He could have started at Lauren's office, but decided he'd better bite the bullet and go to the police station and request a copy of the medical examiner's report. Like swallowing a frog first thing in the morning, nothing worse would happen to him all day.

Most of the personnel on duty knew him. The guard that ran him through the metal detector and made sure he was properly checked in. A police officer or two who stopped to ask and see how he was doing. Zachary was awkward, unsure how many of them knew that he had been dating Kenzie and how many knew that they had recently broken up. And he'd been on the news a bit too much for his liking the previous few months. Good for publicity, not so good for his ego. Not when it exposed his private pain.

He tried to greet everyone warmly and to assume that they didn't know anything about what he had been through recently. It was easier that way.

Pressing the down button for the elevator, he was drawn back to the day, over a year previous, when he had first met Kenzie. She had been pretty, interesting, and had smiled at him and treated him with respect. He'd liked her right from the start. With her wild, dark, curly hair, her deep red lipstick, she was cute and pretty and very unlike Bridget.

That had been important.

But they were no longer together. Now, she knew too much about his rocky past and the emotional issues that he struggled with every day. She was no longer an outsider looking in and curious about what kind of a person he was and if they would make a good couple. Now she knew that they couldn't, and that she had been wasting her time.

Who knew what she might have told Dr. Wiltshire and her

other colleagues about the relationship and about Zachary himself? Women liked to talk, and one of the issues he'd had to confront with Kenzie was the fact that she had discussed details of their intimate relationship. He didn't like to think how much she might have told her co-workers about Zachary and his issues.

Before he reached the desk, he could see that Kenzie was on duty, staring at her computer screen as she worked through whatever tests and requests she had to do. She didn't look at him immediately. She liked to concentrate on what she was doing until it was a good time to take a break, and then she would turn her full attention to her visitor.

After a minute of concentration, she looked away from her computer screen to Zachary's face. Her lips tightened. She said nothing.

"I have a new case," Zachary said, wanting to assure her immediately that he wasn't there for personal reasons. He wasn't going to try to talk her into giving him another chance. Kenzie had given him countless chances. He knew that. She had done more than anyone could have been expected to do.

Zachary was too damaged to be able to carry on a normal relationship. He should have learned that from his marriage to Bridget. Kenzie had been so different, he had thought that maybe he had a chance with her. But he had only been fooling himself.

"Could I get the form to request a copy of the medical examiner's report?"

She delved into her drawer and pulled one out. She handed it to him without a word, her eyes sliding to her computer screen so that she could pretend she was still working on something else, too busy to talk to him.

"Sorry," Zachary murmured, unsure of what to say to her.

Kenzie looked at him. Her lips were still pressed tightly together, but her clenched jaw relaxed slightly.

"Nothing to apologize for," she said stiffly. "You have a job to do. Can't help it if that brings you to the medical examiner's office now and then."

Zachary nodded as he started to fill in his name and address. "I know… I just don't want you to think that I'm here to bug you…"

She shrugged and fiddled with a pen. "You've been good about not harassing me," she admitted. "I wasn't sure how you were going to handle it, to tell the truth. After seeing how stalkerish you were with Bridget, I didn't know what to expect."

Zachary swallowed. His mouth was so dry he could hardly speak. "I'm doing better. I mean, different meds, and seeing my therapist and all…"

"I've been watching for it, you know. Any sign that you've been hanging around, messing with my car, following me. I figured…" She trailed off.

He wondered if it had hurt her feelings that he *hadn't* pursued her. Had she hoped that he would protest her leaving, try to talk her into coming back, beg her and follow her? Did she feel like she must not have lived up to Bridget's level in his eyes? That she hadn't meant as much to him?

He wasn't really sure how to compare the two women or his feelings toward them. They were not at all like each other. He had never been head-over-heels in love with Kenzie the way he had been with Bridget. But he'd felt like their relationship had been more equal, and maybe deeper than he'd ever managed with Bridget.

He'd worshiped Bridget. He'd been devoted to her. But after those first few blissful months, her attitude toward him had changed. As she realized that she wasn't going to fix him and that she couldn't just tell him what to feel and how to behave, her attitude toward him had changed completely. And when she'd been diagnosed with cancer… that had been all the impetus needed for her to boot him out of her life. Get rid of toxic relationships. Put all of her energy into recovery.

With Kenzie, it had been different. She hadn't been abusive or looked down on him. She hadn't been a replacement mother figure. She'd just been… Kenzie. A friend first. Things had gone well for them until the Teddy Archuro case had driven the relationship off the rails.

Not just off the rails, but crashing into an abyss.

"I could put a tracker on your car if it would make you feel better," he told Kenzie, forcing a smile that he didn't feel. "As long as you promise not to take out a restraining order against me. Because that would make it impossible for me to fill out these fascinating forms."

Kenzie laughed and shook her head. Her eyes didn't dance like they did when she was having fun and enjoying herself, but the smile was real. His attempt at humor was appreciated.

"No, I think I'm okay on that score, thanks."

Zachary shrugged, meeting her eyes for a second and then turning his gaze back down to his form. It was going to take forever for him to fill out if he kept getting distracted. And while that had been okay in the past, he didn't want to make things more painful for Kenzie by overstaying his welcome.

"What case are you working on?" Kenzie asked.

He couldn't exactly tell her that it was confidential or wasn't any of her business. She was, after all, the one who was going to process the form. She would know as soon as he handed it to her.

"Lauren Barclay."

"Barclay? The slip-and-fall?" Her tone expressed surprise.

"Yes. Dr. Wiltshire hasn't made a finding yet, has he?"

"No, but he will before long. It's a pretty routine case."

"I know. I don't expect to find anything, but as long as I've got a paying client… I'll do what I can to check out all avenues and reassure her that it was just an accident."

"How could it be anything else? I mean, the woman was found alone, floating in her own bathtub. No forced entry, no signs of violence, just fell and cracked her head. Sad, but it could happen to anyone. Who is your client? Family member?"

Kenzie was creeping into the confidential with that question. He didn't need to tell her anything about who had hired him. But he missed talking with her about cases. He enjoyed pulling out medical examiner's reports to discuss over dinner. Not romantic by any stretch of the imagination, but how many other women were there who would be okay with looking at gruesome pictures over dinner?

"Not the family."

"Well, good luck. I don't know how you're going to make any money on the case. How much can you charge for reading the report and talking to the detective?"

"If that's all there is, that's all there is. I'm not trying to pull something over on her. She wants someone to look into the death, so I will. I warned her there might not be much I could do."

"At least you're not the kind of guy who is going to take advantage and rack up the charges."

Zachary nodded his agreement, glad that she recognized he had standards. He was sure there were people who would take advantage of Barbara, but he wasn't one of them. She hadn't balked at his rates and, looking at the address of the apartment she had given him, he saw that even if she'd had to share the rent with Lauren, she couldn't have been hurting too badly. But he wasn't going to take advantage of her wealth.

"Is she pretty?" Kenzie asked, after a period of silence, during which she had been looking at her screen and occasionally scrolling down.

"Lauren Barclay?"

She rolled her eyes and shook her head. "Not Lauren. I've already got a good idea of what she looks like, and it's not pretty. Drowning victims never are."

"Oh. The client." He realized that he had used 'she' when talking about Barbara, so Kenzie knew the client was female. And if she was a friend of Lauren's rather than family, then probably a young woman of her general social circles. "Uh… hard to say."

"Hard to say? I'm not exactly going to be jealous if you say she's hot."

Zachary's ears burned. He filled out Lauren's name on the form.

"It's not that… she wasn't in very good shape. Disheveled, swollen and blotchy, running nose. I had a hard time judging what she normally looks like."

"Oh. Fair enough." Kenzie scrolled down a couple more times, waiting for Zachary to finish dating and signing the form.

Zachary handed it to her and swallowed. "Thanks, Kenzie."

She dropped it into the wire basket on her desk. "Take care of yourself, Zachary."

4

Making inquiries upstairs, Zachary was advised that the detective assigned to Lauren's case was Detective Robinson. Zachary had seen him before, but had never worked a case that he was on. He was a thin man with very thick glasses. He made Zachary think of a praying mantis peering at him, triangular head cocked slightly, big eyes taking in every movement.

He was unimpressed by Zachary's interest in the case, doing the best he could to get rid of him.

"I'm afraid there's not much to tell you, Mr. Goldman. It was an accidental slip-and-fall, an open-and-shut case. Nobody else around, no suspicious circumstances. Just a home accident, like thousands of others. We're not wasting resources on it."

"No, I wouldn't expect you to," Zachary agreed. "You have cases that require your attention. I'd been hired to look into this case, so I can afford to spend a little time on it. Just look at it from different angles to see if I can find anything concerning."

Detective Robinson peered at him, clearly suspicious that Zachary was being sarcastic. Zachary kept his gaze steady and Robinson decided he was being sincere.

"We can't stop private citizens from asking questions, obviously," he said. "But I don't see how it would be in anyone's best interest to spend time on a case that was so obviously an accident."

"Of course. I understand."

"We have released the scene, so the roommate can show you whatever she wants. We don't have anything to do with it."

"I'll be going over it tomorrow. There wasn't anything that stood out to you? Nothing out of place?"

"Nothing. Young working woman. Neat bedroom. No sign of forced entry or violence. Nothing out of place or suspicious."

"Okay. Would you let me know if anything occurs to you? And do you want me to give you updates, or...?"

"I don't need anything from you. Because you're not going to find anything."

"Okay. Sometimes detectives like regular reports, even if I haven't found anything."

"No. I don't expect to hear from you again."

***

That evening, Zachary bounced around the empty apartment for a while, not sure what to do. He worked through a pile of skip traces and added touches to other client reports, but he missed having Kenzie around and couldn't sit down and watch TV or do something else calming without her there. He needed something to keep him busy, but he'd put in a lot of work hours and he needed to do something quieter before bed if he were going to be able to go to sleep at a decent hour. Recently, his brain couldn't decide whether he should sleep all the time to avoid having to deal with his emotional issues, or whether he should be obsessing over every detail of his life, his past, and his failed relationships to the exclusion of sleep, so he swung back and forth unpredictably between the two.

Dr. Boyle had advised him to keep to a regular schedule whether he felt tired or not. Go to the bed at the same time every day. Get up at the same time every day. His body would become entrained to the schedule and his brain would follow.

Of course, that was assuming he didn't need to do any overnight surveillance jobs. Something like that would throw a wrench into the works. But so far, he'd been able to avoid any night surveillance while training his body and brain to a reasonable schedule.

It wasn't bedtime, so he needed something to keep him engaged and help him to unwind. After scrolling restlessly through his email and social networks, such as they were, he double-clicked the Skype icon and selected Lorne Peterson's name.

Even though Mr. Peterson—rarely Lorne, even though he'd told Zachary numerous times that he could call him by his first name—was more than twenty years older than Zachary, he was probably Zachary's closest friend. He had been Zachary's foster father for a few weeks after the fire that had destroyed not only Zachary's family home, but also his family structure. His mother and father divorced and relinquished the six children to social services, wanting nothing more to do with them.

Zachary hadn't stayed with the Petersons for long. He'd celebrated his eleventh birthday while there, the first birthday that had ever actually been marked by a cake and a birthday present. But his needs and behavioral issues had been too much for them to handle, and Mrs. Peterson had insisted that he couldn't stay there, possibly putting the other children at risk, any longer. Zachary had gone on to another foster family, and another, and a long series of homes and facilities for the rest of his childhood and adolescence. But he and Mr. Peterson had stayed in touch throughout.

The call rang for a few minutes before it was answered. Then Mr. Peterson's round, cheerful face was centered on the screen. He patted down his fringe of white hair.

"Zachary! Good to see you! How are you doing?"

Zachary relaxed into his seat. Mr. Peterson represented safety and security for him. The only person who had felt like family until his younger brother, Tyrrell had reached out and made contact with him, followed by Heather, his older sister. He hadn't yet had any contact with the remaining three siblings.

"I'm good. Picked up a new case today. How are you and Pat?"

Pat moved into the frame behind Mr. Peterson, wiping his hands on a dishtowel. He bent down to look into the screen and smiled into the video cam. "Hi, Zachary!" He gave a thumbs-up. "We're fine! Good to see you!"

Zachary nodded and smiled. Pat clapped his hand on Mr. Peterson's shoulder and gave it a squeeze, then he moved out of the picture, off to the kitchen or whatever job he was doing next. Zachary kept his smile in place.

"How is he…?"

Mr. Peterson's smile grew strained. He gave a little grimace. "It's been tough, I won't lie to you about that. But we've been seeing a therapist and I think we're making good progress. His mood is better. But that could be the antidepressants."

Zachary felt a stab of guilt. He would have taken away Pat's pain if he could. But he couldn't bring back Pat's friend Jose, who had been killed by a serial killer. And he couldn't wipe out Pat's feelings of responsibility for what had happened to Zachary because he had been investigating Jose's disappearance.

"Well… he'll get through it," Zachary encouraged. "He's got a strong support system."

Mr. Peterson shrugged, getting a little pink.

"Thank you, Zachary. I'm sure you're right, he'll get through it. We're seeing progress."

Zachary nodded. The words made his apartment seem even more empty and hollow. He tried to focus on Mr. Peterson's friendly features. Zachary still had support too. He might not have Kenzie, but she was not the only person in Zachary's support network. Mr. Peterson and Pat were there for him, as well as his therapist, doctors, and support groups. Young Rhys Salter and his grandmother. Mario Bowman and other friends on the police force and consultants who provided other services he used in his

PI business. Tyrrell and Heather and Heather's husband. He had received a number of calls, emails, and letters of support from previous strangers after bringing Teddy Archuro to justice, both from people who were grateful or impressed by what he had done and by people who understood the trauma he'd been through and offered their support and encouragement.

He had a big circle of supporters. He didn't need to feel alone.

"New case today?" Mr. Peterson prompted, leaning toward the camera.

"Oh. Yeah. I don't know if you would have seen in the news, a young woman named Lauren Barclay…?"

"The intern at that investment company? Yeah, we saw that. I thought that was an accident."

"No determination has been made yet, but yes, the initial word is that it was an accident. But her friend is not convinced and wants someone to look into it."

"Well, great. That's a good case. High profile."

Zachary nodded. "I doubt it will really go anywhere, but I'll see what I can find out."

"It will at least put her mind at ease to know that it was an accident. Even though it seems unfair… I'm sure she'd rather know that it was an accident than to be worried that there might have been some kind of foul play involved."

"Yes, I think so. And maybe she just needs some time to process. It happened so fast, and she was the one to find the body. That's a shock."

Mr. Peterson emphatically agreed. "The poor girl. She must be devastated."

"I think so."

"So you just started on that today?"

Zachary nodded. "Just getting the initial information processed. Stopped by the medical examiner's office to request a copy of his findings when they are published…"

"Oh," Mr. Peterson understood immediately. He and Pat had

met Kenzie. Mr. Peterson cocked his head to the side empathetically. "You saw Kenzie?"

Zachary nodded. "Yeah. It was… weird. She didn't yell or anything, but it was… awkward, I guess."

"Hopefully, some of that will fade. You guys are still going to run into each other, both being involved in crime investigation. You'll keep bumping up against each other. Best if you can be civil, if not friends."

"Yeah. I'd like to still be friends, but she doesn't. Not yet, anyway. I'm trying to … give her the space she needs. Maybe sometime down the road… we can still share a meal together as friends… talk about cases. We don't have to be dating to do that."

"No, of course not. You're probably right about her needing her own space. You don't want to smother her." Mr. Peterson shifted, moving his head the other direction and considering his question carefully before voicing it. "There is no chance of the two of you getting back together again?"

"No… I don't think so. She says not, anyway. I would… I'd like to give it a try. We got together pretty well… I wasn't really ready to break it off."

Mr. Peterson made a noncommittal noise. Zachary looked at the screen and considered the matter. It had been Kenzie who had said that they were over. But he had been avoiding her before that. He had been the one with a problem.

"Or maybe I was," Zachary admitted. "Maybe I knew it wasn't working."

"You need to put work into a relationship," Mr. Peterson said. "It isn't something that just magically happens and is self-perpetuating. Once you're comfortable and committed… things start to chip away at the relationship. Personality conflicts, irritation, other relationships, work… you have to keep building it up to make it work."

Zachary nodded his agreement.

"You have been through a lot. Things that challenged you and your relationship. If you're not willing to put the work into fixing it…"

Zachary opened his mouth to argue that he had been working at fixing it. He had been talking to his therapist, trying to work through his reflex reactions to intimacy since the assault. It had stirred up a lot of old issues, and the avalanche of old memories and emotions had been too much to deal with all at once.

He had been trying. He and Kenzie had been talking about it and trying to work through it together. They'd been making progress.

Until Zachary discovered that Kenzie was talking to Mr. Peterson and Bridget, trying to get details of Zachary's past relationships and abuse. It had been an invasion of his privacy that he couldn't accept. If they were going to have a relationship, then she had to be willing to wait for him to work through his past and share it with her in his own time. For her to go behind his back to talk to his foster father and ex-wife about such intimate issues was beyond the pale.

"I don't know," he said finally. "We were working on it… but I'm just… I'm not what she wanted, Lorne. I can't change what happened to me and I couldn't share it with her… so how could we have the relationship that she wanted?"

To his credit, Mr. Peterson didn't come out with some glib answer or try to sweep away Zachary's feelings. "Maybe not, Zach. It seemed like the two of you were good together. She was a much better fit for you than Bridget ever was. But I can't tell you how to deal with it. I don't mean to imply that you didn't work on the relationship. Just that… when it's the right relationship… it's worth it to forgive and try again. When it's the right relationship —and you're the only one who can decide that. You and her."

Zachary sighed. He had been telling himself that it was all Kenzie's fault. She was the one who had betrayed his trust. She was the one who had then broken it off and didn't want to continue to see each other or be friends. But that was only half of the story. The truth was… he had been struggling and she had been trying to help, in her own way. He had felt betrayed and had shut her out. He had effectively ended the relationship some time before she had come to the apartment to pick up her things. It hadn't been her at all.

"I'll think about it. But I don't think she'd be willing to try again even if I said I wanted to."

"You're the one who knows best. I'm not going to meddle in your relationships."

"Thanks. You've always been really good about accepting whoever I was with, wherever I was."

"And there have been some doozies," Mr. Peterson laughed, and Zachary knew he only meant one—Bridget. "But who am I to say what will work and what won't? A lot of people told me to go back to Lilith. To mend fences and find a way to make it work. But I never would have been happy staying with her. And I never would have met Pat and been able to have the relationship I do with him, if I was still with her."

Zachary swallowed. "Yeah," he agreed, wondering whether Mr. Peterson could see how pink Zachary's face was getting on the camera. Zachary always felt awkward talking about Mr. Peterson's and Pat's relationship. Zachary liked and respected Pat enormously, but he didn't want to know the intimate details of their relationship.

He changed the subject and still didn't tell Mr. Peterson the news about Bridget.

5

Barbara had indicated that Zachary could come to her apartment in order to see the scene of the accident and to pick up Lauren's phone and computer. Then he could get the names of her friends, contacts at Chase Gold, and see whatever else he might need to see in the apartment and her possessions. Not that Zachary expected to find anything, but he'd been surprised before. Most cases, he'd found exactly what he'd expected to. But every now and then, there was one that blew up big, turning out to be something very different from what he'd initially thought.

Barbara opened the door and silently ushered him into the apartment. She stood there, not sure what to do or say at first. Then she took a deep breath.

"I'm going to go out. You can stay here as long as you need, just lock the handle and pull the door shut when you're done. Shoot me a text when you're on your way out. I just—" she looked around the front room of the apartment, "—I really can't be here while you're going through her things or looking at... the accident scene. I don't want to talk to you about it and walk you through it. You already know what happened, between the paper and what I told you. I don't want to relive it."

"I understand. That's fine, as long as you trust me to be here by myself."

"I know how to find you. If something disappeared or I thought you were messing with my stuff, I would go to the police, believe me. But… I do trust you. I'm comfortable around you, and I'm a pretty good judge of character. So I'm just going to go with my feelings, and if I'm wrong… I'll have to deal with it."

"I won't get into your things or make a mess. Just point me at Lauren's room, and I'll proceed from there."

Barbara indicated one of the bedrooms. "That one." She swung her handbag up to her shoulder. "Good luck. I'll talk to you later."

He went to Lauren's bedroom and heard the front door click shut behind her.

He didn't mind the fact that she had left. Far from it; it was easier for him to concentrate without somebody hanging over him. He disliked clients who hovered. With Barbara gone, he'd be able to immerse himself in Lauren's life and learn all he could from her possessions.

The bedroom was remarkably sparse. He'd seen students' rooms before, and they were usually full of clutter. Posters on walls, bookshelves, boxes that hadn't been unpacked, bags shoved under the bed. But Lauren's room was nothing like that. It was like a hotel room, with hardly any personal furnishings. He looked in the closet. Her clothes were neat and well-cared-for. Not much by way of casual blue jeans and tees; she mostly wore black skirts with white blouses. Some workout clothes in the drawers. He checked the bottoms and backs of the drawers and didn't find anything racy hidden away.

Her drug supply consisted mostly of headache pills of various sorts, caffeine and herbal remedies for alertness and mental acuity. No narcotics, no coke, no pot. No seizure medications or insulin.

Though insulin, he remembered, would be in the fridge. He'd have to double-check that for his report.

She had a few pictures. Parents and a sister, it looked like. No cuddly fiance photos or groups of young people out partying.

There were books and notebooks full of scribbled notes on her computer desk. Flipping through them, they were much more complex math than Zachary was qualified to analyze. If he hit a dead end, he might have to find someone who could interpret what she had been working on to see if he should be looking in another direction. Maybe she had discovered some new way of predicting or manipulating markets.

She had a little shower caddy with all of her toiletries in it. Zachary poked through them. Nothing unusual; they all looked like brands he seen at the grocery store or on TV.

He checked all of the usual hiding places. Under the mattress, behind the nondescript artwork on the walls. He unscrewed the plates over the light switch and wall outlets. In the closet, he searched for any hidden panels or safe, checked the pockets of the clothes hanging in the closet—why did women have so few pockets?—and the purses that hung neatly on hooks inside the closet. The purses contained only the usual miscellany. Combs, cosmetics, and feminine supplies, together with coins, gum, tissues, and crumpled receipts.

He went through the room one more time for hiding places. Her computer and phone were on the desk waiting for him, as well as a music player. He left them all there and went to the bathroom.

The scene of the accident.

There was nothing to indicate what had happened there. No blood, no fingerprints blackened with powder. No flower memorials. Just a scrubbed-clean bathroom, like he would find in any other apartment in the building. Probably cleaner than any others. He suspected Barbara had spent several hours cleaning it after the police and paramedics were gone, wiping out every trace of the horrible accident her friend had suffered.

Zachary looked at himself briefly in the mirror. He didn't like to look in the mirror. He was a small man, dark-haired, not particularly attractive, with various scars on his face from childhood accidents and abuse growing up in foster care and institutions. He had shaved for his initial meeting with Barbara, but not since, so dark stubble shaded his jaw.

He pictured Lauren standing there. A pretty girl, as evidenced by her pictures in the news articles and the family pictures in the bedroom. Hair the color of dark honey, tall and slim, probably athletic in high school. But from Barbara's description, Lauren had been wearing thin. She probably had bags under her eyes, hidden as best she could by the miracle of modern make-up, and lines of fatigue at the corners of her eyes and across her forehead. She had probably stood there, wondering how much longer she could continue to go at that pace.

Shower or bath? If it had been him, he would have been worried about falling asleep in a bath. He would have had a shower. A cold one to wake him up, not a hot one that would make him more drowsy. But she'd drowned in the water in the bathtub, so she'd made the opposite choice. Getting ready for work in the morning, knowing she had to get there before her boss, instead of starting the shower and jumping in and out in two minutes, she had drawn the bath to have a soak.

He stepped into the tub. Of course, any evidence of the accident had already been cleaned away. But he wanted to take a closer look anyway.

There were no anti-slip decals, but the bathmat should have prevented a slip-and-fall. It seemed to be in good shape. The tub was larger than the one in Zachary's apartment, and jetted. Not a huge soaker tub, but big for an apartment. Those jets probably felt great on sore muscles and feet at the end of a long day at the office. But she'd had a bath in the morning, not on coming home from work. Or so Barbara had assumed. He'd need confirmation of time of death to be sure.

He looked at the faucet and handles for any tiny spatters of blood, but found nothing, not even hard water spots. No dents. No cracks in the plastic tub surround. He couldn't tell by looking at it what Lauren had hit her head on.

Back in the bedroom, Zachary opened the lid on Lauren's computer. He looked through the papers on the desk and found one with ten-character strings of random characters carefully noted. He typed the last one in the password field and the lock screen disappeared, revealing the desktop and windows behind it.

No biometrics, luckily. Nothing that would require a computer hacker to break. He looked at the apps running along the bottom of the screen, then started the task manager to see how long they had been running and which ones had downloaded the most data packets. He started with the top ones and worked his way down the list, opening all of the "recently opened" documents in each program. Most of it was Greek to him. High finance was not his wheelhouse. He found one app that appeared to be corporate software that pulled Lauren's various social networks and team workspaces and calendars into one program, all neatly tabbed across the top and side.

Zachary browsed through Lauren's internet history and email. He felt a twinge of guilt reading through her corporate email, knowing that it probably contained confidential information that the firm wouldn't want outsiders to see. But most of it he couldn't even follow. He wasn't going to be passing any tips on. He was more interested in the personalities of the people she worked with: bosses, the other interns, human resources, receptionists, and others. Even if he didn't understand the financial jargon, he could glean the attitudes and personalities of Lauren and the others that she corresponded with on a daily basis.

He was amazed at the hours she worked. He had taken Barbara's outline of Lauren's schedule with a grain of salt, but looking at her archived and sent mail, he could see that she was sending out emails regularly, all hours of the day and night. It was rare to see an interval of more than two hours between emails. She had been keeping a brutal schedule. And it was apparent that the other interns were too.

He glanced over at her laundry basket, where he could see colorful workout clothes waiting to be washed. How had she found the time and energy to follow any kind of exercise routine? He couldn't imagine her finding the energy to walk home, let alone for a stationary bike or aerobics.

Zachary browsed through the last few emails that had come into Lauren's inbox following her death which had not, of course, been dealt with. The first few were just routine emails, giving her information she had asked for or giving her instructions on files. Then there were a number of emails with increasingly stern or frantic tones wanting to know where she was and why she hadn't returned to the office. He wrote down the names of those who had been looking for her. He made a short notation as to which ones were concerned, which were angry or bullying, and which were routine or frivolous. If Lauren's death had been something other than an accident, then the person involved could have sent her an email during that interval to establish an alibi. *I didn't know she was dead, see? I was sending her emails at the time.*

After he had checked out the initial things he wanted to look at on her laptop, he did the same thing with her phone—which luckily Barbara had known the unlock code for—making notes as he went through the calls, text messages, and notifications in any other apps. He wrote down her calendar schedule both before and after she had died. Her task list was enough to make him sick. He thought he had a lot to do running his own business and keeping up with medical appointments and the various different cases he was working on? He had nothing on Lauren, whose lists of tasks to be done was dizzyingly long. How could one person be expected to do so much?

He jotted notes about the files she had and the types of tasks that populated her list, rather than trying to write them all down.

It would have been easier to print them all out, but there was no printer on the desk. He would take it back to his apartment and print it out there, but in the meantime, he wanted a short synopsis that he could read and ponder on later. The big picture, not all of the little bits.

Zachary hit the play button on Lauren's music player to occupy the part of his brain that was trying to distract him from writing, seeking more interesting input elsewhere. He expected music. Pop or classical would be his top guesses.

But it wasn't music at all, it was a man speaking. He was reciting market information which, Zachary suspected, was now several days out of date. He looked at the LCD screen and scrolled through her playlist. It was all podcasts. And nothing light. No fiction or entertainment. All financial stuff, dry as a bone.

He felt sorry for Lauren, who apparently found ways to work every minute of the day, listening to financial reports while she worked out, commuted, maybe even while she slept. She hadn't ever been able to leave it behind.

Zachary wasn't sure how the folks at Chase Gold were going to feel about his nosing around and asking questions about Lauren, her last few days, and whether anyone had thought there was anything suspicious about her death. Since the medical examiner had not yet published his findings, Zachary could at least hide behind the pretense of a police investigation—implying that he was with the police department without actually saying so—and no one would be able to say, 'but a ruling of accidental death was already made on that.' But just how far would he be able to investigate at the firm?

He decided to go about it sideways, and when he walked up to the woman in the plush reception area, he didn't try to get into Lauren's office or to talk to her bosses or the principals of the company, but instead asked for Mandy, one of the interns who seemed to have been close to Lauren.

"Will she know what it's about?" the receptionist asked, raising one eyebrow at Zachary as if she guessed that he wasn't one of their usual high-class clients and didn't have any excuse to be there.

"No," Zachary said. "It's a personal matter. I'll discuss that with her."

She eyed him, but she didn't threaten to call security and, after a few seconds' silence, she punched a few buttons on the phone keypad and informed Mandy in a doubtful tone that there was someone waiting for her.

She nodded to the seating area and Zachary obediently picked out a chair and sat to wait. There were magazines and newspapers arranged on the coffee tables. No Cosmopolitan or Reader's Digest for Chase Gold. Not even People. Chase Gold was the center of the financial community—or at least wanted to be—so all of the reading material was high finance. Zachary stared at the abstract landscape painting in muted pinks and grays on the opposite wall, wondering if it was an original work, or whether the things were mass produced for somber reception areas all over the world.

A young woman with a pencil poking into her messy bun sidled up to the receptionist and looked at her questioningly. The receptionist pointed to Zachary, looking as if something in the room did not smell very good.

Mandy tiptoed over to Zachary, smiling pleasantly, with a frown line across her forehead that clearly communicated she had no idea who he was.

"You wanted to see me?"

"Is there somewhere we could talk privately?"

"Uh… yes…" She looked back around at the receptionist and pointed to one of the glassed-in meeting rooms visible from the waiting area. The receptionist rolled her eyes and nodded, reaching for a reservations sheet to write Mandy's name down.

"Come right this way… sir." She was still fishing for his name and why he wanted her. But Zachary waited until they were in the meeting room and Mandy reluctantly shut the door and turned to him. She was taller than he was, in her early twenties, on the slim side without being skinny.

"Miss Pryor. I appreciate you agreeing to talk to me. My name is Zachary Goldman, and I'm investigating the death of Lauren Barclay."

"Oh." Her face turned to a mask, shocked and not sure what

emotion to show. She looked at him, at the table, at the door, and tried to think of how to handle the surprise interview. "You're investigating Lauren's death?"

"Yes. I'm sorry I didn't say something sooner, but I didn't know if you would want me to say something out there…"

"Oh, of course. No, it's alright. Everybody here knows about Lauren… but I don't really understand. It was an accident, she fell down in her tub, so why would anyone be asking questions and investigating it?"

"That's what we do."

Mandy bit her lip, nodding quickly. "Of course. I'm sorry, it's just a bit of a shock. We were all so shocked when we heard about her accident. And that she died… just a freak accident like that… it's really kind of scary."

Zachary nodded understandingly. He sat down on one of the big padded chairs and motioned for Mandy to take one of the others so they could talk to each other at the same level.

"It is so shocking when someone close to you dies so suddenly and unexpectedly. It seems… unfair and arbitrary. You can hardly believe that it's really true."

"Yes," Mandy nodded vigorously. "Yes, exactly. I think we're all still in a state of shock, to tell the truth. We're all trying to go on and work, but it's very difficult. It's hard to concentrate on your job when you're dealing with something like that."

"Does your company offer any counseling? Maybe something outsourced, if they don't have someone in house?"

"Of course. They've offered; there's someone we can talk to if we need to. But it's not… I don't know. It doesn't seem like the thing to do. We should be… taking a few days off, talking to each other, grieving properly, going to her funeral. Right? You don't go to therapy just because someone dies. Everybody dies sooner or later, and it wasn't like she was shot or murdered. She just… slipped and fell. It's tragic, but not traumatizing."

"You could take a day or two off, I'm sure…"

Her lips tightened and she shook her head in a definite 'no,' even while saying, "Yes, I suppose I could…"

"I gather that you and Lauren were pretty close."

"Well… we were friends, yes, if that's what you mean. We didn't know each other before we started working with the company. We just started at the same time and we had similar personalities. Helped each other out a bit, joked around together."

Zachary raised his brows. He looked around, making a wide gesture to indicate their surroundings. "Joked around? Here?"

Mandy gave a little laugh. "I know, right? Pretty serious place. But you've got to let off steam every now and then. We would all be having nervous breakdowns if we didn't have a way to… express our frustrations now and then."

"Sounds like a healthy attitude."

"They're really big on employee health around here. Like, we all have to get in a certain number of hours of exercise every week. There's an on-site gym, so that we can take a break and do it whenever we need to. Clears your head, gives you an energy boost without caffeine. You know how many studies there are on how dangerous it is to be sitting at a desk all day. So they make sure that we get up and take care of our bodies."

"Ah. I noticed Lauren had workout clothes and wondered how she managed to fit it in."

"There's so much work to do, it's really hard to break away to do it, but you feel so much better when you do. Better health, better wealth!"

"That's good to see. I wondered, when I heard how many hours Lauren was putting in, if the company cared about their employees' health at all."

"It's only while we're interns. Once we have our permanent positions, it won't be as many hours. Right now… it's kind of like a competition. This is our Everest. If we can get over the top… then it gets easier."

Zachary wondered if she knew how many people died on Everest.

"That's good. So you don't feel like they work you too hard here?"

Mandy's eyes went to the side, like she was afraid someone might be listening. She put on a brighter smile. "No, of course not," she assured him earnestly. "Sure, you'll catch us complaining about the hours, but it really isn't that bad. I pulled all-nighters in college all the time and it didn't hurt me. One or two now… it's nothing to worry about."

"So most nights, you don't sleep under your desk."

"Oh, no way. That would be so against company policy. Sometimes… maybe you put in a few extra hours to get a project done that you need for the morning, but nobody is allowed to sleep here. You have to go home and get a good rest."

What Zachary had read in Lauren's private email suggested otherwise. As had Barbara. But he imagined there was an official company policy that said it wasn't to be done, and an unofficial policy that said if you had to, go ahead, but don't advertise the fact. Sometimes it might not even be safe for an employee to leave if they were overtired or it was too late to be out on the street. A person could always get a cab, but even that could be tempting fate for a young woman alone.

He took out his notepad to make some notes, but it was really a ploy to allow Mandy a few moments of distraction, an unguarded moment when she could relax and not worry about what he was going to ask her next. When she looked away, toward the door they had come in, he could see that her eyes were bloodshot, the skin around her eyes pale and stretched-looking. Grief or exhaustion? He couldn't be sure.

He scribbled a few notes about corporate exercise and sleep.

"What is the company's policy on overtime? Are you paid hourly? Do you get more if you work longer hours?"

"No, we're all monthly salaries. Doesn't matter how many hours we put in. Officially, we're supposed to work nine to five, but…" Mandy laughed once. "Believe me, I've never put in a nine-to-five day. Lauren either."

"Yeah. I got that impression."

"But we're just banking it for the future. You know, once we're permanent employees, we won't have to put in those kinds of hours. It will be a lot better."

Zachary opened his mouth to answer her. A man had walked up to the door, and he opened it, sticking his head in. "Mandy, do you know if Jack—" He cut himself off, eyes going to Zachary. "Sorry, I didn't know you were—" Then his eyes got wide. "Zachary?"

7

Zachary stared at Gordon Drake. He scrambled to his feet.

"Gordon? What are you doing here?"

"What am I doing here?" Gordon stared at him and gave a slight head-shake. "My name *is* on the doors."

Drake, Chase, Gould.

Gordon Drake.

Zachary was still flabbergasted. He stood there staring at Gordon. Bridget's new partner. The man who had replaced Zachary in her life. He opened and closed his mouth like a fish.

With everyone calling the company 'Chase Gold' as a joke, he hadn't even focused on the Drake. He didn't know a lot of Drakes. In fact, he only knew one Drake. Gordon Drake.

Gordon pushed the door open the rest of the way and stepped in. Zachary tensed as the man came toward him, ready for an explosion. Ready for a fist swung straight for his nose. He didn't know what Gordon would think of him being there; he might not be too happy about it.

But Gordon thrust out his hand instead, open, reaching to shake Zachary's. Zachary gave it to him mechanically, not understanding what was going on.

"Good to see you, Zachary. You're looking a lot better."

The last time he had seen Zachary was when Zachary was leaving the hospital after a psychiatric admission. Not the best time for him. Better than he had been before the stay, on his way to better health, but still a bit wobbly on his new legs.

And before that… Gordon had probably seen him on TV after his encounter with Teddy, both eyes blackened, his body beaten and degraded. And before that was when Zachary had gone to see Bridget at the hospital, at which time she had told him thank you very much for helping to catch her kidnapper and to make it clear that she never wanted to see him again. As Kenzie had warned him, Bridget had brought Zachary back into her life only to use him and then to throw him away again.

Gordon pumped his hand. "So to what do we owe the pleasure of your company here today?"

Zachary swallowed. He had intended to visit Lauren's office covertly, to talk to her friends and coworkers on the quiet before the management could figure out what was going on. He hadn't counted on one of the owners of the company knowing him on sight.

Zachary slowly pulled his hand out of Gordon's grip, nodding and clearing his throat. "Uh… well… I'm investigating Lauren Barclay's death."

Gordon didn't freeze or go pale. Nothing to indicate any guilt or complicity in Lauren's death. He nodded gravely and patted Zachary on the side of the shoulder, as if to comfort a fellow mourner.

"Lauren Barclay. So tragic. It was such a shock for all of us here, wasn't it, Mandy?"

Mandy nodded. "Yes. That's what I told Mr. Goldman. I just couldn't believe it."

"Lauren's death has left a great hole in our company," Gordon said, and his prose didn't sound at all fake or insincere. "We are all going to miss her smiling face and can-do attitude."

There were a few seconds of silence. Zachary wasn't sure what to say about the investigation or Lauren's death. He licked his lips uncertainly.

"You feel free to talk to whoever you need to," Gordon told him without prompting. "I know you'll be discreet and won't upset people. Unfortunately, there is a lot of work that must be done, so we must all go on even in Lauren's absence. And her work will have to be divided up among the other interns." He raised his brows at Mandy in good humor. "Like you don't already have enough."

Mandy gave a little laugh. "I'm sure we can handle Lauren's work between us, sir. There's a lot to do, but we'll take up the slack, sir."

"Good girl," he said approvingly. And such praise from Gordon never came across as patronizing. Zachary himself had felt warm and appreciated when Gordon had told him 'good man' in the past. Mandy smiled and looked a little embarrassed.

"I appreciate you letting me talk to people," Zachary said. "I really didn't even realize this was your company, or I would have come to you first."

Gordon laughed. "Somehow, people always seem to leave my name out. I'm never sure quite what to think of the habit. I can assure you that I am by no means a silent partner. If you need anything, you feel free to come to me. I'll help you out any way I can, in order to put this matter of Lauren's death to rest. Such a lovely young lady. Very smart and a hard worker."

"I'm impressed that you knew her so well, when she was just an intern."

"Just an intern? They are the lifeblood of this company. We couldn't do anything without all of the hard work they put into it. It's too bad that we can't hire them all on after their initial term is up… unfortunately it is a very competitive business, and if we are going to continue to forge ahead as we have been, we need to be a little bit hard-nosed about it, recognize the realities of the situation. I know every employee in this company. Right down to part-time file clerks. I'm a hands-on leader. No sitting behind a desk drinking my tea and letting everyone else do the work. I'm out there like everyone else, closing the deals."

"Well… very good. I'll let you know if there is anything I need from you. You might be able to give me a little bit of background… the corporate culture, your philosophy here at Drake, Chase, Gould. If you can think about anything about Lauren or her work here that you think I should know about."

"Come by my office when you're done. Say…" Gordon looked at his watch. "Five o'clock? Maybe you won't be here that late. I need to leave at six for dinner with a very important woman you and I both know, but any time before then. If I'm not in my office, my assistant will be able to track me down."

When Gordon left, Zachary turned his attention back to Mandy, trying to determine his best course of action.

"I'd like to meet with the other interns that worked with you and Lauren," he said slowly. "It would be best if I could meet with them one-on-one, I guess… There's no need to take everyone away from their work at the same time or to disrupt things with a big meeting. People will find it easier to talk about things one at a time, I think…"

Mandy shrugged and looked out through the glass wall. "I should be getting back to work. I don't like to lose too much time, especially when we're going to be expected to absorb Lauren's work." She sighed.

"If it's too much, you should have told Gordon that, shouldn't you? He doesn't have any way of knowing how much of a burden it is if you don't tell him."

Her eyes widened. "I would never tell Mr. Drake no."

"He's a reasonable man, he wouldn't fire you for saying that you had too much on your plate."

"Maybe not, but one of the VPs or managers might, once word got around. I don't want to put my job in jeopardy."

"But you need to protect your health too. If you put yourself in hospital or end up on long-term disability, you're not going to achieve your goals either."

"I'm not going to end up in hospital." She stood and drew herself up as tall as possible. "It's been nice to meet you, Mr. Goldman. I guess you have to investigate and ask all of these questions if it's your job, but you're not going to find anything out. Lauren just had an accident. It wasn't anything to do with anyone here at the office. She was at home, alone. That's what happened."

He nodded and shook her hand in thanks. "Would you have one of the other interns come and see me…"

She looked like she would say no, but looking in the direction Gordon had gone, she nodded grudgingly. "Yeah. Sure."

"I appreciate it."

8

Most of the interns were men. The one who came to the boardroom next was Aaron Morgan. Zachary saw him stop for a moment outside the door and wipe both hands on his pants. When he entered and approached Zachary to shake his hand, Zachary could still see lines of fatigue around his eyes. His complexion was pale, but it was possible that he was just fair-skinned.

"Aaron Morgan," the intern announced, and gave Zachary's hand a perfunctory pump.

"Zachary Goldman. Thanks for agreeing to meet with me."

Aaron shrugged with one shoulder. "I was under the impression it was required."

Zachary let that go, keeping a friendly smile pasted to his face. "Why don't you have a seat? I expect you're pretty tired."

Aaron sat. "Why?"

"Why what?"

"Why do you think I'm tired?"

"You are all working long hours, and I don't imagine that's going to be shortened by Lauren's death."

"Yeah. Doesn't sound like they're going to be hiring someone to replace her."

"How many hours have you been working?"

Aaron looked at him, blinking and either trying to decide whether to answer truthfully or calculating the number of hours. "I guess… fifty-something straight. I had a report that had to be presented this morning."

"Are you presenting it?"

"No, one of the VPs. I just do the grunt work, I'm not worthy of client interactions."

"I'll bet you'll be the one taking the heat if there is anything wrong with the report."

Aaron gave a short bark of laughter. "You don't have to tell me that."

"So now that your report is prepared and handed in, are you going to go home to take a well-deserved rest?"

Aaron shook his head and yawned at the thought.

"No, can't go home during office hours. That would be a big problem. I'll just have to push through until tonight. Then I guess… get a few hours of shuteye, if I can still remember how."

Zachary nodded. "You must be exhausted. I can't imagine staying up that long on purpose."

"Well, people do it for medical tests or all kinds of other things, right? So I can handle it. It's not the first time."

"What makes it worth that kind of effort? You must feel like crap."

"Yeah? Try going seventy-two hours straight."

"Have you done that?"

Aaron started to answer, then shook his head. "I don't see what this has to do with anything. I thought you were here asking about Lauren."

"I'm wondering what kind of physical shape she was in… seeing you and Mandy, I have to wonder how many hours she had put in before she died. If she was that tired, it could have had an impact on what happened."

Aaron shook his head firmly. "I saw her when she left here.

She was just fine. She wasn't a zombie. She was just going to go home to catch a few winks and a shower, and then come back."

"But then she never did."

Aaron nodded his agreement, shrugging. "We all got here in the morning, and she was nowhere to be seen. Mandy started calling her after a while, but there was no answer. Eventually, we just gave up. And then we heard after that how she had died in her bathtub. I thought… what a waste. All of that work for nothing."

Zachary thought Aaron meant that all of the work Lauren had done had been for nothing, because she died before she ever saw the benefits of it, but his supposition was dispelled by Aaron's next words. "All of the effort spent competing with her, trying to beat her out… and then she ends up eliminating herself. Unbelievable."

Zachary raised an eyebrow. He wrote a few words in his notepad. "Is it that cutthroat?"

"We're all competing for the same position or two. They do it intentionally, getting more interns than they need, so that we have to win the right to stay on. And in the meantime, they've squeezed all kinds of work out of us. Good for their bottom line."

"I assume you must track your hours."

"Yeah, we have to."

"So they know that you're putting in several days in a row, without any kind of rest in between."

"Well…" Aaron made a face and tried to come up with an answer. "I guess they know what kind of hours we're putting in, because they see us here at work."

"Sure. So… how well did you know Lauren? I know that she and Mandy were close, I imagine because they were the only two female interns. How did the rest of you get along? Did you do things together, or were you too competitive to socialize with each other?"

"There wasn't time to socialize."

"But you need to eat, joke around to break the stress and tension. There must have been times when you were just too brain-dead to continue working on a project and had to put it to the side until you were fresh again."

"Yeah… we did do some of that. Buy pizza and everybody would dive in, take a few minutes to pig out before getting back to our projects. Or sometimes after a big deal closed, go out to the bar and just wipe away the cobwebs. Not very often, but sometimes."

"So you must have known Lauren pretty well."

"No. Just to talk to. Like, I know that she lives in an apartment with another girl to pay the rent. I know she was good with numbers and was the top of all of her classes—but we were all the top of our classes. She had a sense of humor, I guess. She and Mandy would giggle together about things."

"You didn't go out with her?"

"Like a date? No."

"Like anything. Did the two of you go out for a drink together, just the two of you? Or a bite to eat? Or crashing at her apartment because it was closer than yours?"

Aaron clearly didn't like Zachary's line of questioning.

"If you think that I went back there with her one day and drowned her, you're crazy. Why would I do that? I knew I was going to beat her out. She wasn't my most serious competition."

"Oh. Who was your most serious competition?"

"Well, it had to be the men, right? It wasn't like the partners were going to pick a girl over us."

Zachary let the words hang in the air for a few minutes, thinking about them.

"Why is that a 'given'?"

"Because girls… women… they get distracted. Just when they hit the top of their career, the biological clock starts clicking and they have to have babies. And then they've got to stay home to take care of them, for like a year. For each one. And then if they ever get back into the workforce, they've lost their position, and they can't get to the top again. They'd have to intern all over again, and who would hire a thirty- or forty-year-old intern? No one wants someone that old."

"Is that really the way they see it?"

"Of course. They have to take on women interns, but they're never going to get the top positions, because they have the whole biological imperative."

"There must be female investment bankers. It's not all just a men's profession."

"Sure, there are a few. Even here at Chase Gold, there are a couple. But they don't last and everybody knows it. So they hire someone they can downsize a few months or years down the line. Get what they can out of them and then let them go."

"Did Lauren know this?"

"Sure. Everyone knows it. Lauren was talking about getting her tubes tied so that she couldn't have any kids. That would show them she was really serious about working for the company."

Zachary couldn't believe anyone would give up the opportunity to have children just to work at a place that was so demanding. Barbara had said Lauren wanted to be wealthy. Did she want it badly enough to give up any chance of having children?

Of course, tubal ligations could usually be reversed. And people could adopt. Or foster. Or end up getting custody of a deceased relative's children. Would Chase Gold really only have accepted Lauren on equal footing with a man if she had opted for sterilization?

"Wow. That's pretty dedicated. She really wanted to get a permanent position here."

"Yeah, she did."

"It didn't worry you, this talk of getting her tubes tied? Did that put her ahead of you in the competition?"

Aaron clenched his jaw. "I would still have been ahead of her," he insisted. But Zachary had a feeling that the young man was, in fact, pretty worried about the possibility. And what would he have been willing to do to protect his position?

"So, I didn't catch whether you had ever been out with Lauren, or to her house."

"We didn't date."

"No. But did you ever go out anywhere together?"

"With the group, maybe."

"Ever by yourself?"

Aaron hesitated.

"Come on," Zachary gave Aaron a conspiratorial grin. "Are you telling me that the two of you never spent any time alone together? She was a nice-looking girl. She didn't have anyone else. She didn't have time for any real dating. All she could do was flirt a bit with the men at the office. Maybe go out together for drinks. I can ask Barbara; she said that Lauren sometimes saw men from the office, maybe even brought them home."

"Okay, maybe once or twice," Aaron admitted grudgingly. "It wasn't dating. It wasn't anything serious. It was just letting off steam at the end of a long day, or a long week."

"You've been to her apartment?"

He again hesitated, but Zachary waited him out this time, and Aaron conceded. "Yeah. A couple of times. She was close by, like you said. Going back to my place would have added an hour of commuting time. And going back to the office and sleeping on the floor… that wasn't any way to live. Not when I could just stay at her place and be comfortable in a bed."

"Sure."

"But I'm telling, you, it wasn't anything serious, and it was only once or twice. And I wasn't with her the day that she died. I didn't go home with her. We didn't do drinks or anything that night."

"Did anyone else?"

"What?"

"Did anyone else go home with her that night? Just because you didn't, that doesn't mean no one in the office did."

"No… I don't think so. No one left with her."

"Nobody left at the same time? Followed her out a few minutes later? It could have been covert."

"No." Aaron frowned and shook his head. "A few people went home, but… no, I'm sure no one left with her."

"Okay. Just thought I'd check. She didn't have any health problems that you knew about?"

"No. She would never have made it here if she was sick. You gotta be able to work all the time. Even through a cold or the flu. If it was something worse than that… no way. They'd have her out of here. We aren't permanent employees yet; they can terminate us at any time for any reason. If she was a risk because she was sick, they could just boot her."

"What about substance issues? Did she drink? Abuse pills? Something to help her stay mentally alert?"

"Well, everybody has caffeine. Like, all the time. We're drinking coffee and energy drinks like there's no tomorrow. And NoDoz."

Zachary nodded. "Lauren too?"

"Sure. As much as any of us."

"What about coke? Meth? Adderall?"

"I don't know anything about that. Not around me."

"What about you? It's out there, right?"

"It's out there. I don't know who does what. I don't do any prescription drugs or anything hardcore. Just the caffeine, to help stay awake on a day like this. Perfectly legal."

"Not necessarily safe, though, if you abuse it. You can still do some real damage."

"Nah. We're young and healthy and it's not like we're shooting the stuff. A drink to pick you up when you start to get sleepy. That's all. People all over the world drink it every day."

"They do," Zachary agreed. "I'm just saying, it can still be dangerous."

"Anything can be dangerous. We're trying to make a life for ourselves here. If you had the last twenty years to do over, what would you do? Would you try something more daring? If you knew you could be where you wanted to be right now instead of…" He wobbled his hand back and forth, expressing his opinion of Zachary's job. "What are you, detective? If you could put in a few years at a higher-octane level, and instead of being that, you could be… private security or something else you liked, making ten times the money? Come on, you'd do it, wouldn't you?"

Zachary smiled blandly and didn't give Aaron any information that he didn't already have. He'd found it useful in the past to have people underestimate him.

"Maybe I would," he said noncommittally.

"Yeah, exactly. I'm putting in my time now so that I don't have to be stuck in a dead-end job later. No offense. I have my life planned out. I know where I'm going and what I have to do to get there."

9

Blair Bieberstein was a little man who made Zachary think of a hyperactive squirrel. And as a small, ADHD man himself, that was saying something. Bieberstein seemed so hyped up and on edge that Zachary assumed he'd either just drunk every energy drink in the fridge, or he was dipping into the illegal stuff. He looked Zachary up and down and stood back, gazing at him, his whole body vibrating.

"So it's you, huh? You're the one investigating Lauren's death? This is just so crazy. I never thought that anything would happen to Lauren. She was always so grounded, so down to earth, you know? I never expected her to die like that. And then to have the police investigating it. You have to do that with accidents? Because no one was there when it happened? Is that why?"

"I was asked to look into it," Zachary started, keeping his voice pitched low and slow, trying to bring Bieberstein down. But the man didn't give him time to even start an explanation. He just nodded vigorously, as if he knew the whole story, and started to shift his feet back and forth. Zachary didn't know whether he had to go to the bathroom, or to pace, or if it was some kind of tic. Or a combination of all three. Bieberstein seemed like exactly the sort of person who was wound so tightly he was just going to spring apart at the slightest provocation. He was not the type of person Zachary would have pictured as an investment banker. He seemed way too out-of-control to be any kind of financial planner or to be able to plan anything ahead of time. They must have had a reason to hire him, but Zachary wasn't sure what it was. Maybe he was related to somebody. An idiot nephew that Chase or Gould had to give a chance to in order to get his sister off his back.

"I don't think I know anything that could be of any use to you," Bieberstein said, shaking his head rapidly. "Lauren and I weren't close or anything. We never went out together or snuck into the storeroom together, like some of the guys around here might have done. She wasn't my type. Or I wasn't hers. Doesn't really matter, because none of us have any time to be messing around while we're working here anyway. I don't need any more distractions in my life."

Zachary could see that. He could just see Bieberstein racing off down some rabbit trail when he was supposed to be preparing a report. His manager would find him days later, curled up under his desk with three laptops, typing and laughing maniacally.

"If we could just sit down for a minute to go over things, I'm sure it won't take very long."

Bieberstein looked at the chairs and the boardroom table. "I don't sit. I have a standing desk. I pace. I have a lot of nervous energy. I don't sit."

"Well…" Zachary was prepared to argue that he must sit down at some point, even if it were just to eat, but that really wasn't the point. Bieberstein probably didn't sit down to eat, either. He hovered over the computers, devouring Danishes, getting crumbs between all of the keyboard keys. He must be a menace to work with. "Okay, then," he said. There was no point in a battle of wills or trying to force Bieberstein to sit down.

Even if he were to succeed, Bieberstein would not be able to talk or focus once he was forced to sit still. Much like Zachary had felt as a kid when he was told he had to sit at his desk to do all of his schoolwork or homework. He wanted to get up and move around and think about it, work things through with his body. Once he sat still, everything fled from his brain and he couldn't explain why.

At least he was better than that now. He could—and frequently did—sit at the computer for hours to do research or compile reports, working through the puzzles that he had been tasked with solving. Sitting at the computer was, he knew, bad for his eyes, his heart, his posture, and everything else, but once he got into a project, it was hard to break off to do anything else, like getting up to walk around and give his eyes and body a break.

"Did you and Lauren work on any projects together?"

"Yeah, of course. I work with all of the other interns on their files. If they need research on markets, or need some numbers crunched, or whatever, I'm your man. Their man, I mean. That's my thing. I don't do my own files or projects, I'm a resource for others."

"Oh. So does that mean that you're not in competition with the others for a permanent position?"

Blair rocked back and forth and twisted his head around, thinking about it. He gave a wide shrug. "I don't know. Who really cares? I don't think so. I'm pretty sure that no matter who else they pick to go full-time permanent, I'll still have a place here. I don't think they're going to be getting rid of me anytime soon."

Zachary pondered. Although the others had not said anything about Bieberstein getting one of the permanent positions, they had made it sound like there was only one opening for them to fight over. So maybe Bieberstein did have a locked-in position, and it was everyone else who was trying to get that last chance. If they already knew that somebody had one space, it would make them all the more desperate to get the last one.

Bieberstein started to pace. He drummed his fingers against his legs and looked up at the ceiling, but he obviously wasn't counting ceiling tiles or avoiding Zachary's questions. His mind was busy on something else. Something that was far away and totally separate from what was going on in the boardroom.

Bieberstein had heavy, bristly whiskers, as if he hadn't shaved for three days. Maybe he hadn't, or maybe he was just one of those men who grew facial hair really quickly. He had the same blood-shot eyeballs and dark bags under his eyes as the others, clearly working the same brutally demanding schedule. Zachary wasn't sure how Drake, Chase, Gould could get away with working them for so many hours. There had to be laws against it. Was there any regulation of investment bankers or other office types? There had to be laws in place to prevent them from getting used as slave labor, as the interns clearly were.

"When was the last time you saw Lauren?" he ventured.

"Two days ago, ten thirty-five," Bieberstein said crisply, not even looking at him.

Zachary hesitated a moment, wondering if he was joking. But he didn't appear to be. "Morning or night?"

"Night. She went home. Had to get some rest so that she could work on a project Mr. Drake had given her the next day. So she went home to sleep. Then she never came back. You should have seen, everybody was going absolutely nuts around here trying to call and text her and find out what had happened to her, how she could have just stayed home and not come back in like she was supposed to. I wondered if she was dead. I wasn't surprised when the police came around and said that she was."

"You weren't surprised?"

"No. Why else wouldn't she answer anything? Even if she was sick, she would have at least sent a text back explaining that. But not a word…? No communication at all? That's just not the way we work. That's not the way Lauren was. She was always sending emails and texts out at all hours. That was how she got as far ahead as she did."

"I suppose so. I just didn't think that anyone would have thought 'maybe she's dead.'"

"Maybe not, but I don't always think the same way as other people do."

That much was clear.

"What did you think of Lauren as a person?"

"She was nice. She wasn't rude to me. She'd tell me to push off sometimes, but sometimes I need to be told that. That's okay, there's always something else to do around here."

"And what do you think happened? How do you think she died?"

"You already know how she died, don't you?" Bieberstein challenged. "She just fell and hit her head, drowned in the bathtub. That's what they're telling us. Unless everyone is lying and something else happened."

"Let's say something else happened. What are the possibilities?"

Bieberstein seemed unperturbed at being asked this. His chin jutted up toward the ceiling as he tipped his head way back and ran through scenarios. "She slipped in the bathtub. She stepped on something in the bathtub. She slipped or tripped on something outside the bathtub and fell into it. Someone pushed her and made her hit her head. Someone hit her over the head. Someone forced her into the tub and held her head under the water."

Zachary swallowed. That was a pretty good list of possibilities. And Bieberstein clearly wasn't concerned that anyone might think that he was the party who could have hit Lauren or held her head under the water. He wasn't connecting the possibilities to the dead girl personally, she was just a variable he was trying to solve for.

"If someone hurt her, who would you suspect?"

"If someone hurt her? But someone didn't hurt her. The police said that she slipped and hit her head. If someone hurt her..." He paced across the room, head back down, thinking, then walked back across the room again, backward this time, but avoiding the chairs and the corner of the side table without looking to see where they were. "It could be any of the interns. Everyone left at the same time. All of them wanted the job and knew she was probably the first in line for it. Most of the rest of the staff was gone, but there were still a few people around. Mr. Drake was still here, I know, because he'd just given Lauren the new assignment. I don't think any of the other partners were in. Receptionist goes home at six. Night security man was on, but he wouldn't have followed her home; he has to stay here to make sure that no one tries to break in. Or it could be someone who we don't know. Just a random burglar or junkie. There's nothing to indicate that it's anyone from work. It could be someone from her family, too; I don't know how close she was to them. Then there's that roommate. Is she really telling the truth? Or is she the one that knocked Lauren out and drowned her, and then just called in a report to say that she had found her, to throw suspicion off of herself? Nine times out of ten, it's the lover, a family member, or the person who reported it. Most fatal accidents occur in the home, so that was the best place to set something like that up. Lauren had to go home sooner or later. At most, her roommate would just have had to wait a couple of days."

Zachary felt like he was stuck in the middle of a whirlwind. He liked Bieberstein. He liked the way that he thought and that he didn't care whether Zachary thought he was crazy or guilty or just weird. He liked that Bieberstein didn't hold back, but just poured everything out, where they could both look at it and analyze it.

An older man poked his head into the boardroom. It was the second time that someone had done this to interrupt one of Zachary's interviews. It was irritating. The more senior members of the firm obviously felt like it was their domain and they could interrupt a meeting whenever they wanted. Gordon had been gracious about it and had been happy to see Zachary. But having another man stick his head in and act like whatever Zachary was doing was unimportant got his back up.

"Biebs. Hey. I need you. You done in here?"

"Yeah," Bieberstein nodded, switching directions to leave the boardroom. "What do you need?"

"Hey—we weren't done yet," Zachary protested. "Can't it wait for a few minutes?"

"I don't have anything else to tell you," Bieberstein said. "I don't know anything about it and I've told you everything I could to help. Maybe one of the others will be able to give you some more insight. I'm not really good with people. I'm better at numbers."

"Maybe we could meet again later and finish up…"

"I don't think I have anything else to contribute," Bieberstein said dismissively.

The man who had come to fetch him nodded his head in agreement. "It was just an accident. What's anyone here going to know about it? None of us know anything."

"Who are you?" Zachary asked, holding up his hand for the older man to wait.

"Not part of your investigation. I have work to do. I'll see you around."

He left, taking Bieberstein with him.

10

"I know you're trying to talk to everyone," Kelly Pierce, one of the supervisors of the interns said. "They're just all busy right now. You can wait until their time frees up, but they're all working on vital projects right now. Maybe you could make an appointment and come back later when things are quieter."

Zachary studied him. "If I can't see any of the other interns, maybe I could talk to someone in human resources. Do you have a Manager of Human Resources I could follow up with?"

"We do… I don't know if she'll be busy right now…"

Zachary waited, and eventually the supervisor realized that there wasn't anything he could do other than make a phone call and ask. Zachary wasn't going to go away and wasn't going to offer any easy outs. Pierce rolled his eyes and pulled out his cell phone. He searched his contacts and found the person he was looking for. Obviously not someone who was on his favorites list.

"Bev… hey, we've got a bit of a situation here that I wonder if you can help with. I don't know if you've heard, but we've got this detective up here who's looking into the Lauren Barclay accident… yeah… and he wants to talk to someone in Human Resources. I guess that's you, so… tag, you're it! Do you want to come upstairs to the boardroom, or do you want me to send him down there?"

He spoke for a couple more minutes, mostly just listening to Bev on the other end, watching Zachary and looking around the room restlessly. "Yes… yes… I know. But we've been told to cooperate."

More commentary from Bev in human resources, with Pierce nodding and uh-huh'ing, waiting for her to finish.

"So… you want me to send him down?"

He was finally able to hang up the call and rolled his eyes at Zachary. "Just be warned you're going to have to hear all of that for yourself when you get down there."

Zachary chuckled. "Okay. Thanks for the heads-up. Where do I go from here?"

"I'll walk you down," Pierce sighed.

"I can find my way."

"We have to be careful of security. The door down there is locked. She said she would let you in, but…"

"Well, I appreciate you looking after me."

They headed out to the lobby and onto the elevator.

"Everybody seems to get along pretty well here," Zachary commented. "I expected the interns to be a lot more… antagonistic toward each other."

It surprised Zachary how close-knit the employees seemed. Since they were competing against each other, he would have thought that they would have shown animosity toward each other, have talked behind each other's backs and made accusations or tried to direct him against their enemies. But everyone seemed to consider themselves part of the team.

Pierce raised his brows and nodded. "We try to foster a strong corporate identity. A unified, supportive culture. It's important in a place like this. People have to work so hard, and if there isn't any kind of intrinsic reward—and monetary reward just doesn't cut it —then people are just going to burn out and leave. If you want to reach people, you need to… inspire them."

"How do you do that?"

"Bev can fill you in on that kind of thing. That's one of the jobs of Human Resources."

"Okay. You like it here?"

"Of course I do, I wouldn't stay here otherwise. Like I said, money isn't the be-all and end-all. You have to get something deeper out of it. Something more… spiritual."

Zachary couldn't help the skepticism that entered into his tone. "Spiritual?"

"That's maybe not the right word, but I'm not sure what word to use. Fulfillment. Satisfaction. Wholeness."

"Out of an investment banking company?"

"You can find your zen anywhere. We happened to find it at Drake, Chase, Gould."

"Okay. Well… good for you. That's pretty amazing."

They got off on a lower floor, and Pierce led Zachary over to a plain brown door. Closed and, as he had said, locked. They both stood there for a moment, looking at it. Pierce sighed and pulled out his phone again. He tapped the number and stared up at the ceiling as he waited for Bev to answer.

"We're here, Bev. Yes, already. Waiting for you."

He hung up again, shaking his head.

"You don't have a key?" Zachary asked.

"I'm not part of the department, I'm not supposed to be letting people in and out without approval. Gotta make sure we know who is where and have some kind of security."

Zachary nodded. They waited a few more minutes, and eventually, the door opened.

Bev was a tall woman, black hair pulled back, liberally streaked with gray. She towered over both of them. Her face was smooth and unwrinkled in contrast to her hair. Maybe the hair was colored. Though Zachary didn't know why a young woman would want to color her hair gray.

"So you are…"

"Zachary Goldman." He held his hand out to her, and she

hesitated for a few seconds, then offered her hand and let him squeeze it, offering no firmness in response. The quintessential dead fish.

"Come this way, I suppose. Thank you, Kelly."

Pierce nodded and made a little gesture to Zachary that he interpreted as, 'you asked for it, and now you got it.' He went back to the elevator to ascend to his own floor, and Zachary followed the tall, stern woman. She took him, not to a meeting room, but back to her own office. It wasn't big. The walls were lined with metal file cabinets, a few paintings on the walls, some inspirational posters and awards. Stacks of paper on her desk and on the visitor chair, which she had to remove with a sigh before Zachary could sit.

"Thanks so much for agreeing to see me," Zachary said. "I know it's inconvenient…"

"It is," Bev agreed. "And there's no reason for it. I don't understand why the police are investigating Lauren's death. It was obviously an accident. Why would you waste your resources on this?"

"I was asked to," Zachary said simply, not correcting her impression that he was with the police. If she knew that he was a private investigator, he had a feeling that she wouldn't help him, even with the instruction coming down from Gordon Drake that they were to help Zachary.

Zachary flipped a few random pages in his notebook, thinking.

"Pierce said you could tell me about the corporate culture you have here at Drake, Chase, Gould. It seems like you have a really close-knit community. I thought it would be… cutthroat. But people seem to get along with each other, for the most part."

Bev studied him, the lines of her face softening a little. Starting with a compliment always went a long way to getting some cooperation.

"Yes, we've worked very hard to develop a real community. A team where people help each other out, rather than trying to steal files from each other or to talk each other down. Kind of unusual in this industry. But it's something that we've consciously worked on."

"Do you have some literature on the company? And can you tell me about some of the stuff that you have done to build it up that way?"

Bev looked at him for a moment as if to make sure that he was really serious. Then she bent down and opened a drawer, where she went through a number of folders, taking one item out of each to put on the desk in front of him. A company handbook, pamphlet on their health and welfare program, some glossy brochures on retreats and team-building volunteer days, various items that they had put together showing what a wonderful company new employees were coming to work for.

Zachary picked up the handbook and opened it up to one of the first pages, reading the big, bold headlines.

Drake, Chase, Gould

Building wealth, building community

A world leader in investment banking.

He didn't spend a lot of time browsing through the handbook, just reading a section heading here and there throughout the book and looking at the pictures of happy employees doing various things. He'd spend more time on the handbook later, when he had the time to read it without someone hovering over him.

"This looks really good, thank you."

He turned to the health and welfare brochure, and saw that it outlined information about the company gym and their activity program, as well as a few other headings about counseling for substance abuse issues, benefits for things like massage therapy and acupuncture, and a corporate dietician to help employees work through meal planning, weight loss, and other issues.

"One of the interns mentioned your gym," he said. "I think it's great that you have something on-site where employees can go to get their workouts. When you've got people working as hard as your employees do, it's such a great idea to have something right on-site so that they can take a break whenever they need it, get their workout, and go back to work fresh."

"That's right." Bev nodded vigorously. "Exercise is absolutely vital for employee health. And we've gone one step further. Not only are they allowed to take breaks to go get some exercise, it's actually prescribed. They have to log a certain number of exercise hours a week at our gym. And not all on a Saturday or Sunday, either. They have to be working out regularly throughout the week. We want to make sure that people are getting the exercise they need, that they're getting away from their desks and actually doing something physical."

"You track their workout hours?"

"Absolutely. And if they are not putting in the hours they need to in order to maintain peak health, then their supervisor is going to be talking to them. It's very important to us."

"Wow. That really is forward-thinking. I've never heard of a company doing that."

"Our employees are important to us. If we don't take care of their health, then we're going to end up losing a lot of hours that they could have been working dealing with sick leave and disability. We don't want to have to deal with downtime. We schedule workout time so that they have the best possible chance of maintaining peak health."

"Do you require a physical when they start? They always say that you have to consult a doctor before beginning a new exercise program. I mean, what if you had someone who had a bad heart and they got on the treadmill, and…"

She chuckled. "Well, we don't want to have to deal with that kind of liability. So, yes, we do have employee physicals, both before they begin working here and annually, so that we are up-to-date on those kinds of issues and can head off problems before they really become an issue. If you can see a problem developing and refer the person to the corporate dietician to get them back on track, why wouldn't you do that? So much easier to deal with it at the beginning than once it becomes entrenched."

"So everybody would have a physical before they start working here."

She nodded her agreement.

"I'd like to see the report on Lauren's physical, if I could."

Bev stared at him. She didn't move. She didn't get up to go to one of the banks of file cabinets and pull out Lauren's personnel file or a file on employee physicals.

"We don't have one for Lauren."

"Not for Lauren? Why not?"

"She wasn't a permanent employee, she was just an intern. If she had stayed on with us, we would have had a physical done then. But we don't do them for interns. Why would you waste your time and money on a handful of employees who are not going to stay with the company? Once they've been put on-track as permanent employees, then we do the physicals."

"But they were required to go to the gym."

Bev's mouth twisted into different shapes as she tried to find a way to explain this discrepancy. "Well… an intern isn't actually required to attend at the gym, but they do have access to it. It's at their own discretion. They are allowed to, but they don't have to."

Zachary frowned, thinking about that. He made a note to go back to it later.

"That makes perfect sense," he told Bev. Her face relaxed, relief showing through. "Why would you spend money on temporary employees who were only going to be here for a few months and then move on to something else?"

She nodded her agreement.

"So what do you do when an employee has heart problems or high blood pressure or some other issue that precludes them from exercising?"

"You'd be surprised. There aren't really a lot of conditions that would bar someone from exercising. They might have to start off easy, limit what kinds of exercise they did at the start, but most people can do some kind of exercise. It's just a matter of finding out what it is and starting slowly."

"Okay. Sure. That makes sense."

"We have a portable v-fib machine in the gym," she said proudly. "And we have staff who are trained in how to use it and in CPR and first aid. All that kind of thing. They are on-site to handle any issues, from a sprained ankle to heart attack. We're investing in our employees' futures."

It sounded like another slogan. Zachary looked down at the brochures and saw the same tagline written across the front of the health and welfare brochure. *We're investing in our employees' futures.*

"That really sounds good. I wish other companies would do that." He fidgeted with the edges of the brochure, running his eyes over the headlines again. "Do you have a lot of issues with substance abuse? I would imagine you must have a few employees who... abuse caffeine... maybe drink too much on weekends when they get away from the grind."

"There are issues in any company. I don't think we have any more than is normal in any other company. And we are dealing with it right away, with counseling and keeping track of employees through their annual physicals. I don't think you could say the same about most companies. That's just not normally done. We're way ahead of the curve there."

"And how about overwork? It seems like your interns especially are racking up some crazy hours..."

"No, certainly not. We have policies on how many hours they're allowed to work. We know that the type of people who become investment bankers tend to have those type A personalities and really get into their work. So we have policies to guide them on how long it's reasonable to work, and then they need to go home and get some sleep. These self-starters, they will run themselves into the ground if you let them. You have to be strict and say they aren't allowed to work more than a certain number of hours in a day or a week."

"Really. Do you have a written policy?"

She went to her drawer again, and pulled a single sheet out of a folder. Zachary looked it over. It was an infographic with numbers and graphs and little pictograms showing how employees needed to log their hours and ensure that they weren't working too many days or hours per month. On the back was a daily time log that could be photocopied. As well as an internet URL showing where they could download a tracking app on their phones or computers.

"So they actually have to clock in and out."

Bev nodded.

"Could I get a copy of Lauren's logs? And the other interns' that she worked with?"

"That's private employee information. I really can't share that with you."

"I'm going to need to see it," he said firmly. He pressed a little harder, working on her assumption that he was a police officer. "Am I going to have to come back here with a warrant? Gordon told me that I would have the company's full cooperation."

"Well, of course I am cooperating, but this information is private…"

"I see." He wrote 'warrant' slowly and deliberately in his notepad. He didn't know how well she could follow his pencil movements and tell what he was writing down, but he figured that even someone who had no talent for cryptography could tell that the word started with a W.

Bev was looking distinctly uncomfortable. Zachary looked down at his page, and wrote down 'call Gordon' in his slow, awkward printing. She shifted in her seat. Her forehead was creased with frown lines. Finally, she decided to cooperate with him.

"Okay, okay, you don't have to do that. I'll get you Lauren's log."

Zachary sat back and waited. She looked back at him. She clearly expected him to go on with the interview, and she would track down and send him Lauren's work log later. Or not at all, hoping that he would forget to follow up on it. He just looked at her, waiting for her to produce the log.

Bev finally turned her attention to her computer and tapped on the keys, logging into their time tracking program and searching up the employee and report that she wanted. She printed it off and handed it over to Zachary, her nose wrinkling like Zachary smelled bad.

"I really don't like this. I don't think I should be compelled to give you confidential employee records…"

Zachary looked over the columns of numbers. He would have to study it at home later, when he could really focus and see whether Lauren had been working the hours that her roommate claimed, or whether that had been untrue.

"And the other interns' logs?" he pressed. He had waited until he had Lauren's log in his hand, not wanting her to backtrack and end up hiding the information because he'd asked for too much.

"It's one thing to give you Lauren's. She is dead and you are investigating her death, but the other employees… I really don't think that I can justify that. I might have to talk to our lawyer…"

"I see." Zachary put down Lauren's time log and sat back in his seat. He looked at the other handouts that Bev had given him. "Why don't you tell me about the employee retreats?"

11

"I'm sure you've seen or been to corporate team-building events before," Bev said, looking over at the flyers she had handed to Zachary. "Inspiring speakers, building trusting relationships, working together for a unified goal, camp type situations where everybody eats together, sleeps in communal cabins or cottages. We work on visioning, corporate cheers, personal goal-setting, or dream-mapping. We're really invested in developing a sense of community and loyalty to each other. Not just to the company brand, but to their coworkers and the company's vision."

"Well, from what I've seen, it's working."

Bev nodded her agreement. Zachary didn't point out that she was the only one so far who had resisted being a team player, trying to get out of talking to him. While the lower-level workers were loyal to the company, he wasn't sure that management had the same attitude.

"You don't ever get anyone who refuses to participate or comes back with a bad attitude? Maybe mocking the whole team-building process? Because it seems like you always have the one guy…"

She rolled her eyes. "One clown who has to mock everything and act like he's above it. Yes. We have had one or two of those.

But you know what? If they don't come around in a session like that… your best course of action is to get rid of them. Give them notice when they get back to the office and have them out of there in two weeks or sooner. You don't need rabble-rousers like that who aren't going to fall into line."

"So I assume you never got that kind of attitude from Lauren."

"Heavens, no. And not from any of the other interns either. They all know that if they want to stay with the company, they'd better show us what they're made of. There's no skepticism tolerated with the interns. Fall in line or you can go home. Everybody else is working their butts off to earn a place here."

"How many intern positions are open?"

"Two or three, depending on the needs of the company. It does change a bit from one season to the next."

"The current batch of interns? How many are they fighting over?"

"Two."

"Blair Bieberstein seemed to think he has one of them tied up."

Bev pressed her lips together.

"Would that be accurate?" Zachary asked. "Is Bieberstein already picked for one of them?"

"I don't know that I would put it in quite those terms… but he is a serious contender."

"You haven't been told that he's been picked already?"

"There's been talk. But policy says that they don't get finalized for another month."

"So maybe he's an unofficial pick?"

Bev shrugged. "Call it what you like."

"Was Lauren at the top of the list for the other one?"

Bev shook her head. "I don't think I could say that. She was definitely up there, but we have some extremely capable and hard-working interns. It is going to be a close race."

"Would she be picked for the other slot, being a woman? I got the feeling that male interns are preferred, because they don't have the inconvenience of childbearing to worry about."

She tapped the end of her pen on the desk, considering what to say.

"It's a tough world out there for women," she finally said. "Men don't really understand what it's like to have avenues closed because of the fact that they might become parents. For women, it is a reality. Even if you keep working right up until you go into labor, and return as soon as you can be on your feet, there is still a prejudice that you are going to miss a lot of work with baby illnesses and when your childcare falls through, or school gets out for a snow day. For the next ten to twenty years, you have another priority. And if you keep having children… even worse."

"Is that a consideration here?"

"It is everywhere, whether they will admit it or not. Women of childbearing or child-rearing years are second class. Whether they are married or single. Even if they tell you that they don't plan on having children. Everyone has been burned at some point by a woman going on mat leave."

"Lauren was talking about getting her tubes tied. Would that have made her a better candidate?"

"It would certainly help, not only in showing that she wouldn't accidentally get pregnant, but also that she was willing to put the company before family. Definitely a step in the right direction. The board had been getting pressure because of the gender inequality in the company. You get one woman on the board, and suddenly you have to address why there aren't women everywhere in the company, on an equal basis with men. Why aren't we hiring more women? Why are their salaries smaller? We need to be proactive in putting women before men until the inequality is evened out. It's one thing to have women as secretaries or in human resources," she indicated herself, "but that's not the same as having them as investment bankers or vice presidents."

"So you were actually under pressure to hire a woman rather than a man."

Bev shrugged and didn't confirm it in so many words.

"So the male interns didn't really have much of a chance of getting a position once Bieberstein and Lauren were locked into place. Unless one of them… dropped out for some reason."

"That's probably overstating the situation. There was still plenty of competition for those positions. Nothing was—or is—set in stone. It's still an open audition."

"But a little less competitive than it was a few days ago."

"Of course. But I don't think anyone is going to go through all of our interns, knocking them off until there are only two left. No one did anything to Lauren. She slipped in her tub."

"Perhaps. Or maybe she had a little help."

"You don't have any proof of that," Bev challenged, leaning forward in her chair. "I really don't understand what's going on here. The girl didn't die under suspicious circumstances. Everything I read and heard said it was an accident. I don't know why there's any investigation going on at all. It doesn't make sense."

"We want to know what happened. What really happened. Don't you?"

"Of course I do. Lauren seemed like a nice girl. But to imagine that there was anything… suspicious going on is ridiculous. There wasn't anything going on."

"Will Mandy Pryor get the position, since Lauren isn't in the running any longer? Because she's the only other woman?"

Bev's nose wrinkled, clearly projecting her feelings. "I don't think Mandy has what it takes. Not like Lauren did. She's a good, capable candidate… but she doesn't have that extra luster. And I don't think she'd ever promise not to have children. With someone like that, who would eventually leave you in the lurch… it's better to say no now than to pick her up and then be scrambling to fill her position another year down the line. We would go back to that original pool of interns to replace her. Why not just replace her before it ever becomes a problem?"

"By not hiring her in the first place."

"Yes."

"So much for equality in the workplace."

"I wish I could say it wasn't true. But society has a long way to go before we get to the point where women are not held back by childbearing and childcare. Maybe like one of those dystopian books where the children are all grown in vitro and then raised and trained by the state instead of their parents…"

Having spent much of his youth in the care of the state, Zachary didn't have much confidence in the government's ability to raise all of the children without the interference of loving parents. They would all turn out to be psychopaths.

"I really need to get back to work," Bev said, looking at her watch.

"I appreciate you spending the time with me. Before I go, would you mind getting me those time reports for the other interns?"

She froze. "I told you, that isn't going to be possible right now."

"You want to talk to a lawyer."

"I don't want to, but sometimes you have to. I can't just give you confidential company information."

Zachary worked his phone out of his pocket. "Do you have Gordon Drake's direct line?"

She stared at him without responding. Zachary waited, and she still didn't offer any help. Zachary turned his attention to his phone and found a web listing for Drake, Chase, Gould. He reached the receptionist and asked for Gordon.

"It's Zachary Goldman. He asked me to be put through to him directly."

"I don't know if Mr. Drake is in his office right now."

"Give it a try. He said his assistant would help if he wasn't in the office."

Bev stared at him as he waited for the receptionist to put him through to Gordon. Her eyes moved back and forth around the room as she tried to come up with a strategy to deal with him, and probably to figure out whether he was really calling Gordon directly to overrule her or whether he was just bluffing. Zachary gave her a pleasant smile while he waited. The receptionist put him on hold, which was a combination of easy listening music and commercials for the firm. He'd heard the same commercial about five times when the receptionist finally came back on the line.

"I'll put you through to Mr. Drake now," she said in a tone that pretended to be pleasant, but she was clearly not happy with this outsider who could just call any time he liked and get put directly through to the big boss.

There were a couple of rings, and then Gordon picked up.

"Ah, Zachary. How is it going? Are you getting everything you need?"

"Everybody has been very cooperative," Zachary assured him. His eyes were on the human resources director, her complexion pale as she looked at him. "There's just one issue. Your human resources department has concerns about releasing information to me."

"What information? We do have to protect employee privacy of course. We'd be in trouble if we just released confidential information to you. As much as I want to help you, you're not the police, and there are no court orders compelling us to turn information over to them."

"I'm looking for the time logs for the interns."

"Time logs?"

"When they clocked in and out. How many hours they were putting in. What time everyone got off the night before Lauren's accident."

"I don't see a problem with that. Give me to Beverly."

Zachary offered Bev the phone. She took it from him, her eyes wide, handling it like it was a live snake. One that might whip around and bite her at any moment. She put it up to her ear.

"Hello?" She listened for a moment to Gordon on the other end. Zachary couldn't hear that part of the conversation. "Yes, sir, everything is fine. I've been doing everything I can to help. Though I really can't understand why…"

She stopped talking and listened some more.

"Yes, sir. If you really think that's okay, but isn't that breach of confidential information? I wouldn't want to have to defend against a lawsuit for disclosing private employee information… Yes, sir. Okay. Yes. I'll see to it. Okay."

Eventually, she pulled the phone away from her ear, and after checking to make sure the call had ended, handed it back to Zachary. She swallowed and looked at him.

"It may take me a few minutes to get you everything you need. You just want the few days before Lauren died? And just the interns?"

"If I could get all of the time they've logged since they started here. It's only been a couple of months, right?"

"Yes."

"Give it all to me, then, if you could. That way I can track patterns."

"It will take me some time." She looked at her watch. "Do you want to come back after lunch, and I'll have it ready for you then?"

Zachary thought about this. He hadn't expected it to take her more than a couple of minutes to tell the computer which employees she wanted to see the timesheets for and what dates she wanted to cover. Why would she need an hour to print that out? She obviously wanted time to review the information to make sure that there was nothing that would show the company in a bad light.

"I thought you just had to tell the computer… like you did for Lauren's…"

"I know, but going back through previous pay periods is stupid on this computer. They've already been paid out for those months, so the information all gets archived, and you have to query in a different database and…" She searched for further explanation. Zachary shook his head. He was a private investigator. He knew the way that computers worked, and none of the mainstream payroll programs were going to make it complicated to print timesheets. There was no special procedure to go through to get the previous months, other than to tell it the dates you wanted and that you wanted already billed information. Whatever else she wanted to do, she wanted him out of her office for a while.

He weighed whether he should go back to Gordon again, but didn't want to press his luck. She would complain and give him a sob story about how Zachary was asking her for things that couldn't be done, that he was going beyond what he needed to for the investigation, that he was being rude or unreasonable in his demands. Zachary didn't want to risk getting on the wrong side of Gordon. For more than one reason. The investigation into Lauren's death was only part of it. Gordon had always been pleasant to Zachary and treated him with respect, trying to keep Bridget calm when she got angry with Zachary.

Gordon had been the one to call Zachary when Bridget had been kidnapped. Had called him even before the police. He had made sure that Zachary was involved in the investigation, no matter what anyone else had to say about it. He trusted that Zachary would be able to find Bridget, and Zachary had. He'd tracked her down and he'd saved her. Another day, and they wouldn't have been so lucky. Even a few more minutes… Zachary knew that the kidnapper had been trying to give her an injection before abandoning her in the remote shack in the woods. Zachary didn't have any doubt that it hadn't been a vitamin shot.

Gordon had been open and honest with the police investigator who was in charge of investigating Bridget's disappearance, protesting when the police had suspected Zachary of being complicit. He had told them that Bridget and Zachary's rocky relationship and bitter divorce had not been Zachary's fault, but Bridget's, putting the blame squarely on his own partner.

And Gordon would be the one who either kept Zachary up-to-date on Bridget's pregnancy or blocked him out. Since it was really none of Zachary's business how Bridget was doing, the only way he was going to hear anything was if Gordon had positive feelings toward him.

He got up and left Bev to whatever subterfuge she was up to, giving her a friendly nod. "I'll be back after lunch, then."

Zachary decided to have a look around the more public areas of Drake, Chase, Gould to glean what he could of the corporate culture and what other issues might be present that he wasn't aware of yet. People would be gossiping about Lauren, and gossip could provide valuable information about whether her death had merely been an accident or there was someone in particular—one of the interns or someone else altogether—who might have wanted to see Lauren dead.

There was an employee cafeteria, which no one had mentioned in their interviews. Zachary suspected that most of them probably ate at their desks, whether they bought their food in the cafeteria or somewhere else. He just hoped that the food wasn't so bad that nobody bought it there, and that was why they hadn't mentioned it.

There was no guard at the door to make sure that only employees of the company could eat there, no security passes required to get into the lines, so Zachary took a look over the offerings and got himself a small soup and a sandwich.

Far from being the bland, over-processed foods that he would see in a hospital cafeteria, the Drake, Chase, Gould cafeteria seemed to focus mostly on fresh, unprocessed foods. Lots of fresh salads, sandwiches, soups, beans, and stir fries. There were a few more processed offerings such as Jell-O dessert and Rice Krispies squares, but that was to be expected. There were also baskets of ripe fruit, granola bars, and other easy-to-grab snack foods.

Zachary looked around for a place to sit down to eat. There were lots of available seats, but he couldn't see any of the interns he had already talked to. He was pretty sure that they were still at their desks, whether they had popped downstairs for something to eat or not. Working the long, arduous hours they did, they wouldn't be willing to give up an hour, or even half an hour of wasted time sitting in the cafeteria doing nothing.

He sat at a table that had several empty chairs so that he wouldn't be sitting too close to anyone else or, hopefully, taking anyone's favorite seat without leaving an acceptable alternative. He took the lid off of the soup and was peeling the plastic wrap off of his sandwich when someone sat down beside him.

"That doesn't look like a very satisfying meal," the man said, putting down a large, well-stuffed hamburger, a carton of chocolate milk, and a chocolate pudding for dessert. The hamburger was surrounded with thick-cut fries and he had a small cup of gravy to dip them in or to pour over them. Zachary raised his eyebrows.

"I don't think I could get all of that down," he said, turning his eyes to the owner of the voice and the burger. To his surprise, it wasn't a big, overmuscled body builder, but a slim, almost skinny man with a pencil mustache.

"I can pack it away with the best of them," the man said, laughing.

Zachary shook his head. "You must have a hollow leg."

"Or two."

Zachary chuckled. "You must."

The man sat down and inhaled the fragrant steam coming off of his burger and fries. "So you're the detective who's asking questions about Lauren Barclay's death."

"Yes. Word gets around fast."

"Corporate grapevine. Faster than a speeding bullet."

Zachary took a bite of his sandwich. "Did you know Lauren?"

"Sure. Worked with her on a number of projects. She was one of the interns that I managed."

Zachary held his hand out to him. "Zachary Goldman."

"Oh, sorry. Daniel Service." Daniel shook hands with him, then dug into his meal.

"So how was she as an employee? Everybody seems to agree that she was a hard worker. Maybe at the top of the list for a permanent position."

Daniel nodded his agreement. "She was really driven, that one. And that's a good thing around here. It's a tough atmosphere for anyone who wants to take it slow or needs a long time to ramp up. Lauren got into the swing of things right away and had what it took. Very impressive."

"How are the other interns? Anyone else that measures up to her?"

Daniel ate a couple of french fries, swirling them in the cup of gravy first and then chewing them slowly.

"Maybe not quite," he admitted. "I mean, there's Bieber, and he's absolutely unmatched. No way we would want him going to another company. The others are good, don't get me wrong, they're just not... outstanding. It won't be easy to decide which of them is going to stay and which will have to go." He shrugged. "At least they've had the experience of working for Drake, Chase, Gould. I really believe there's nothing like it in the industry. It's going to be a world leader within a couple of years. Really, it is now, people just haven't recognized it."

"You think so?" Zachary thought about what he knew about the company. "I mean, it's a big company for a town like this, but on a world scale? How are you going to compete with Goldman Sachs and JP Morgan? They have thousands of employees worldwide."

"And we will too. What we're doing here is scalable. Everything is done with expansion in mind. The program the interns are in, company policies, infrastructure, communications, the health and welfare program, everything. You could take this office and replicate it in any city around the world. You could have a new office set up in days and up and running efficiently within a couple of weeks. It's brilliant."

Zachary took out his notepad and put it beside his plate, making a couple of notes.

"What can you tell me about the health and welfare program?" he asked. "Obviously, it's a huge step forward to have your employees working out in the company gym and eating in a cafeteria with its focus on healthy foods like this." He made a gesture to indicate the room and the people around them. "What else is involved? And how do these high-finance types react to being told that they have to work out a certain number of hours a week?"

Daniel chuckled. "I'm not one for organized exercise myself. It's not easy to get into the mindset that whatever you do during the day, walking to work or running back and forth all day long, isn't enough, and that you need to log a certain number of workout hours on top of that. I like to incorporate my exercise into my life, but you can't log that. But… yeah, I know it's good for me, so I do it, and I try not to whine too much about it. Some of the managers and VPs, they really think they should be excused from the workout requirements, but Mr. Drake says they knew what they were getting into when they signed on, and if they didn't like it, they shouldn't have joined the company."

"Ouch."

"Maybe they thought they would be able to get away with not working out, that it was just a throwaway clause and no one would be tracking them. But it is included in everyone's contracts, which means that Chase Gold can enforce it. Do what you promised to do, or you're out the door."

"Do you think it has made a difference in absentee rates? Is there a noticeable reduction in sick days or in people having major health problems?"

"You'd have to talk to human resources to find out what our

rates are like compared against the industry. I don't know… we still have our fair share of people with high blood pressure, heart disease, and all that. We had a VP who had a stroke a few months back. Went down right at his desk in the middle of a big deal. That really refocused management on making sure that people were logging their workouts and getting to their annual physicals. And if there was a major problem observed in their physical, they have to be seeing their regular doctor or specialist every month and bring in a signed note confirming that they have."

"And people don't complain about that?"

"Oh, they complain about it. But would you rather have people complaining or going down at their desks? Management is of the opinion that it's more important to be sure people are seeing their doctors, taking their meds, and getting in their exercise than worrying about whether they like it. You have to do what's best for the company. And for the machine to work, you need to make sure that all parts are running efficiently."

Zachary nodded. He sipped a couple of spoonfuls of soup, which was surprisingly good.

"And these retreats and team-building days that are part of the health and welfare program, what do you think of those? Is it a waste to take time away from the office? Or is it worth it?"

Daniel didn't take long to consider it. "A corporate community is very important. If you've got a bunch of politics to deal with, people who won't work with others, employees who haven't bought into the company's policies and procedures, that damages productivity. It cripples communication. If you can get everybody onside, that's worth a day or a weekend or a few days for a retreat."

"You're able to make changes like that in a day or two?"

"We're always working on it when we're here at the office too. It's not like that's the only time we're working on company productivity. But a retreat is a lot more intensive, you can make more headway with difficult cases in that setting."

Zachary had a couple more bites of his sandwich and soup, but he was about finished. He didn't have a good appetite with the meds he was on. He had to make an effort to eat enough to get back up to what his doctor would consider a healthy weight.

"You like working here?"

Daniel gave him a broad smile. "There's nowhere like Drake, Chase, Gould. It's a privilege to work here."

He'd only spent a few minutes of the hour Bev had asked for in the cafeteria, and Zachary was interested in seeing a little more of the employees away from their desks. He found his way to the on-site gym. While he wasn't exactly inconspicuous, with everyone else in their workout gear, he tried to look natural and relaxed. He had been given permission by one of the owners of the company to go where he wanted to and ask the questions he needed to. There was no reason for him to feel like he was doing something sneaky.

The gym was not big. There were no running track or squash courts, but there were plenty of stationary bikes and ellipticals, treadmills, weight machines, and some free weights at the ends of the room. Everything the employees needed to stay in shape. Not every machine was occupied, but it was a busy place over the lunch hour.

The music that was being piped into the room, with a quick, pounding beat, was interrupted momentarily by a recorded message, praising the employees for being there to take care of their health, giving a short message about getting good nutrition and sleep, and ending with the phrase 'better health…' which the employees responded to with 'better wealth!' It was an automatic response, not emphatic, but also not with eye-rolling and a groan. The way they answered immediately, in unison, reminded Zachary of some of the church services that he'd been forced to attend growing up, living with foster families who were devout, or who dragged him along for a funeral or Easter Mass. Never Christmas, because he was usually at Bonnie Brown or the hospital Christmas

Eve. He couldn't face Christmas Eve with a family since the fire that had devastated his life, and he certainly couldn't have gone to a service with lighted candles.

But the services that had required certain responses from the congregation always fascinated him. He tried to predict when they were going to prompt a response and to memorize the appropriate replies. He'd never had any particularly spiritual feelings about the practice, he just found it immensely satisfying to be part of a group and to know what response was expected of him. There were few other times when his behavior was explicitly scripted so that he knew exactly what he was supposed to say or do. He always felt like he was doing the wrong thing and was going to be caught and punished for it. Probably because all too often, that was the case.

The music started up again, and Zachary just watched the employees for a few minutes, their legs and arms moving with the beat of the music, faces shining with sweat, focused and intent on what they were doing.

"It's Detective Zachary again," a voice observed.

He looked over to the nearest treadmill and saw Blair Bieber-stein, in all his hyperactive squirrel glory, knobby knees showing under long shiny shorts.

"Oh. Mr. Bieberstein. Good to see you again."

"Are you here to work out? No, probably not, because you're not an employee and you're not dressed for a workout. You know that the rest of us have to put in workout time every day? They want to keep us healthy and happy." He kept up a brisk walk on the treadmill, not quite running, but definitely hustling.

"Yes, I heard about that. How do you feel about being forced to work out?"

"It's good. It shows that the company cares about us and our health. They don't want us to just have a heart attack or stroke one day. They're trying to keep everyone in good shape. Healthy employees mean a healthy bottom line."

"Better health…"

"Better wealth," Bieberstein chimed in, and grinned. "You got it. And I'm all for better wealth, aren't you?"

"I am…" Zachary said slowly, "but I wouldn't want to give up my lifestyle for it. Working the crazy hours you guys are… I don't think I could ever do that."

"You give up some time on the front end so that you can enjoy yourself more later in life." Bieberstein shrugged. "Either way, you want to be healthy to enjoy it, right?"

Zachary looked at a few of the other employees working out, then returned his eyes to Bieberstein. "But are you?" he asked. "You look… exhausted. Pale like you haven't seen the sun in a month, and your eyes are red and have bags under them. I know you're competing for the permanent positions but are you sure you're not pushing it a little too hard?"

"Best shape I've ever been in," Bieberstein declared. "Never did any sports or exercise before. Exercise is better than sleep. Refreshes your brain and gets it revved back up again when you start to get tired."

"Do you take anything to help you stay awake? Caffeine? Energy drinks?"

"Sure. Everybody around here does."

"Did Lauren?"

"As much as anyone else, yeah. Everybody has to do something to stay awake. It's like being in the army. When they had to stay awake for long periods of time and still be alert, then they gave them amphetamines. Tried out different drugs on them to see what worked best. Where do you think meth came from?"

"Meth?"

"It was developed by the army to help keep troops alert and focused when they couldn't sleep. That's what it's for."

"You use meth?"

Bieberstein gave him a grin. "I didn't say that."

"Would you consider it?"

"Maybe. Under the right circumstances. Using it the right

way, like a prescription. Why shouldn't we use every tool at our disposal?"

"Because it's illegal and dangerous."

Bieberstein kept up his brisk pace. "Did you find everything you were looking for?"

"I wondered… everyone seems to act like this is a pretty good place to work. You talk about them in positive ways. You seem to like your coworkers alright. Here's this company that has a great health care program… but what about the other side of the coin?"

"The seamy underbelly?" Bieberstein asked in a joking voice.

"Well… *is* it the perfect place to work? Would you recommend it to all of your friends? What do you really think of it?"

Bieberstein walked, his feet pounding in time with the music. He shook his head. "It's no utopia," he admitted. "But when you apply to work at a place like this, you've got to know that. The high finance community is known for being pretty harsh. It would be like applying to be an air traffic controller and thinking it wouldn't be stressful. Or like training to be a doctor and thinking that you could just keep whatever office hours you felt like, right from the start. You know what you're getting into."

"So tell me a little about that side of it," Zachary suggested, finding a spot where he could lean against the wall to talk to Bieberstein, and be out of the way of other employees coming and going.

Bieberstein considered, looking up at the ceiling, but miraculously not losing his stride. "Where to start… there's a lot of egos here. Everybody thinks they're the best. You got managers and other bosses who think that you only work for them, and if you don't get something done on their arbitrary schedule, look out. I don't think I've ever been anywhere that I've been cussed out so much. I've had grown men totally lose control and full-out scream at me, red-faced, trying to shame me in front of everybody else. Just because of some arbitrary deadline, or because they didn't like my conclusion—even though it was right."

"Yikes. I think that would be it for me. I'd be out the door."

"I'm a pretty hard guy to offend. I look at idiots like that and think, 'what a schmuck,' and then go on and do my own thing. But the girls, and some of the other interns, I've seen them break down. Tears, talking about quitting, harming themselves, everything. I hate seeing girls cry, I really do."

Zachary nodded. It was something he couldn't bear either. He never knew what to do. And he had a lot of women cry around him. Not because he was nasty to them, but because they came to him with their stories of heartbreak and loss, asking for his help when they were at their most vulnerable. Like Barbara, crying while she told him about finding Lauren dead in the bathtub.

"Sometimes, I think they actually do it on purpose. Like they want to break us down before they build us up. Like they're seriously trying to hurt us as much as possible. Completely destroy everyone's egos, and then you have something to work with. Once you've reduced someone to mush, then you can sculpt them into what you want."

Zachary frowned, thinking about it. Knowing Gordon as he did, he couldn't imagine him approving of anything like that going on in his company. Did he know about it? He had always been calm around Zachary, even with the problems that he and Bridget had, and Gordon had always been the first to give a compliment or register approval. He had welcomed Zachary at Chase Gold, hadn't he? He wouldn't have done such a thing if he thought that Zachary might discover abusive behavior toward employees.

"I'm used to people not liking me," Bieberstein said conversationally. "I get on people's nerves. But you know, I don't care. I would rather be in a place like this, where they can use my talents and I can spend my days playing with numbers than in any other place where they are nice but expect good social behavior in return. I can't be bothered."

Zachary nodded, chuckling a little. Bieberstein was nothing, if not unfiltered. He would always be someone who would attract criticism for his hyperactive, in-your-face communication style.

"And then there's the hazing."

"Oh? What kind of hazing?"

"Same kind of thing that goes on in any closed society," Bieberstein said with a shrug. He hit a button on the treadmill console to check his progress, and kept going. "They want you to earn your position. You'll be loyal to the society if you had to work to get into it. And if you know things about other people and they know things about you. Shared secrets, ordeals, proving yourself. You know."

"I know what hazing is… but it isn't usually something you see in corporate culture. Usually military or college. I don't think I've ever heard of it in a company like this."

"It's the same thing, though."

"So you went through hazing? What did you have to do?"

"Lots of drinking involved. Running messages from one place to another. Doing stupid, dangerous stuff just because it's on a list of things to do. Like a scavenger hunt."

"What kind of dangerous stuff?"

Bieberstein looked sideways at him. "That's the kind of stuff that you promise never to tell. You have to keep other people's secrets, and they have to keep yours. You show that you're willing to go above and beyond what would be considered reasonable. You make them believe that your soul is theirs and you would never tell."

"So you're not going to give me an example?"

"You don't need an example. You said you know what hazing is. So you already know the kinds of things I'm talking about."

"And was this… who was in charge of this hazing? Do the owners know about it? Is it just one department or the whole company? Does everyone go through this? Or just the interns?"

"Ah." Bieberstein raised one finger. "I neglected to say, there were masks, hoods, and blindfolds involved. So you couldn't identify who was there and who wasn't. You don't know who you can talk to, because they might be watching you, reporting on your activities."

Zachary let out his breath. Hazing? Was Bieberstein pulling his leg, or was it the truth? Had he been pranked by some of his fellow interns? Did the bullying come from his direct manager or someone else? Bieberstein's expression was open and unconcerned, untroubled by what had happened or by the fact that he had revealed so much to Zachary.

The treadmill gave a beep, and Bieberstein leaned on the handrails as he read the display, relaxing his posture so that Zachary saw how exhausted he was. He might comply with the company policies and declare that the exercise gave him the energy and clear mind that he needed for his work, but he didn't look alert and refreshed after his powerwalk. He looked like he was ready to pass out.

Bieberstein punched a few buttons on the console and, as it started to slow, held on to the bars and let out a deep sigh. Then suddenly he clenched his hands tightly around the bars and let out an animal-like howl. Zachary took a step away from him, startled and confused. Bieberstein's feet stopped moving on the treadmill, and that meant that the treadmill, still moving, pulled the lower part of his body toward the end of the treadmill while his upper body remained anchored by his clenched hands to the handrails.

Zachary couldn't do anything, had no idea what was going on and what Bieberstein was trying to do. Was this some kind of ritual? A bizarre dismount?

For a moment, Bieberstein's body was suspended over the treadmill, supported by his hands, while his feet dragged to the end of the treadmill, and then his arms sagged and he fell face-down onto the treadmill.

Zachary tried to pull Bieberstein off of the treadmill when his brain processed the fact that Bieber had passed out, but his body was slow, his feet not responding to his brain's directive to jump in and help. In the time it took for him to get into a position where he could grab Bieberstein and try to pull him off of the machinery, Bieber had been pulled to the side and got a nasty gash on his head as it collided more than once with the side of the treadmill. He hadn't been wearing the emergency shut-off clip that would automatically stop the treadmill as soon as he fell, so the machine continued to run through its cool-down routine.

Zachary managed to grab one of Bieberstein's elbows and jerk him off of the running treadmill. It was a good thing that Bieberstein was a small man. Zachary had a hard time wrenching the dead weight off of the machine.

There were shouts and exclamations around him, people gasping and asking what had happened. Zachary tried to move Bieberstein into a natural position on his back so that he could be examined. He expected Bieberstein's eyes to open, confused by his momentary loss of consciousness, but instead Bieberstein's body was rigid and started to shake wildly while Zachary tried to get him into position. A full-on tonic-clonic seizure.

"Someone should call an ambulance," Zachary said, releasing his grip on Bieberstein and hoping that he wouldn't hit his head on anything else while in the midst of the seizure. Someone reached over and shut off the treadmill so that it wouldn't present a further hazard. People gathered around, talking and making suggestions. One man brought over a small suitcase and opened it up, and Zachary saw the small v-fib machine that Bev had mentioned.

"I don't think you need that," Zachary said. "It's a seizure, not a heart attack."

"You don't know that. Are you a doctor?"

"Uh… no."

"I've been trained on this thing. It will tell us if he needs to be shocked or not. We just have to stick the pads on him."

"But he's…" Zachary motioned to Bieberstein, at a loss for words. How exactly were they going to do anything while he was in the midst of the seizure?

The other man moved in and attempted to pull Bieberstein's shirt up over his head, which did not work with him thrashing around, and Zachary wasn't about to try to hold his arms still to assist with the operation.

"We need scissors," the other man said, "so that we can cut his shirt off. I need to be able to put the sticky pads on his skin."

"You're not getting close to him with scissors while he's having a seizure," Zachary warned, prepared to defend his position. He might not be a doctor or have much experience with seizures, but he knew the recommended approach—leave the person alone other than trying to make sure he couldn't hurt himself while seizing. No forcing a spoon into his mouth or using sharp implements to cut off his shirt.

There were noises of agreement from the rest of the employees gathering around. The man looked angry.

"I'm the one who's been trained in first aid. How many of the rest of you have been certified?"

A number of them raised their hands, taking a bit of the wind out of his sails.

"Has someone called 9-1-1?" Zachary asked, looking around at them. Some of them had their phones out to video the episode or were tapping away, maybe tweeting the moment, but not one had his phone to his ear talking to an emergency dispatcher. Zachary pointed at a woman with a bright blue halter top. "You. Please call 9-1-1."

She rolled her eyes, looking put out.

"It's just Bieberstein," one of the onlookers joked. There was a ripple of laughter, but then the disapproval that was leveled at the jokester made everyone sober up.

The woman tapped on her phone and held it up to her ear. Zachary turned his attention back to Bieberstein and left her to the call, watching for any sign that the seizure was slackening. His head wound was bleeding, the movement of his seizure spreading the blood around grotesquely, making it look much worse than it was. Zachary had seen enough childhood mishaps to know that scalp wounds always bled profusely. He wasn't going to be able to press anything over the wound until the seizure stopped.

"They're on their way," the woman informed Zachary. "They shouldn't be too long. We're pretty close to the fire station."

Every second that ticked past seemed to take forever. By the time the paramedics got there, the seizure had stopped and Zachary was pressing a towel over Bieberstein's head wound. Once the seizure stopped, he could see that there was something wrong with Bieberstein's arm too. It was bent where it shouldn't be bent, and while there was no bone sticking out through the skin, it was pretty obvious that it was broken. Zachary breathed deeply, trying to slow the wild beating of his heart. He was feeling nauseated, regretting that he'd just eaten. Seizures, blood, and broken bones were not exactly his forte. He preferred to stay out of the way and let other people step in when something like that happened, but he wasn't about to let the determined first aider bully his way in and end up cutting something other than Bieberstein's shirt with a pair of scissors.

Bieberstein's breathing was even and when Zachary had felt ineptly for a pulse, he'd been able to feel the beats of Bieberstein's heart racing away under his fingertips. No need for CPR or the v-fib machine.

"Make some room," one of the paramedics advised, motioning the crowd back. "Who here saw what happened?"

Zachary made a motion with his free hand. "I was talking to him."

"Great, why don't you walk us through it?"

Zachary did the best he could to describe each movement, not wanting to miss anything that might require special treatment. The paramedics could see that Bieberstein was bleeding, had at least one broken bone, and was no longer seizing. What else they could tell on a quick visual examination, Zachary wasn't sure. He moved out of the way so that one of the paramedics could get in to sneak a look under the towel. He grunted and nodded, and the two of them worked through an examination of Bieberstein.

"Anyone know if he has epilepsy?"

There were head shakes from the crowd. No one offered anything. The paramedics looked for a medical bracelet or necklace, but didn't find anything. One of them took a few long seconds to examine Bieberstein's arms, and Zachary realized after a delay that they were checking for needle marks.

"Has he taken any drugs? Does anyone know if he takes anything?"

More head shakes. Zachary spoke in a low voice, not wanting to spread Bieberstein's business to all of the spectators.

"Caffeine for sure. He was acting really jacked up earlier. I don't know if he was on anything, or just hyperactive. He's probably short on sleep, I don't know if he might have taken anything else… he was talking about meth, but he didn't say that he took any, he was just saying… that it was intended for mental alertness, and wasn't dangerous if it was taken like a prescription, like they would use for soldiers…"

"Then it could be an overdose. We'd better get him in and have his blood levels checked. We'll need the heart monitor," the man told his partner, who nodded agreement.

"I don't know that he *did* take anything," Zachary warned, not wanting to mislead them. "I'm just saying we were talking about it…"

"That's good enough for me. We'll take him in. Does someone here want to come along? Know who to contact in case of an emergency?"

No one volunteered. The paramedic looked at Zachary.

"I just met him today," Zachary said, his face heating. "This was only our second conversation."

"Fair enough. We'll see if he has an ICE contact on his phone." The paramedics looked around. Someone found a phone on the floor beside the treadmill and handed it over to them. There was a crack in the screen, but it still appeared to be operable. The paramedic did a couple of clicks and swipes to bring up Bieberstein's emergency ID screen. "Okay, thanks for your help. We'd better get him in to get checked out."

Zachary had been hoping that Bieberstein would wake up before the paramedics took him away, just to reassure him that he was going to be okay, and that he hadn't just had a seizure and slipped into a coma, from which he would never awake.

Everybody watched the paramedics get Bieberstein onto a gurney and remove him from the gym, murmuring quietly to each other. No one jumped immediately back into their workouts. One of the health and welfare commercials played, and while a couple of people said 'better wealth' at the appropriate juncture, no one seemed to have much enthusiasm for it.

When Zachary checked the time on his own phone, he saw that more than an hour had elapsed since he had seen Bev, so hopefully she'd had enough time to get the timesheets for the rest of the interns printed off for him. He went back to the human resources floor and knocked, but that didn't raise any response. He called the main switchboard number again, and got the receptionist to put him through to Bev. Her line rang a number of times before going to voicemail.

He muttered to himself and left her a message. But he didn't have any appetite for standing there in the elevator lobby waiting for her to pick up his message and let him in. She knew when he was supposed to be getting back, and she should have been ready for his call. If she had decided to go off for a late lunch while he hung around waiting for the information that he had requested…

Zachary went back up to the main reception desk. The receptionist gave him a wary look. Zachary did his best to paste a friendly smile on his face.

"Hi. I'm trying to track down Bev in human resources. She doesn't seem to be answering her phone. She was expecting me."

"You'll have to wait until she can get back to you. I can't do anything from here to make her answer her phone. I know that we did have a medical emergency, and she's probably dealing with getting in contact with family members or providing medical records. You'll just have to wait."

"I know there was a medical emergency, I was there when it happened—"

"Then you know that I'm not just trying to put you off. You'll have to wait until it's been dealt with." Her tone was stern, brooking no argument, and Zachary couldn't argue that it was unreasonable to make him wait while they dealt with Bieberstein's care and his family.

He went over to the reception chair he had waited in that morning and sat down once more.

14

Zachary decided it was a good time for him to check on his email messages and go over the notes he had made so far in his notebook. There were a few inquiries in his email that would need to be followed up on. There were always more cases to look into and work to be done. He immersed himself in the notes he had been making about Drake, Chase, Gould and Lauren's death.

Was he getting distracted by the work environment at Chase Gold? Was it really relevant to his investigation?

If Lauren had simply slipped and hit her head in the tub, then it had nothing to do with the company. Was it even remotely likely that one of the other interns had gone to her apartment and killed her because they were fighting over the same permanent position? He felt their desperation to get one of those coveted spots, to beat each other out to get the one remaining opening. Was it a matter of life and death for them? Would they really go so far as to harm the other competitors in order to get it?

Of course, with Bieberstein's accident, maybe they were back to two openings again. A seizure wasn't usually fatal, he knew, and even though Bieberstein hadn't woken up before the ambulance had taken him to the hospital, he would probably wake up with only the concerns of his broken arm and lacerated scalp to worry about, and everything else would go back to normal. Unless the management decided that, like a woman who might get pregnant at any moment, someone who had seizures was too much of a risk for the company to hire. They wouldn't have to fire him for his medical disability. They wouldn't have to put him on leave. He was only there in a temporary position, so all they had to do was to make the decision not to hire him; he was too much of a risk.

That would be good luck for the other interns.

But was it just luck? Was it possible that someone had drugged him or done something to cause the seizure?

Who would kill off all of the competition for a permanent job opening? There were jobs to be had at other companies. And no one could just keep eliminating the other interns in the competition without making everybody suspicious. Two of the interns had now fallen victim to accidents. Any more, and people would start to get suspicious. Two could just be bad luck. Three would arouse suspicions.

So who was the next in line for those positions? If two positions had now opened up, then the next two remaining interns could get in. He couldn't picture Mandy Pryor as a murderer. He knew that you couldn't tell by looking at a person whether or not they had what it took to kill someone. Or multiple someones. The serial killers were always charming, easy to make friends with, seemingly harmless.

He resisted the urge to think of Teddy Archuro. Of Pat's words that he would never do anything. *He's been around for a long time. He's harmless.*

But Archuro hadn't been safe. He'd been around for years and he had been killing for years, managing to stay below the radar. Everyone thought him charming, a perfectly nice guy. Entirely trustworthy.

Zachary felt himself sliding back into darkness. Seeing Archuro looming over him. Feeling the drugs take hold of him so that he couldn't fight back. Teddy Archuro's greedy eyes and crooning voice as he began his sadistic rituals, telling Zachary what he was going to do, wielding his weapons while Zachary lay there lifeless, but conscious, unable to even protest.

"Zachary?"

He heard the voice, but couldn't believe that it was real. How had he slid from flashing back to the assault by Teddy to hearing Bridget's voice? What did *she* have to do with the memory? There was no connection other than that Bridget too had been abducted. They had both had to face opponents who had been intent on killing them.

"Zachary!"

He jolted at the second call, looking up from his notebook to see Bridget standing there staring at him. One hand was over her lower abdomen. He couldn't tell by looking at her that she was pregnant, but for some reason her unconscious reaction to seeing him was to cover the baby bump, to hide her pregnancy from him or protect her baby from his eyes.

She looked better than she had the last time he had seen her. She had been so nauseated that she had looked like she was on chemo again. Her color was back. The shape of her body had not yet changed and her slim form still fit into the stylish professional dress she wore. She didn't look happy to see him there, but when was the last time she had been happy to see him?

Other than when he had rescued her from certain death, of course.

"What are you doing here?" Bridget demanded.

"Oh… uh… Bridget."

She looked around, as if expecting someone to jump in and explain to her what her ex-husband was doing sitting there in the lobby of her current partner's company. Or was she looking for an audience? Or making sure that there were no witnesses?

There was no one else sitting in the waiting area. Only the receptionist looking up from her work to see what was going on.

"I asked you what you're doing here! I can't believe this. You said that you would stop. You said that you wouldn't track me, wouldn't show up in the places I go to. First I see you at the gas station, and now here! At Gordon's work! And don't try telling me you're interviewing for a job or something stupid like that. I'm going to call the police and report you for stalking. This is just too much!"

She pulled out her phone and tapped the screen, glaring at him, just daring him to fight back. Zachary supposed she expected him to leave, to run away from Gordon's office and never return. But he had a legitimate reason to be there. There was no restraining order against him, so Bridget couldn't claim that he was breaking the law by being there. She would just have to accept that he had the right to live in the same town as she did and to occasionally bump into her around town.

So he just looked at her, waiting for her to make the next move. Bridget put her phone to her ear, looking at him, her expression pinched and sour. Zachary leaned back in his chair, trying to look comfortable and unmoved by her threats. He looked back down at his notebook, trying to pick up his earlier thread.

Not Mandy. Statistically speaking, serial killers were hardly ever women.

Though poisoners were more often women than men. Maybe she hadn't meant to kill. Maybe she only intended to disable the competition. Maybe Lauren was only supposed to sleep too long, riling her bosses by not getting back to the office when she was due. And Bieberstein hadn't died. It might be dangerous for him to have a seizure while walking on a treadmill, but no one could have foreseen that that was where he would be when the attack hit him. Or maybe they could. Maybe he was on that treadmill every day at the same time. People like Bieberstein often had strict routines, so it wasn't a stretch that he would have insisted on doing the same workout at the same time every day.

Maybe neither one was intended to die, but only to be removed from the running for the permanent positions.

And what about the other interns? If it were one of them, would Zachary be able to figure out which? They all had the same motive. They all had opportunity, working closely together in the same office. He hadn't seen their desks, but he knew from experience that students and interns were likely all jammed like cattle into small cubicles. They would have access to each other's water bottles. Someone took a run to the restroom or the coffee machine, and their bottle could be spiked. Or one intern could bring coffee to the others, spiking one of them in the kitchen. Or he could be poisoning all of them by degrees, and Lauren and Bieberstein were merely the first to succumb, due to lower body weight or faster metabolism.

What could they have been poisoned with? A sedative? Something known to cause seizures? Was it intended to kill or only to make the other interns less productive and competent?

"Gordon?"

Zachary looked up from his notepad as Bridget's call apparently connected. Her face was flushed. She did not appreciate the fact that Zachary was unconcerned by her phone call.

"Zachary is here! He's in the reception area."

She listened to his response, her mouth tightening and going white around the edges. She was still staring daggers at Zachary, angry that he was there in her domain and furious that he wasn't cowed by her appearance. If he were there just to spot her or to stalk Gordon, then he would have been worried by her discovering him there. He would have protested and given excuses and run away. But for once Zachary didn't feel the need to justify himself.

"He can't do that. He's not supposed to be here. He's not supposed to be anywhere around me. You need to get rid of him."

Zachary couldn't hear Gordon's responses, but he could imagine them. Reassuring her that Zachary wasn't there because of anything to do with Bridget. That he wasn't there because he was harassing Gordon. He wasn't there trying to talk Gordon into stepping aside and giving Zachary the chance to woo Bridget once more.

Zachary would have loved that. It wasn't going to happen, of course, but if Gordon had been frightened off by Bridget getting pregnant, if he were the type who didn't want to be responsible for a child, Zachary would have been only too happy to step back in and take care of Bridget and her child. It didn't matter to him that the baby wasn't his. He would go back to her in a second.

Bridget pulled the phone away from her ear and turned it off, her thumb tightening convulsively over the hardware button. She didn't tell Zachary what Gordon had said to her. She didn't walk away or try again to bully him into leaving. She just stood there looking at him.

15

Gordon walked into the reception area. He gave Bridget a squeeze around the shoulders. "Hello, my dear. Why don't we all go to my office where we can have this discussion privately?"

"I don't care who hears it," Bridget snapped.

When Zachary and Bridget had been together, Bridget had always kept her fights private, or confined to certain close friends. She dropped caustic comments to Zachary with a vicious smile he came to dread, but kept anything further private. But once they had separated, the gloves came off. The more witnesses to her disparagement, the better.

"This is my office. A certain level of decorum would be appreciated," Gordon told her.

Bridget didn't argue with that. Gordon twitched his head at Zachary to follow, and they all took the short walk down the corridor to Gordon's large, bright, corner office. He ushered them in and shut the door.

Rather than sitting behind his desk with the two of them standing or sitting in front of it, Gordon motioned to a small grouping of chairs and a couch on the opposite end of his office.

He sat down with Bridget on the couch and Zachary sank down into an upholstered chair.

"He is not allowed to be here," Bridget insisted.

"As I said, he is here with my permission. He is investigating the death of a young woman who worked here as an intern." Gordon's face was appropriately sober.

"You hired him?"

"No, I did not. But I do not object to him looking into it. We have nothing to hide. Let him reassure her family and friends that there was nothing they could have done to prevent it and that it was, in fact, just a tragic accident."

"What else would it be?" Bridget looked at Zachary, sneering, "You think it was murder?"

"Bridget," Gordon reprimanded gently. "Who did you go to when you thought there was something suspicious about Robin's death?"

She pressed her lips together as if she didn't want to remember a moment of weakness.

"And who did I go to when you disappeared?" Gordon went on. "Zachary is a good investigator. I wasn't expecting you to come by today or for him to be in the lobby, or I would have called to warn you ahead of time. I'm sorry for any distress this has caused you."

Bridget was silent.

"Why were you sitting in the lobby?" Gordon asked Zachary curiously. "You weren't waiting to see me, were you?"

"No. I'm still waiting for those reports from human resources. Bev said it would take an hour to get them together, but now she's not available, so I'm just waiting for her to get everything sorted out."

"Bev is 'not available'?"

Zachary shrugged. "There was an accident in the gym over the lunch hour. I'm told that she's dealing with the hospital or his family on that, which of course takes precedence over handing over the reports to me."

"An accident. I'm afraid I've been out of pocket. What accident?"

"Blair Bieberstein. He had a seizure while working out on the treadmill. Fell on the machine while it was still running, cut open his scalp and broke his arm."

"Good heavens. Is he okay?"

"He didn't wake up before the paramedics took him away, so I don't know any more than that. I imagine Bev will be able to give you an update."

"Just a moment." Gordon walked over to his desk and hit a button on the phone. He gave instructions to his assistant to put Bev straight through if she happened to call, then returned to the couch to sit down by Bridget. He patted her knee absently, frowning. "You were there?" he asked Zachary.

"Yes. I was talking to him when he went down."

Gordon shook his head. "What a bizarre accident. I wasn't aware that he had a seizure disorder."

Zachary shrugged. "It didn't come up in our conversation," he said lightly. "I got the impression from talking to him that he is… neurodiverse… and people who are wired differently are more likely to have seizure disorders. But I don't know anything about his health. Bev said that your company does employee physicals before hiring anyone permanently, but not the temporary positions like interns. So there wouldn't have been any reason for it to come up, unless he happened to talk to someone about it."

"Well, it sounds like that is a policy that needs to be revisited. I will bring it up, once we know how Blair is doing."

"If he does have a seizure disorder, would that stop you from hiring him for the full-time position?"

"Oh, no. If he has the skills that we need, an occasional health problem like epilepsy shouldn't come into it."

Zachary would withhold judgment on that. While Gordon seemed as open and generous as ever, Zachary was beginning to have some concerns about Drake, Chase, Gould, and he doubted that Gordon could be unaware of all of the bullying, hazing, or overtime issues.

"If you don't have anything you want to discuss with me, I guess I'll let you go back to waiting for Bev," Gordon told Zachary. "Or if that's the only thing you're waiting for, she could certainly email them to you when she gets back to her office. You don't need to wait around for them."

"I'll give it a bit longer." Zachary stood up. "And there may be issues that I need to pursue after today…"

"Really? Well, whatever you need, of course. Just let me know. Do you have my cell number?"

"No."

Gordon got up to get a business card from his desk for Zachary. He clapped Zachary on the shoulder in a friendly goodbye.

"Zachary *is* investigating this matter," he told Bridget in a calm, detached voice. "I am sorry that you ran into each other accidentally, but I'm sure it won't be an ongoing problem. You wanted to see me, my dear?"

Bridget wasn't quite willing to let it go at that. "You know what he's going to do, don't you? He's going to dig up anything he can that throws you or your company in a bad light, and then he's going to publicize it far and wide. He's trying to destroy the company you've built, all out of petty jealousy."

Gordon spread his hands wide. "I have nothing to hide. I am not the least bit concerned about what he might find in the course of the investigation."

Zachary eventually left the building without the additional timesheets for the interns. He didn't know where Bev had disappeared to, but he eventually got tired of waiting and left her a message before heading home. It had been an interesting day and he needed to ponder on what he had heard before he was sure what to think of it.

Once settled at home, he called Heather, his older sister. They had only recently been reunited and he was still building a relationship with her. It was a strange feeling, knowing someone and yet not knowing them. He knew her and her personality from when he was little, before the family was split up, but he hadn't been in contact with her during all of the intervening decades, and she had grown up and had experiences that had changed her. Every now and then, he caught a glimpse of the old Heather, like the sun coming out from behind the clouds. But then the moment would pass, and he'd be looking at a stranger again.

But he was trying, and so was she.

"Hi, Zachary."

"Hi. How's it going?" He forced himself to start with an inquiry about her health and some small talk, rather than launching directly into the reason he had called. She wasn't just some contractor he had hired; she was his sister, and he needed to take the time.

"Really good. When am I going to see you again?"

"Uh… I don't know right now. We'll have to set something up."

"Yeah. I'd really like to see you again."

"Maybe… next weekend, if I'm not too busy with this case?"

"You got a big new case?"

"Well… I don't know whether it's going anywhere, but it will take some time before I know. Maybe something, maybe nothing."

"What kind of case?"

"Accidental death."

"An insurance case? Are you doing accident reconstruction?"

"No. Someone who thinks… maybe it wasn't so accidental."

"Hmm. One of those. What do you think?"

"Too early to tell."

"Okay." She obviously recognized that he wasn't going to give her any details. It was still confidential; he didn't want word of the investigation getting out to Lauren's family or the media. It needed to stay under wraps until he had a better idea of what he was dealing with. "So what else is going on in your life?" she inquired. "Anything interesting?"

He thought fleetingly of Bridget and her pregnancy and running into her at Gordon's office. And Gordon's connection with his current case. So far, he hadn't told anyone else about those details. Other than Kenzie. He had told Kenzie about Bridget's pregnancy the day they had broken up. He'd been so shocked with the news that he'd had to tell someone.

"Well, I've had a few things come into my inbox, and I was wondering whether you wanted to help with some skip traces."

"Sure!" Heather's voice was warm and eager. Zachary had been training her on some of the basic detecting skills he had learned over the years, and she was enjoying it. She hadn't had a hobby or a job in all of the time that she'd been married, and she needed something to keep herself occupied now that she was an empty-nester and was recovering from events that had kept her a near-recluse for so many years.

"Great. I'll send you some names and details, and you can see what you can find. That would be a real help. Keep track of your time and bill me."

"It really doesn't seem like I should get paid for it. I'm just playing at being a detective."

"You're not playing, you're doing actual detective work. So you should get paid for it. If you were working for any of my competitors, you'd get paid for it. I don't want you leaving me to go to someone who gives you a better deal."

Heather laughed. Zachary knew she wouldn't even consider it. But maybe in a few years, she'd have the confidence to go somewhere else. And if she did, that was good for her. He'd be happy. Until then, he was happy to use her for some of his overflow work. He could take on more than he could otherwise, and help her out while he was at it. A win-win.

"Well, feel free to shoot them my way. I'll see what I can track down."

Zachary nodded to himself. That would clear out some of the work in his inbox. "That's a big help to me. Let me know if you need any help with getting your license, right?"

"I will. So far, it's just paperwork. I keep worrying someone is going to show up at my door and ask me who I think I'm kidding. Me, a private investigator? Whoever would have thought?"

"You'll make a good investigator. You relate well to people. You're interested in solving puzzles. That's all you need. It isn't like on TV, you don't need to carry a gun and drink hard and challenge organized crime figures. A lot of it is just computer work. Knowing where to look for the information you need."

"I suppose. Have you talked to Tyrrell lately?"

"Uh… no. It's been a little bit. I'll have to get to him soon. Maybe we should invite him for next weekend."

"That would be nice."

"I could bring some doughnuts?"

"Sure. Of course."

Zachary wasn't sure if she planned to bring Grant. Zachary and Tyrrell wouldn't be bringing along dates, but it would be rude to ask her to leave her husband at home. Especially when they were growing so much closer to each other than they had been in the previous years of their marriage. Grant was a nice guy and Zachary got along with him okay.

Maybe one day, he would have a girlfriend to bring to dinner with his siblings. And Tyrrell should be dating. Zachary couldn't see any reason for him to be holding back.

One day, maybe they would all have happy families.

He thought longingly of Bridget and her unborn child. The child that he had hoped for while they had been together. And of Kenzie, giving up on him. It wasn't her fault. He had driven her away. He had pushed her until she had finally given in.

But someday. Maybe.

He had another call to make, and he knew it wouldn't go as well as the call with Heather. He kept putting it off, telling himself that he had other things he had to get done before that. But he knew that he was just procrastinating because he didn't like the job at hand.

Eventually, he forced himself to stop puttering around with less important tasks and called Kenzie's number. One of the only numbers that he knew without looking it up or using his phone directory.

It rang a few times, and he wondered if she was just going to let it go to voicemail. She probably didn't want to talk to him. Not now, when she was out of his life. He wasn't sure if he should leave her a voicemail. Probably, if he ever wanted to get an answer. Or send her an email, but that might just end up in her spam folder.

"Zachary." Kenzie sighed.

"Uh, hi. I'm sorry to bother you, but—"

"I'll call you when I have anything to tell you. I do know your number. And if I didn't, it's on the form."

"No, it wasn't about that. I know you'll get me the information when it's released. This is completely unrelated, and you're the only one I could think of to call. I don't really know any medical doctors…"

"Aside from the ones who prescribe you your meds?"

Zachary winced at her sarcastic tone. "Uh… right, I guess so. But I don't know if they would have any insight into this…"

"Well, you've got me on the phone, so you might as well ask. What is it?"

"I had a request come in from a doctor who does organ transplants. He wants someone to investigate potential recipients. Weed out the ones who are a bad risk for transplants. You know, alcoholics who are waiting for a liver transplant. People who engage in high-risk sports. Things like that."

She was silent. Zachary gave her some time to think about it before prompting her. "Kenzie?"

"Why would you ask me about that?"

"Uh… I don't know. I just figured that being with the Medical Examiner's office, you would have some insight into things like organ transplant and risk management. Your education is recent, so you could maybe tell me what you think of the ethics of something like this that an older doctor wouldn't be up to speed on…"

There was another silence. At least she wasn't railing on him like Bridget would if he asked her something that was out of line, but because she said nothing, Zachary wasn't sure what the problem was or how to fix it.

"Is there someone else I should talk to?" he asked. "Maybe you know a doctor or professor who would be interested in talking to me?"

"I just want to know why you picked *me* to ask about it."

"Just… what I said. I figured you'd know something about it."

"Is this something to do with my dad?"

Zachary was floored. He sat there with his mouth open, trying to formulate an answer. Kenzie rarely even mentioned her parents. He knew that they were both still living, but she didn't spend much time with her family, even on holidays, and didn't like to talk about them. He didn't think that she'd had a bad childhood, but for some reason, she just wasn't in close contact with her parents.

"I don't know anything about your dad," he assured her. "Is he waiting for a transplant? I didn't know. I'm sorry if I hit a sore spot. I didn't have any idea."

"No, he's not waiting for a transplant," she snapped.

"Um… okay. So I'll find someone else to talk to about it. I really didn't mean to say anything to upset you. It was just a random inquiry. I don't want to accept the case if it is unethical."

"Yeah, why don't you ask someone else about it?" she agreed. "Call up one of your own doctors, or call the Medical Board and ask for the Ethics Committee."

"Okay. I'll do that. Thanks for pointing me in the right direction."

"Sure. Happy to help," she snapped. But she clearly did not want him to repeat the blunder. He was not to call her and ask her something like that again. He didn't know why transplants were a sore subject for her, but he was kicking himself for bringing it up.

"I'll let you know when Lauren Barclay's results are in," Kenzie said.

She hung up. Zachary gazed at the phone as he set it down on his computer desk. He didn't know who Kenzie's father was, but he was itching to do a little investigating to find out. Would it be crossing a line if it were just for his own information, so that he wouldn't make that same mistake again?

Zachary looked through the fridge for something edible. He needed to be able to show some increase in his weight, no matter how slight, before he saw his doctor again. He always lost weight before Christmas and then had to gain it back again over the following months. It was a familiar pattern. But the last Christmas had been particularly bad, and the trauma of his encounter with Teddy Archuro afterward had not helped matters. He didn't want Dr. Carter threatening to refer him to a feeding program, so he had to make eating a priority.

He had a few microwave dinners left, so he put one into the microwave and set the timer, then went and sat down in front of his computer again. Trying to keep his mind off of Kenzie's reaction to his call, he pulled out Lauren's timesheet. He ran his eyes down the columns of numbers, and frowned.

He was better at math than most other subjects, but he had to be reading the timesheets wrong, because they didn't make any sense. He got out a highlighter and read each column heading carefully. He highlighted alternating columns to make sure he was following the columns down properly and not drifting from one to the next without realizing it. He looked down the left-hand side, translating the numbers into dates. He looked at the heading at the top to make sure that it was Lauren's timesheet and not one for the receptionist or another member of the staff.

He had Lauren's computer, so he opened the lid, tapped in the password, and pulled up her email. He started with the day before she died, and worked his way backward, comparing the times of her emails against the hours that the timesheet said she had worked. It didn't take long to confirm that the timesheet was a complete fiction.

Zachary didn't need to keep comparing the emails against the timesheets. He knew they were wrong, and likewise he knew that the timesheets he was going to get for the other interns were going to be wrong. But who was falsifying them? The interns themselves? Their supervisors? Human resources? He had no idea what level they were being changed at. The interns clearly worked long hours, far longer than could be expected of any employee, and probably longer than any labor laws would allow. So the company just changed the timesheets and then they were in compliance. The computer clearly showed that Lauren had been working all hours of the day, with only a few hours off here and there for sleep.

He started browsing through the subject lines and contents of the emails for more information. Anything that looked like it was a specific client project, he didn't open, or if he had opened it to preview the contents, he quickly closed it again and went on to the next one. He was looking instead for personal emails. Communications between Lauren and the other interns, or her supervisor, or the human resources department. He wasn't interested in the projects that she was working on, but on what else she had to say.

There were a couple of emails with her manager, Daniel Service, asking about time off for a family event or a break. But it soon became obvious that Daniel had no intention of giving her any time off for such frivolous activities. No one had died. She could fit her family events into her own personal time. Even if she didn't have any. Exactly when was she supposed to get together with them, at two o'clock in the morning?

She had communicated with human resources regarding a note from her doctor saying that she had been ill and needed time to rest and recover. The request was quashed. She was to get back to the office as soon as she was physically able and, in the meantime, to do what she could from home. If she wanted more time off than that, she was going to need to submit test results that showed that she had some disease or disability that required treatment.

Obviously, being exhausted or having the flu were not on the list of approved reasons for missing work.

Lauren wrote to Mandy about her problems, how tired she was and how run down her body was getting.

"I can't even run on the treadmill anymore. I'm so tired I can barely do anything but walk. I feel like I'm going to pass out any minute. I keep falling asleep in the middle of eating, because that's the only time that I stop and relax. How can anyone keep up this pace?"

Mandy had commiserated, but she was going through the same thing too, and however she was handling it, she didn't give Lauren any tips. Was she constantly taking caffeine? Another performance enhancer? Was she taking the opportunity to sleep at her desk when she was supposed to be working? Zachary had fallen asleep at his own computer numerous times. It really wasn't that hard to sleep sitting up if you were really tired. Lauren was trying not to fall asleep on the job, but maybe the answer was in falling asleep wherever and whenever she could. Could Mandy appear to be working, but hide the fact that she was sleeping covertly? Working so closely with the other interns, would she be able to keep it from them?

Zachary scribbled down a few thoughts and continued to look for more personal mails.

There was a desperation in Lauren's emails. She was obviously at the end of her rope, fighting illness constantly as her body's immune system was defeated by stress, too tired for the physical activity she was supposed to be logging, trying to remain alert and on top of her files and keep the information flowing to her supervisor and the other employees she was doing work for.

But the human resources department continued to block any attempts to take time off. She was expected to be there the hours she had agreed to, and unless her doctor could provide something other than that Lauren was tired or fighting a virus, there was no way for Lauren to get approval to take a few days off.

There were a few personal emails with her family or friends as she dashed off quick notes to them to let them know that she couldn't make it to some planned event or that she was okay, or promising she'd be able to spend more time with them once she had a permanent position.

"It's just too risky right now," she explained to her mother. "I'm pretty sure that it will be Blair and me, and then once I've got it, I can schedule some down time. But right now, if I slack off, they'll say that the other interns are more productive and I won't be able to get in."

That confirmed Zachary's suspicion that she and Bieberstein were lined up for the permanent positions. Had someone intentionally caused their accidents, hoping to clear one or both of those positions to allow him—or her—the chance at one of them? Was it really that important for them to get the jobs they were fighting for?

There were some general emails from the company. Newsletters and notices of policies, days that the building would be washing windows or carpets, and other routine administrative matters that every company sent out. Zachary skimmed through them, not expecting to find anything important there.

He opened one email that was apparently from the company's legal department. He wasn't sure at first why an investment banking firm would need a legal department, but it soon became apparent. There were updates on a number of pending matters; some files where clients had sued the company claiming that they had been given bad advice and lost money. And one that appeared to be the firm suing a former employee, Cody Russo. Zachary tracked the spare sentences across the screen. He frowned, trying to parse their meaning. The company was reporting their success in the lawsuit against Russo for breaking the confidentiality clauses of his contract, revealing the company's trade secrets and making defamatory statements about it.

He thought about what that might mean, and came to the conclusion that Russo might be a whistleblower. Someone who had tried to speak out about what the company was doing to its employees. Or maybe some other practice. And for being courageous and telling what he knew, Drake, Chase, Gould had retaliated by suing him for talking about the company.

Could they do that? Could they sue him if what he said was true?

First, he would have to prove that it was true, and then he'd have to prove that he was not revealing confidential information about the company. If he really did have a confidentiality agreement that said he couldn't talk about the way things were run at Drake, Chase, Gould, that would be pretty difficult. Zachary wrote down the name of the defendant. He could order the court documents and see what it was that the employee had revealed, and then read through the company's defense.

But aside from whatever had happened, he got the feeling that the reason the legal department had circulated the memo about the lawsuit was not to reassure the employees that all was well and the company was defending itself. They had circulated the memo as a warning to anyone else who had thoughts about talking about the company. If you talk about Drake, Chase, Gould, you will be sued. Whether the allegations were true or not didn't really matter. What really mattered was that they could crush anyone who got in the way of the firm. It wasn't going to be David versus Goliath. It was a human being stomping on a bug or slapping a mosquito. The rest of the mosquitoes had better watch out.

When he went into the kitchen to get a glass of water, he could smell the remains of his dinner hanging in the air. He looked at the sink, but there were no dirty dishes in the sink. He took a peek under the sink and there was no recently-opened microwave tub discarded in the garbage. He stepped toward the living room and looked around to see if he had eaten his dinner in front of the TV or left it on his computer desk.

Nothing.

He ran the water and filled a glass of water, frowning. Finally, he reached over to the microwave and popped it open.

What a detective. There was a freezer meal, sitting in the middle of the microwave turntable. He touched it, and it was room temperature. Not cold from the freezer, not warm from heating it up. It had obviously been sitting there for long enough to either thaw out or cool off.

As he took it out and dumped it into the garbage, he tried to remember when he had heated it up. It didn't smell like it was going bad, so it had probably been in the past twenty-four hours. He had left dishes in the microwave until they started to go rotten before, so he knew what that smelled like.

He needed a new microwave. One that kept beeping to remind him that there was something in it so that he didn't forget to eat what he had heated up.

Zachary was directed by a receptionist to the unit and room that Blair Bieberstein was in, and found his way through the maze of corridors at the hospital. It was never as easy as it seemed it should be, almost always resulting in some backtracking to correct wrong turns, even though he thought he knew the hospital fairly well.

He knocked lightly on the open door before entering to let Bieberstein and whoever else was in the same room know he was there.

The first bed was occupied by a large, red-faced man who looked at Zachary like he was invading his private space. Zachary nodded hurriedly and went past the privacy curtain to the second bed. Bieberstein was there, sitting cross-legged in the middle of the bed, staring up at the ceiling and snapping his fingers.

"Hey, how are you doing?" Zachary greeted.

Bieberstein didn't look at him.

"Bored to death. Ready to get out of here, but the doctor doesn't want me to go yet. Wants me to have a bunch of tests. Wants me to talk to their counselors and to get therapy or something. I don't need to do any of that. But I'm in the hospital and they're saying not to leave, so I may as well take advantage of it and get a bit of a break. Catch a few winks and get away from exercising for a day or two. Sounds good, huh?"

"I never feel exactly comfortable in the hospital. I'm almost always jonesing to get out before they want to release me."

Bieberstein nodded. "Yeah. Not exactly a restful resort vacation. Always noisy. People coming in and poking me and wanting to know my vitals and pain level and why I'm not sleeping and all of that. I'd sleep better at home. But once I'm home, I need to go back to the office, and that wouldn't be restful."

"Did you ever talk to Lauren about that? It sounds like she had been sick a lot lately and wanted to take some time off, but human resources said no, she couldn't get it off, even with a note from her doctor."

"Well, Lauren didn't have a seizure, a lacerated scalp, and three broken bones."

"Three?"

Bieberstein nodded. "Two in the arm, and one rib," he explained, tapping each in turn. He pulled his gaze away from the ceiling and looked at Zachary. "So what are you doing here? You got everything you needed from me, didn't you?"

"I guess so... but I wanted to see how you were doing. Make sure you were okay. Seeing you fall down and have a seizure like that was kind of a shock... I've been worrying about you."

Bieberstein laughed. "No need to worry about me! I'm just fine. Hunky-dory. Better than fine." He gave Zachary a slightly-loopy smile.

"What have they got you on? Painkillers?"

"Maybe a few. I should be sleeping. But I'm not. Been awake since they brought me in."

"You have? I can see why the nurses keep telling you that you should be asleep. Aren't you exhausted?"

"They think maybe I'm having a paradoxical reaction to the painkillers. Normally they are sedating, but in my case, they seem to be hyping me up."

"I hope you can get some sleep soon. That must be frustrating."

"Frustrating is having nothing to do. I asked Aaron if he would bring me my laptop from work, but so far, he hasn't shown up. Doing his own work, I suppose. But I need that computer. I need to be working on something."

"Do you have a seizure disorder? Have you had this happen before?"

"If I had a seizure disorder, they wouldn't be keeping me here saying that they just needed to do one more test. And one more after that. And another one after that."

"They're testing for epilepsy?"

"Epilepsy. Sleep disorder. Toxins in my blood. Maybe I've been licking lead paint or something. But I haven't."

"No. You do seem pretty hyped up. Are you taking meth?"

"They already tested me for that," Bieberstein said, waving the question away with his non-injured arm. "They would know if that was the problem. Of course, my caffeine levels are off the charts, but what do you expect with Drake, Chase, Gould?"

"So could that have caused your seizure?"

"Maybe. They haven't said they think so and keep looking into other things so it might be a contributing factor, but they seem to be looking for something else."

"You said that they were looking for toxins, so I assume they would know if you'd been poisoned…?"

"Poisoned?" Bieberstein shook his head at Zachary. "Why would I poison myself?"

"No, I don't mean you poisoned yourself, I mean… what if someone put something into your water bottle or coffee cup at work? What if someone wanted you out of the way so that they had a better chance at getting a permanent position? Or maybe someone had a grudge against you for some other reason. Have they checked for any poisons?"

"No," Bieberstein shook his head quickly, irritated. "They haven't checked for poisons. Other than… whatever else they test for in their blood tests. I don't know all of what they were looking for. What would cause seizures?"

"Whatever caused Lauren to fall down and not wake up. Or maybe something different, so that it wouldn't be too suspicious."

"You think that someone tried to kill both of us off? That would be a pretty bold move."

"You don't think it could be a possibility?"

Bieberstein considered it only briefly. He shook his head.

"Why don't you think so? The competition at Chase Gold seems to be pretty fierce."

"But I wasn't really competing against the others. I was… my talents are totally different than any of them. None of them could really outplay me."

"Exactly. So how else would they get you out of the way and open up the position for one of them?"

That made Bieberstein think for a little longer. He shrugged uncomfortably. "Someone trying to kill me at the office? That's just ridiculous. Pushing me in front of a speeding car, maybe, but spiking my drinks? I don't see how anyone could do that. If they hated me for being there, or hated the work that I was doing, thinking I was showing them up… it would have made more sense to have me just disappear. Or to start undercutting me by telling stories about me. Stories that aren't true," he was quick to tell Zachary. "But they could make up anything about lifestyle or what I thought of them, or that I was selling company secrets behind their backs. That would get me out of there a lot faster than poisoning."

"Not if you'd died right away. Or had been too injured to get back to work right away."

"Hmmph." Bieberstein still didn't seem to think it was likely. "What were the chances that I would have died from it? Whatever it is? I had a seizure… hit my head… woke up in the hospital. That didn't even come close to killing me."

"But it could have, with you being on the exercise equipment. If you'd been going faster… or maybe it was supposed to do something to your heart when you were in the middle of your exercise routine." Zachary thought of the man who had wanted to use the portable v-fib machine on Bieberstein, when he didn't have any reason to think that there was anything wrong with Bieberstein's heart. *Or had he?* Had he known what Bieberstein had been given? Was it supposed to stop his heart? Mimic a heart attack?

"Maybe you just didn't get enough," Zachary suggested. "Maybe there wasn't enough in your drink, or it's something that is supposed to work on you over time. Who knows? It could be something slower-acting, so they're hoping that you won't notice any symptoms, and then by the time you realize that you really are sick… it's too late." He thought about all of the health issues that Lauren had been complaining of. "Have you had anything lately? Flu symptoms? Headaches? Malaise?"

"You mean like being tired?" Bieberstein laughed. "Everybody is tired."

"But they could have been giving you something over time that took away your energy. If it's something they wouldn't normally test for…"

Robin Salter, Bridget's friend in the cancer ward, had been poisoned with an iron overdose by her own sister. And no one would ever have known if Zachary hadn't taken on the case at Bridget's request. They all would have laid Robin at rest, thinking that she had just died from her cancer or from the chemo treatments. No one would have known that she'd been poisoned with iron.

"Nobody has been poisoning me," Bieberstein said firmly. "I would know."

19

There were noises in the hall. Zachary and Bieberstein both stopped talking and looked toward the door, trying to decipher the voices. There was an increase in volume, a female giggle, and then it sounded like they were grouped outside of Bieberstein's door. Zachary and Bieberstein both looked toward the door, waiting.

Zachary was alert for trouble, but he knew he probably didn't have to worry, since the voices had not sounded threatening, and the woman had giggled. But bad things could still follow when people were laughing and in a good mood. Sometimes, bullying or pranking someone was the funniest thing in the world. If someone had evil designs on Bieberstein, they could be planning something that would hurt or humiliate him.

Zachary's muscles tensed, listening to the quiet, whispery voices outside the door and waiting for the arrival of the visitors. Maybe they weren't even there to see Bieberstein. Maybe they were there to see the dour man in the other bed. Or they were checking names outside the doors looking for the person they actually wanted to visit. It might be nothing at all to do with Bieberstein.

At least Zachary wasn't worried that they were targeting him. No one had known he was planning to see Bieberstein.

After a few expectant seconds, the visitors finally entered, streaming into the hospital room. Mandy and the other interns from Drake, Chase, Gould. Other faces that he didn't recognize. Bev. And, of course, Gordon. Gordon Drake himself, main owner of the firm, had deigned to come and visit Bieberstein, following through on his comment that the interns were the lifeblood of the company, that he knew everyone by name, that they were all important to him.

Bieberstein's eyes were wide. He looked from one person to another, his body language tense, movements jerky.

"We came to tell you to get better soon," Mandy told him in a high-pitched voice. She handed him an oversized card. Bieberstein took it from her, and looked at the other visitors warily, as if expecting one of them to jump out and assault him. Zachary knew the feeling. He didn't like crowds, and he didn't like this crowd in particular. It all seemed too phony. These were people who worked hard for hours, who couldn't take time off for their own sickness or family events, but they could all get time off at the same time to visit a lowly intern? Someone that most of them probably didn't even like, hyper and annoying, socially indifferent.

Bieberstein opened the card awkwardly, the cast on his arm keeping his elbow at the wrong angle. He tore the envelope and pulled out the card. He barely looked at the cartoon picture on the outside, the punny greeting on the inside, or the scribbled get well soon messages that everyone had penned inside. It had obviously moved from desk to desk at the office, everyone required to put some happy, encouraging message on the inside for him. Some of the signatures overflowed onto the back. It was crowded with their well-wishes.

Bieberstein looked back at the mob of people. "This is really nice," he said. "Thank you. I'll be back to the office as soon as I can. I don't like to miss…"

"Oh, this is for you," Aaron said, reaching out with Bieberstein's slim, silver laptop in his hand.

"Now that, I need," Bieberstein said eagerly, lunging a little to grab it from him, as if fearful that he might pull it back again at the last moment. He gripped it in both hands, clearly precious to him.

"We wanted to tell you how much we miss you," one of the other employees, who Zachary didn't recognize, told Bieberstein. "You're very important to the company and we're sorry that you got hurt. We want you to get better again soon."

"Yeah, thanks," Bieberstein said with a quick nod.

"You're one of the smartest people that I know," Aaron said. "How you manage to do what you do with numbers… in your head… it absolutely amazes me. You're brilliant."

"We're going to be very happy to have you on permanently," Bev said, giving him a quirky smile. "If you are one of the ones to get the position, of course." But her words left little doubt that he had, in fact, earned one of the full-time positions.

Bieberstein grinned. "You're not going to be sorry," he said. "Drake, Chase, Gould is one of the up-and-coming investment banking firms, and they're going to be able to compete with the biggest and most elite firms in the world. I'm going to make sure of that."

"Yes, you will," Gordon agreed, beaming his beneficent smile on Bieberstein and then on everyone else. "It is people like you who will make Drake, Chase, Gould a household name. When they are writing biographies fifty years from now on the most influential men of the century, your name will undoubtedly be one of those on the list."

"Yours too," Bieberstein said, looking uncomfortable.

"Well, if I'm lucky, but I'm not counting on it. I'll more likely be one of the men behind the scenes who saw which way things were going and got on the train before it was fully up to speed. I'll be there, but I don't know that I'll be one of the influencers. It is minds like yours that will be counted when all of the votes are in."

Bieberstein was getting red. Zachary worried a little that his emotion over Gordon's praise might throw him into another seizure, but nothing untoward happened. He just clutched his laptop to himself and stared up over their heads.

"That's really nice," he said, "I don't know if it's true, but thank you."

The visitors started to talk to each other instead of Bieberstein, taking some of the pressure off of him and leaving him to get his equilibrium back. Zachary watched him covertly, not wanting him to feel like he was under the microscope, but concerned.

Someone offered to tape the 'get well' card to the wall for him, as if there were going to be a lot of cards on display there. Zachary supposed that he should have brought one as well, but it hadn't even occurred to him. Someone else had a bunch of flowers, someone else a vase, so they filled the vase with water and added the flowers, displaying them on the small shelf that acted as a bedside table.

Mandy sat on the edge of Bieberstein's mattress and made jokes to him, most of which seemed to fall flat, either because Bieberstein didn't get them or because her nervousness was making her muff the punchlines. Zachary didn't actually get most of them. He would have been worried if they hadn't been financially-themed jokes.

After a while, he caught Bieberstein's eye. "I'm going to sneak out," he said, motioning to the door.

Bieberstein nodded. "Okay. Thanks for coming by."

"Let me know if you think of anything... if you want to discuss anything," Zachary said. He didn't want to say too much in front of all of Bieberstein's coworkers. "If you get anything back in the results..."

"Yeah. I'll let you know."

Zachary met his eye to make sure he realized that it could be important. If someone were trying to kick him out of the running, they were obviously going to have to try harder. Gordon and the others who were in charge over at Drake, Chase, Gould were not going to just drop him because he'd been put in the hospital for a couple of days. They obviously thought a lot of him.

Bieberstein wasn't going anywhere.

After leaving the hospital, Zachary ran a few personal errands. He needed more groceries. Gas in the tank. All of the grown-up, adult things he was supposed to be doing to take care of himself. At the store, he had to stop himself from buying the things he normally got for Kenzie. She wasn't there anymore. There was no point in filling the fridge with the things that she liked if he wasn't going to consume them himself.

He was still thinking about her when he got home and shoved the newest frozen dinners into the freezer. When the phone rang, he knew without looking at it that it was going to be her. He didn't think the medical examiner's report would be in yet, so he didn't know why she would call him when they were broken up. It probably wasn't her. He just thought of her when it rang because he'd already been missing her.

He pulled out his phone and looked at the screen. It *was* Kenzie. And from her cell phone, not the office. Zachary closed his eyes and took a couple of breaths before answering it.

"Kenzie, hi!" He tried not to sound too eager. Or like her call was unexpected. He had wanted to stay friends with her, and friends called each other now and then. He couldn't expect too much from it. Even so, he wished he *had* bought the treats that she enjoyed from the grocery store, so he could tell her that they were there waiting for her now, whenever she was ready to come over.

"Zachary. Yeah, hi." She sounded down. Depressed? Or just tired after a long day? "Uh… listen… I was a little harsh with you yesterday. More than harsh. That was unwarranted. I'm sorry. You didn't do anything wrong, you just called to ask me a medical question and I jumped to conclusions."

"I am sorry," Zachary said. "If I had a medical ethics question, then I should have just gone to the Ethics Committee to start with. I don't know why I didn't. I didn't need to bother you with something like that."

"I don't want you to think that you can't still talk to me and ask me for advice. Really. We're not together anymore, but that doesn't mean that we can't ever talk to each other again."

"That's good. I wouldn't want that."

"My family is sort of a sore spot with me. Especially my dad. So when you were talking about transplants, I just automatically got defensive."

Zachary didn't say anything. If it was a sore spot, then asking her *why* would probably not be the right thing to do. She needed to know that he could just accept that it was off-limits.

"My dad… our family has some history with transplants, and he and I don't see eye-to-eye. He thought that after I finished my medical degree, I would agree that he was right about everything, but… well… I don't."

"Okay. I won't ask you about it again. I didn't mean to trigger any bad feelings. Sorry about that."

"Not your fault. You'd think that I'd be able to handle it better by now. But those feelings are still raw. I try not to hold it against him, but…"

"Do you want to come over tonight?" Zachary offered. "Just to relax and hang out?"

There were a few seconds of silence during which he thought Kenzie might actually be considering it. Or maybe she was just startled by his asking and how inappropriate it was.

"No, Zachary," she said with a sigh. "I think that would just be asking for trouble. We both need to move on. Try out some other relationships. We just don't work together."

"I think that we could. I've just been going through some stuff… you know with my therapy… everything that I've been dealing with lately…"

"I don't see things getting better anytime soon. I can't keep putting my energy into a relationship and not getting anything back."

That stung. Zachary had put a lot of effort into the relationship too. Kenzie didn't have any idea how hard he had tried, how far he had gone out of his comfort zone to do things for her. Even as far as going back into therapy to try to deal with their relationship. That had all been for her.

Kenzie had done a lot for him and had stood by him through some very tough times. But he had been working on it too. He had thought that she was getting something out of it.

20

He was still thinking about the call with Kenzie when he went to his therapy session that afternoon. It rankled. He kept making the arguments in his head, but had no way to get them out and see how they resonated with her. With Bridget, at least he'd been able to make his arguments. She might have screamed at him and mocked his arguments and dismissed his feelings, but at least he'd been able to tell her, to try to talk her into getting back together again.

With Kenzie, she didn't even want to hear his arguments. She didn't scream. She was calm and reasonable, but she didn't want to hear what he had to say and he was left arguing with himself and imagining what Kenzie would say to him in response.

Of course, even in his head, she didn't agree with him, and he could still hear her repeating herself in that calm, reasonable voice. "We're just not good together."

But they *had* been good together. He had enjoyed having her as a friend and someone to bounce ideas off of and to discuss any medical issues he was trying to sort out with her. They had moved slowly to a more intimate relationship, and he had felt good about it. Until Teddy. That had blown everything all to hell.

"You're not looking too happy today," Dr. Boyle commented

as he sat down and shifted around in the chair, trying to get comfortable.

Zachary didn't have a naturally happy face, so he must have really been scowling for her to notice the difference. He rubbed his forehead, not wanting to overwhelm her with the avalanche of words that threatened to come out, burying her beneath their weight.

"I guess… I'm just having trouble getting used to being alone. To not being with Kenzie anymore."

"It is hard to get over a relationship like that. The two of you had been together for a long time. You were close friends and cared about each other."

Zachary nodded. Dr. B waited, watching him. She knew there was more to come out and she was not afraid to use silence to draw him out. She got paid the same amount whether he spent it talking or brooding in silence. He was the one who would get less out of it if he didn't address the issues.

"She called me today."

"Uh-huh?"

"Not because she wanted to get together, nothing like that."

"Why did she call, then?"

"She called to apologize. I called her the other day about a medical question and it made her upset. So she called to say sorry for snapping at me."

"That was nice of her. It can be hard to admit that you were in the wrong, especially when you're dealing with emotional issues."

"Yeah. It was nice of her. But… I asked her if she wanted to come over."

"Did she give you some sort of sign that she would be interested in coming over?"

Zachary thought about it. He was a good observer of human behavior and he was good at reading people. Body language and tone of voice told him a lot. It was a skill that he had honed through his years in foster care and as a private investigator.

"No… I guess not. She said that she still wanted to be friends and to be able to talk to me, that it was okay if I called her about things that I had questions on. So I just… I guess I jumped ahead and thought that maybe it would be okay if she came over and we just hung out… watched a movie or had a chat. I didn't mean that we had to jump right back into being a couple again. Just that we could… be friends… spend some time together."

"And she probably saw it as something more. She knows your history, that you might have trouble letting go."

"I just don't understand… why she left. She just gave up on us. I was having problems, and she decided that she'd had enough."

"Do you think that she should have put up with your issues for longer? Or handled them differently?"

"I…" Zachary thought about all that had happened. Kenzie had stayed by him through all of it. He had thought that they could weather any problem together. She had seen him through injuries and depression, through the initial aftermath of the attack. She had put up with a lot of things that he hadn't really had a right to expect that she would. "I don't know. I guess she couldn't keep doing it forever, when she wasn't getting anything out of the relationship."

He said the words with a bitter edge. Dr. Boyle studied him, waiting.

"I thought she was. I thought I was giving her something too. But she said that she didn't get anything out of the relationship."

"Does her saying it mean that it's true? Is it a fact or a feeling?"

"I guess… maybe it's a feeling?"

"What do you think? This is your relationship. I don't know Kenzie."

"It *isn't* a relationship. She made that clear."

"She made it clear that it's not a romantic relationship. She said that you could still talk to her, that you could still be friends. Do you think that's true, or was that just words to make the two of you feel better?"

"I don't know."

"If she's willing to still be friends and to talk about your investigations and medical matters with her, then obviously those are things that were important to her. She was getting something out of the relationship, or she would not have been willing to continue those things."

"But she wasn't getting anything out of our romantic relationship?"

"Maybe not. What do you think?"

"I was trying. I was working it through, talking to you about it, talking to her about it."

"And…?"

"I think… I think we were both getting something out of it."

"Then why did it have to end?"

"I didn't end it, she did."

Dr. Boyle was silent.

"I contributed," Zachary admitted, "But she was the one to call it off. She was the one who decided that it was over."

"Did she decide it was over? Or did you?"

"She did. That's what she said."

"You hadn't pushed her away? We've talked about this before."

"I… yes, I was trying to work through her talking to Mr. Peterson and Bridget about our relationship. She was trying to dig into my past. Talking about intimate things with other people. Things I wasn't ready to share. How would you feel if you found out that your husband had been talking about your sex life with his friends? Or not with his friends—with your friends!"

"That would put me in a very difficult position. But I think you need to consider her intent. Was she talking to your family about your intimate relationship because she wanted to brag? Or because she wanted to put you down? I understand you being embarrassed and worried about what details she might have revealed to them. But you need to consider her intent."

Zachary put his hands over his face, cupping his eyes. "I know she was doing it because she wanted to work things out. I know that she meant well. But she shouldn't have done that. She shouldn't have gone to them, asking them about my past relation-ships. She went behind my back."

Dr. Boyle made an encouraging noise.

"I would have talked to her about it and gotten it smoothed out eventually," Zachary said. "I just needed to work it out in my brain first. I was going through a bad spell."

"When would you have gotten to it, do you think? How long would she have to wait in limbo while you worked it out and figured out how to talk to her about it? And would you have decided that it was okay for her to go to alternate sources when you couldn't talk to her about these issues, or would you have decided that it was wrong?"

"It was still wrong. But… I just got out of the hospital. I could have used another day or two to get settled back into my life. Then we could have discussed it."

"Until then, she was just supposed to sit back and wait for you to work it out and decide to talk to her again."

"I think she could have waited a few more days."

"I'm sure she could have. But she didn't know how long it would be. A few more days, or would it be weeks or months? And in the meantime, was she still in a relationship with you, or were you on a break? How long should she wait until you were ready to talk? And would you make that move on your own, or would she have to prompt you and talk you into it?"

"I don't know. Because she didn't give me that chance."

"How long did she wait?"

Zachary scratched at a seam in the upholstery of the chair he was sitting in. "What do you mean?"

"I mean, how long had she already been waiting when she decided that the two of you were done?"

"Uh…" Zachary considered, trying to construct the timeline in his head. The time between when he had learned that Kenzie had been talking to Mr. Peterson about the relationship until he had gotten out of the hospital and she had come by the apartment to clear out her things. "It was… a few weeks, I guess. A couple of weeks before I was admitted, and then a couple while I was in the hospital."

"So probably a month…?"

"Yeah. Something like that."

"A month without you talking to her at all?"

Zachary cleared his throat. He looked down at the carpet. "We talked a few times… just to say… that I was busy and couldn't get together. She was busy too, I wasn't the only one. We had lunch… a couple times…"

"But a month with no significant contact or time together."

"Yeah."

"Do you think she should have waited more than a month? Maybe two?"

"A month is a pretty long time."

"Yes, it is."

"She would have waited if I was away on vacation or a work trip for a month."

"More than likely, yes. But that's something that you would have defined. And during your vacation, you would have kept in touch with her. The two of you would have talked to each other, shared what you were doing, even if it was only once a week. Don't you think?"

"So you're saying she was justified. That she should have split up with me because I didn't talk to her while I was going through a crisis."

Dr. Boyle gave him a tolerant smile. Zachary knew that he was dramatizing, that he was just trying to get her on his side. He wanted to be told that he was right, not that he had screwed up.

Zachary returned to the offices of Drake, Chase, Gould to pick up the timesheets for the other interns, even though he knew that when he looked at them, he would find the same thing as he had looking at Lauren's timesheet. That it was completely untrue. He took the reports from Bev and put them away in his bag before challenging her about them.

"I suppose these have been sanitized, just like Lauren's?"

"What are you talking about?"

"That Lauren was working eighteen- or twenty-four-hour days. And her timesheets show that she was working a regular nine-to-five job, with occasional hours of overtime at either end. You know that isn't true, and that her computer records would show that they are lies."

Bev stared at him.

"I assume there are laws that you have to follow in the way that you treat your employees. You can't let them—or force them to—work for twenty-four, forty-eight, or seventy-two hours straight. You can't deny them medical leave when the doctor says that they need it. You can't deny them the ability to take an evening or weekend off or to do other things."

"I don't know what you're talking about."

"I've seen her computer and her emails. I know she was working all hours of the day, just like her roommate says. I know that you denied her any time off, even for medical reasons."

"Lauren didn't have any medical issues. She was a perfectly healthy young adult, and if I had allowed her to take time off every time she had a cough or a sniffle, then pretty soon all of the interns would be faking sick after the weekend. Or whenever they wanted time off to mess around with friends, go on dates, or have dinner with their favorite aunts. We needed them to show that they could be dependable and do what they had promised to. Lauren was very smart and got along well with her superiors and coworkers. But she had a problem with putting in the time. She was always looking for a way out."

"She put in the time. I can see it from her computer."

"You're misinterpreting what you see. Are you making an arrest? You think that I went to her house and pushed her down in the tub and held her underwater?"

"I'm not making any arrests. I'm asking you whether these records are true, or whether you were just making them up."

"I resent the suggestion that we would do anything unethical or illegal. We cared for these interns like they were our own kids. If they put in timesheets for too much time... we would correct them. Nobody wants to get into trouble with labor policies because they don't know how to fill out their timesheets."

"How were they supposed to fill out their timesheets?"

She motioned to the reports that she had given Zachary. "Like those. You can't fill out a sheet alleging that you have been working for twenty-four hours at a time. That's just going to get people in trouble. And they weren't working for that whole time. They would take breaks for meals, exercise, or gossiping. They would nap at their desks. They weren't working for that long. So we would correct them to the time they were actually working."

"I see."

So she admitted that she, or someone in her department, had been involved in making the changes to the timesheets.

"What other records do you change?"

"What do you mean?"

"I mean… you change the timesheets to bring them into alignment with your policies. Did you find it necessary to change other records as well? Are there other things that they would get wrong? Because they didn't know what they were doing? Because they were new to the employment world and didn't know the right way to fill them out?"

"I don't appreciate your implications…"

"I'm asking a question. Did you change other records as well?"

"If they were wrong, yes, of course we changed them. If someone put down the wrong address, birthdate, or social, wouldn't you fix them?"

"Sure. If they were wrong."

"It's the same with the rest of their human resources records."

"If they made a mistake, you would fix them."

"If they were wrong," Bev agreed. "That would be our responsibility."

When Zachary left the human resources department, he saw an atrium where several people sat around looking at their phones or typing on their computers, on benches surrounded by cobblestone pathways and lush plants. Obviously, another part of the "health and wellness" programs offered at Drake, Chase, Gould. He wouldn't be surprised to find a spa somewhere, just another way of ensuring that the employees were in the peak of health. The trouble was, everything was being counteracted by an environment where the employees were expected to work long, arduous hours, where there were bosses who were alternately abusive and approving, and where their needs were actually being subverted in the name of productivity.

He remembered the reading he had done when he'd been investigating the ABA programs at the Summit Learning Center.

How being angry and abusive toward a child and then later showing love and approval, you could bond the child to you and get better compliance. The same way that spouses convinced their partners and children to stay in abusive relationships. The same way that gangs initiated their members and cults controlled theirs.

He'd heard from Bieberstein the way that the interns were abused and humiliated about their work, and how they hazed the new employees. He'd seen the love-bombing of Bieberstein at the hospital, how emotional and appreciative he became at the excessive praise. He had been overwhelmed, as anyone would have been, at Gordon's praise. They had gushed over how much they loved him and handed him his computer. *We appreciate you and get back to work.*

Zachary sat down on an unoccupied bench in the atrium. He kept his eyes down, looking at his phone and then at his notepad as he checked his email and jotted down some of his thoughts. He was watching the employees who were enjoying the atmosphere of the atrium out the corners of his eyes.

One of the men balanced a laptop on his knees and stared unblinkingly at the screen, intent on whatever it was he was doing. He pecked with the index finger, middle finger, and thumb of his right hand. His left hand was beside his leg, and he plucked at his pant leg as he read through whatever he was reading. Pluck, pluck, pluck, in a steady rhythm. Zachary looked away, studying the next employee.

While he had expected the employees other than the interns to look better, less tired and well-rested, he didn't find that to be the case. The receptionist looked okay and Bieberstein had declared that she left at six o'clock every day. So she was one person who wasn't expected to work the ridiculous overtime hours that everyone else was, and she had looked fresh and well-rested. The face of the company, it was probably important that she not look like a zombie. The other employees, even those who were sitting in the paradisiacal setting of the atrium, looked fatigued. They had red eyes and heavy lids. Some were falling asleep where they sat, eyes slowly closing and heads nodding, losing the battle with the work they were trying to get done.

One man was holding a heavy, thick binder and, as he drifted off, it slipped from his grip and fell onto the flagstones below him with a crash that sounded like a gunshot.

Everybody in the atrium was instantly awake and alert, eyes wide as they looked around for the source of the noise. The man sitting on the next bench to Zachary's right leaped to his feet, his face a picture of panic.

"What the hell was that?" he shouted. Looking around, he spotted the binder and the owner picking it up, red-faced. "What are you doing? Don't you have any consideration for anyone around you? This is supposed to be a quiet place to study, not a war zone!"

The woman sitting between them muttered under her breath. "You're the one making this a war zone," and in a louder voice, "Just chill, Chris."

But Chris was just getting ramped up. "Why should I chill? He's the one causing a disturbance. Can't you be quiet?"

"He made a mistake. He dropped something. People make mistakes sometimes. Just go back to your work."

Chris took a few steps toward the man who had dropped the book and Zachary shifted anxiously, worried that it was going to escalate into a physical fight. This was what constant stress did to people. Lack of sleep and the pressure to produce made them so anxious and hypersensitive that they couldn't respond in a logical, reasonable way. Chris was acting like he *was* in a war zone ready to take down the enemy, instead of in a quiet atrium.

"I'm sorry," the other man said. "It just slipped out of my hand. I didn't mean to startle anyone."

"People think it's so funny to scare others. So funny to see how they react," Chris snarled.

Zachary could remember bullies at school or Bonnie Brown who had thought it was hilarious to make him jump. He was so tightly-strung, so hypervigilant, that they were guaranteed a really good reaction. Zachary couldn't help it. He would be running or fighting to protect himself before he had any idea what was going on.

He had once hit a teacher who had decided to wake him up when he had fallen asleep at his desk by slapping the ruler down on the desk next to his head. He had been terrified upon realizing what he had done, fleeing the room and hiding in a toilet stall until they had managed to find him. That had been while he was at the Petersons', and Mrs. Peterson had been ready to send him on his way that day. It had taken Mrs. Pratt a long time to talk her down, and she only succeeded in getting Zachary a few more days there while she looked for another home to transfer him to. It had been the last straw for Mrs. Peterson. Any boy who would hit a teacher was not a safe person to have in her home. Not with other children to consider. She wouldn't take the chance that he could hurt one of them if they happened to startle him.

"It wasn't on purpose," the man with the binder said again. "Really. I'm not laughing. I don't think it is funny to scare anybody. Hell, *I* just about wet my pants!"

Chris stared at him, then finally was able to give a little smile, nodding his head. He forced a chuckle. "Yeah, okay," he said finally, his voice shaking a little. "Sorry to overreact. I just… I don't like being scared like that. I don't know what I thought was happening, but it scared the crap out of me."

His opponent nodded eagerly. "I know, I know. I'm sorry. Guess I'd better head back to my desk. Reading in here wasn't such a good idea after all."

They gave each other space to maneuver, and both ended up leaving, the atrium falling into silence once more. Zachary took a few breaths, long and even, trying to calm his own body back down. No need to get anxious about a little accident.

Holding his phone in front of his face so that it would look like he was reading something, Zachary looked around at the others who had stayed behind. Everyone was looking pretty shaken. It was incredible that the stress level in the building could be so high, especially in a calming environment like the atrium. The plants and the sounds of a waterfall in the distance should have made it a paradise of peace, but all it took was one mistake for everyone to turn on each other.

<hr>

Zachary put a frozen dinner into the microwave, mentally prompting himself not to forget it was there this time. After considering for a moment, he told his phone to set an alarm for him, then went to his computer to do a quick email check while the dinner was heating up.

He had cleared a few items out of his inbox when his phone rang. At first, he assumed it was the alarm for his dinner, even though he hadn't heard the microwave beep. That wouldn't be unusual; he often tuned out noises like that when he was concentrating on something on the computer. That was why he had set the alarm on his phone. But when he reached for it to turn off the alarm, he realized it was a phone call from Heather. He sank back into his seat and touched the green answer button.

"Hi, Feathers."

"Hi, Zachy," she returned, laughing a little at the use of their childhood nicknames. "Though I'm not so sure I should be calling my boss Zachy."

"I don't think anyone else could get away with it, but I don't mind it coming from you. What's up?"

"I have results on some of those skip traces for you."

"Oh, good." Zachary reached for his notepad. "Will you email them to me?"

"Sure. I did run into problems with one, though. I wondered if you could think of anywhere else I should look."

"Okay, shoot."

She outlined what she had found for the man, and the various databases and searches she had tried. Zachary's phone vibrated in his hand and beeped, and he dismissed the alert, focusing on

Heather's skip and what she might have missed or any creative ways he might have tried to find the man.

"You might want to check with unions," he suggested. "Tradesmen are usually registered with unions, no matter where they go and who they work for. He'll want to keep his membership active so he can use them if he runs into any trouble. There are also some job boards you might try out. If he hasn't landed a full-time job, he might be doing short contracts on one of them."

"Oh, good idea," Heather agreed. He could tell by the way she was drawing out her words that she was writing it down, so he waited until she indicated she was ready before moving on to anything else.

"If we can't find anything else, we might try courthouse searches. If he's disappeared because he owes child support or was found liable in some traffic accident, it would be nice to know that. If there are any court cases, his lawyer might have a current address, or family members to check with."

"Good. Okay. I'll do those too, if nothing else shows up."

"Sometimes people are just very careful not to leave a footprint, but chances are, he won't be able to avoid it, and we'll find him somewhere."

"I'll do my best. How is your accident case going?"

"I'm starting to wonder if there was foul play… there are several people trying to get the same job, and two of them have had accidents in the last week. I don't know if someone is trying to clear their way to one of those positions, or if it's just a coincidence. Or if it's because with how hard the company is working them, they're just dropping from exhaustion."

"Where are they working? Some sweatshop?"

Zachary chuckled. "The modern-day equivalent, maybe. They certainly seem to be taken advantage of. I don't know how you could expect anyone to work that hard."

"More immigrants?"

"No. An investment banking firm, Drake, Chase, Gould. That's in confidence, though, don't go repeating it to anyone. I'd really like to know if any of the other interns bought any poison lately… but so far, as far as I know, any toxicology screens have come up negative, so I could just be trying to find foul play where there isn't any."

"I doubt it. You seem to have a pretty good sense of these things."

"Well, so far I'm not sure that it's anything. Just a possibility at this point."

"If there's anything to find, you'll find it."

He liked her confidence. He wasn't sure that she actually had anything to be confident about, but he appreciated it. He'd had a few cases where he'd made lucky finds. Maybe Lauren's death would be another.

And maybe it was just what it looked like. A woman slipping in the tub and hitting her head. Accidents like that happened every day.

As Zachary thought about the information he had gathered in Lauren's case so far, he thought back to Bev and her admission that they would change whatever records they needed in order to get them to fit the company's reality. By now, Bev had probably realized that that had been a stupid thing to admit to Zachary. And while Zachary had the proof on Lauren's laptop that the timesheets were a lie and that Lauren had repeatedly been refused time off, that information resided in a corporate mailbox, and if they decided to shut down and erase that mailbox, Zachary could lose what information he had.

To preserve it, he would have to be sure not to let Lauren's computer connect to the internet. He had connected to it once via his Wi-Fi router, so to prevent it from connecting again, he delved into the network settings and deleted the Wi-Fi profile. The computer wouldn't be able to connect again unless Zachary gave it the password. After deleting the connection information, Zachary watched it search for another connection and find an open Guest network somewhere in the building. He looked for the settings that would prevent it from searching automatically for networks.

He shut off everything he could, including the Wi-Fi radio. The Bluetooth indicator pulsed, and he saw Lauren's phone wake up. Of course, sometime in the past, Lauren had tethered the laptop to her phone, and it had remembered the connection information. He deleted that profile, telling it to forget the device, and also shut down the Bluetooth radio.

He watched the screen for any other activity. With Wi-Fi shut off and Bluetooth shut off, it shouldn't be able to connect to the internet unless he plugged a network cable into the port. But he was still half-expecting it to find some other way to connect to the internet. The computer was desperate to find a connection and start downloading new information. Lauren had been connected to the information superhighway night and day, always looking for the most recent market information.

There were no more connection icons on the screen. Zachary went to the browser and tried connecting to a couple of sites, but just kept getting 404 errors, and the computer didn't find an alternate route to the internet.

Sure that the company could no longer remotely delete the information already in the computer's mailbox, Zachary again opened the application and browsed through the mail. There were a few more routine mail pieces that had arrived while he had been trying to keep the computer from reconnecting, but nothing unusual and, as far as he could tell, none of the already-downloaded emails had been deleted.

He went to the sent mail and did a screen print of the first page of emails so that he could save the evidence of the times that Lauren had been sending out emails. The printer icon flashed warnings at him and nothing came off on the printer. Zachary looked at it. No connection to printer. Of course he couldn't print anything over Wi-Fi if he had prevented the computer from connecting to Wi-Fi. He could plug it into his network with a cable, but then it would have internet access as well, and he only wanted it to talk to the printer. Which meant he needed a printer cable. Something that he had not purchased since setting up his new system.

Zachary took a look at the connectors on the printer and on

the computer, then looked through the USB cables he had on hand. He had charge cables for various devices, or to connect his phone or tablet to the computer, but they used specialized connections that the printer didn't. He was going to have to get a new cable to connect the computer to the printer to memorialize the information that was currently on it. Unless he could plug into his router but not let the router connect to the internet. Zachary examined the router, tracing the cables visually.

He should also have cloned the hard drive before he'd done anything else. Gerry, his technology consultant, had tried to drill the importance of this into him on more than one occasion. Gerry had given him the hardware he needed to do it. Any time he touched a computer that was not his own, he was supposed to clone the drive before even attempting to log in. Gerry would not be impressed that Zachary had not only logged in without cloning it, but was now worried about losing the information stored on the hard drive and was resorting to printing hard copies to save it.

Clone the hard drive, bonehead.

Zachary didn't know how long he had been working on Lauren's computer and emails when the phone rang. He knew that his eyes were getting sore and gritty, which probably meant that it was late and he'd been spending too much time staring at the screen.

He looked over at his phone laying on the desk to his right. He wasn't sure whose number it was, but it appeared to be local, and it was too late at night to be a telemarketer. He picked it up and answered the call.

"Zachary here."

"Is this Detective Goldman?"

Zachary squirmed a little at not correcting the fiction. "This is Zachary Goldman. Who's calling?"

"It's Blair."

Zachary drew a blank.

"Blair Bieberstein."

"Oh, Blair. Sorry, my brain was somewhere else. How are you feeling?"

"I want to know if you really think that someone could be trying to kill me."

"Well... I don't know. I don't want to scare you, but at the same time... Lauren is dead and you did have a pretty serious accident. If someone was trying to get one of the permanent positions, they could go to great lengths to get what they wanted. So... let's say it's a possibility. But it's also possible that it was just someone who wants the company to see you as a risk, they don't really want to kill you. Or it could just be an accident. A strange coincidence."

"So you think someone is trying to kill me."

"Uh... yes, maybe."

"The hospital said that everything was fine in my bloodwork. There was no reason to think that anyone had poisoned me."

"That's good news."

"You know they don't routinely check for poisons, and there are so many poisons out there, they would have to know which one they were looking for. They don't just assume that anyone who comes in with a seizure has been poisoned."

"I realize that."

"Then why are you trying to scare me? No one is trying to hurt me."

"Okay."

"Okay?" Bieberstein repeated, his voice rising in tone. "It's not okay! What's happening to me? Why did I pass out?"

"I don't know. You haven't ever had that happen before?"

"No, never."

"What did the doctors say?"

"Maybe I'm fighting a virus. Most people who have a seizure never have another one, so it's really nothing to worry about unless I start having more of them. They don't know what's going on, and they don't really care about finding out."

"Are you still at the hospital?"

"No. Checked myself out of there. Too many people watching me. Didn't want to stay there."

"So you went home?"

"I can't go home. Lauren died at her apartment. I don't want them to get me."

"Them?"

"Whoever killed Lauren. Whoever poisoned my water bottle. I don't want them getting me."

Zachary gripped the phone more tightly. "Have you had any sleep, Blair? Where are you?"

"I'm at the office. Can't sleep. Need to stay on top of things."

"I think they can do without you for a day or two until you start feeling better. If you don't get any sleep, you are not going to be able to do your job anyway."

"I'm just fine. As long as I don't let them catch up to me."

"But if they poisoned you at work, wouldn't it be safer to go home?" Zachary reasoned, hoping to be able to get Bieberstein to go home and get the sleep he needed. Who knew how long he'd been awake before his accident, and if the medication they'd given him at the hospital had kept him awake since then, Bieberstein could be putting his health at serious risk.

"No, they got Lauren at home," Bieberstein reiterated. "I just need to make sure nobody can put anything else into my water bottle. That's the trick. I'll keep it with me. Won't let anyone near it."

Zachary heard him take a pull on his water bottle and chug down several gulps of water.

"You're not taking anything, are you?" he checked. "You know that if you take meth or something else to keep you awake, you're going to damage your health further. You need to find somewhere quiet and have a nap."

"Yeah, yeah," Bieberstein said impatiently. "When are you coming back here again?"

"I don't know. I don't have anything else to pursue there right now. I can't just hang out there without something specific to do."

"You need to arrest them so that it's safe for the rest of us."

"Do you know who it is?"

"It's *them*. You told me that. Why won't you do something about it?"

"I'll do something when I have the proof, Blair. If you know anything, you need to tell me. Give me the proof so I can do something."

Bieberstein muttered something in an angry tone and ended the call.

Zachary set his phone back down, pondering the call and what he should do about it. The hospital hadn't found anything wrong with Bieberstein, but that wasn't unexpected. As Bieberstein said, they needed to know what to look for, and it wasn't that unusual to have a seizure without ever discovering the cause.

If Bieberstein were home and resting, that would be one thing, but trying to continue to work at Drake, Chase, Gould while he was in such rough shape was not a good idea. He was sounding paranoid, which he hadn't been when Zachary had talked to him earlier. That could be a sign that his sleep deprivation was getting really serious.

He looked at the time on his phone. It was too late to be calling anyone. If any of the interns were still at Drake, Chase, Gould, they would already know that Bieberstein was having issues. He doubted any of the supervisors would be working there so late, and he didn't have any of their personal cell numbers.

Except for one.

But was it really appropriate to call the owner of the firm about a low-level employee?

Zachary dithered for a while. He didn't know whether to leave Bieberstein alone and just let the other interns deal with him if they were still there, or whether to get involved.

But if his theory of the poisoning was true, which Bieberstein now believed, then the interns would be working against him.

After considerable mental back-and-forth, Zachary finally decided to just bite the bullet. What was the worst that could happen? Gordon would tell him off and say not to call him again. Zachary tapped in the number Gordon had given him, and waited.

He had to allow several rings for it to actually connect, and then there would be a few more before Gordon woke up. Even more, if his phone was on vibrate and he was a heavy sleeper, in which case it might just keep ringing until his voicemail picked up.

"Zachary? What's wrong?"

Gordon's voice was sharp and alert, not like he'd just been awakened from a sound sleep. Zachary looked at the time again to confirm to himself that it was the middle of the night; he hadn't just been confused or misread it.

"Uh, Gordon…"

"Yes. What is it?"

"I just had a call from Blair Bieberstein, and I'm a little concerned…"

"Blair? What was he calling you about in the middle of the night?"

"He's checked himself out of the hospital and he's at the office, working."

"At three o'clock in the morning? What's he doing?"

"I don't know. But he hasn't been able to sleep since he was admitted, something they gave him kept him awake. And who knows how many hours he was awake before that. These interns put in wicked hours."

"We have rules about how long employees can work. We don't want people working themselves to death."

Zachary paused, considering. "We'll have to talk about that," he told Gordon. "But to get straight to the heart of this… I think Blair is having a breakdown. He's paranoid. He hasn't been sleeping. He's afraid to go home."

"You think he could be violent?"

"Violent? Well, no… I'm worried about his state of mind. That he might be harming his health. You wouldn't want any more bad press."

He knew that big corporate types worried about how their organizations were portrayed in the media. What people thought of them. They didn't want people to boycott their services.

"You really think that he's at the office and having a breakdown?"

"Yes."

"Okay." There was a period of silence. Zachary pictured Gordon wiping his eyes and trying to get his brain and body woken up and operating properly. "Thanks for letting me know that, Zachary. I'll see if there is anything I can do."

Zachary decided that it was time for him to go to bed if he didn't want to end up in the same shape as Bieberstein. He wasn't operating on very much sleep himself and he'd been sitting in front of the computer for far too long.

So he did a quick toilet before bed and climbed in under his blankets.

As he tried to settle himself to sleep, he longed to hear Kenzie's voice or to have her in the bed with him, her body stretched out warm along his. He slept better with her there, in spite of any kicking or blanket hogging. It was comforting to have someone there with him when anxiety or nightmares struck.

But he wasn't going to call her at three o'clock in the morning. She was a lot scarier than Gordon and she wouldn't put up with such nonsense.

He had hoped that his tired eyes and headache would mean he could fall asleep quickly for once, but he tossed and turned and couldn't find a comfortable position. He was too hot and too cold and too restless and too exhausted. After an hour, he got up and went to the medicine cabinet for a sleeping pill. Maybe just half of one. He needed something that was just strong enough to take the edge off. He'd been reluctant to take any kind of sleep aid since accidentally overdosing at Mr. Peterson's house during the serial killer investigation. He had been taking painkillers he wasn't accustomed to and had apparently managed to take several pain pills and sleeping pills before falling asleep. The resulting nap had lasted most of the next day.

When he opened the medicine cabinet, he saw Kenzie's note still taped to the back of the medicine cabinet door with the stern instruction to "Call somebody!" with her number, Bridget's, Mario's, and several hotlines or emergency operators. But that was only for when he was contemplating suicide, not when he was just having trouble sleeping.

He took an herbal sleep aid rather than the stronger prescription pills. He would need to be up in just a few hours and he didn't want to be groggy.

Zachary woke up as dawn started to peek in through the windows. He lay in bed for a few minutes, thinking he might fall back asleep again, but he knew that he wouldn't. When he was extra stressed or anxious about something, he could shut down and sleep through the day, but in his normal state, he couldn't sleep more than a few hours at night and then his body and brain were too restless to stay asleep.

He got up, made some coffee, and tidied up the kitchen and any stray dishes while he waited for it to perk. He realized that there were barely any dirty dishes. There should have been more if he had eaten the day before. He checked the garbage for microwave dinner wrappers, and closed the cupboard again slowly. He looked over at the microwave and didn't open the door. He knew he had eaten supper the night before. He had set an alarm so he wouldn't forget that there was something warming in the microwave. He had obviously just laid the box down somewhere he shouldn't have.

He went into the living room and checked the garbage by his desk. He checked under the edge of the couch and any other places he might have put down the remains of his meal and not picked them back up again. He returned to the kitchen as the coffee started to drip into his travel mug, and looked on top of the fridge and behind the garbage in case he had somehow missed the garbage bin.

He impatiently watched the coffee dribble into his mug. He still refused to open the microwave door. He knew that he had taken his supper out of the microwave the night before. He had made sure he wouldn't forget.

Zachary picked up his coffee mug and went to his computer to check his email and read through his handwritten notes. After a few sips, he put the spill-proof travel mug far away from his computer and keyboard. Remembering his discussions with Gerry about making sure that all of his work was properly digitized and stored in the cloud, he took a few minutes to snap pictures of the pages of his notebook and save the resulting files where they would automatically sync to the cloud. Having lost all of his work product once before, he wasn't willing to let that happen again.

The phone rang. Zachary leaned back tiredly in his chair and picked it up. Heather's face was on the screen. He tapped it and smiled at her, holding the phone in front of him.

"Hi, Heather."

"Good morning, Zach!" Her voice was chipper. She shook her head at him. Zachary hadn't shaved or even combed his hair yet, but if she were going to video call him in the early morning, she was going to have to take what she got. "You don't look like you've been up for long."

"Not long, no, but you didn't wake me up."

"That's good. You're sleeping better?"

"I'm sleeping… more regularly." His sleep schedule after the assault had been unpredictable, but since he'd been seeing his therapist like he was supposed to, he was doing better. Not a lot of sleep, but he at least had some idea of when he would be asleep and didn't have to worry about missing client calls in the middle of the day because he'd passed out.

"Good," Heather approved. Zachary didn't imagine he looked well-rested. He tended to have bags under his eyes and to look like a homeless person if he hadn't cleaned himself up, but Heather had seen him enough mornings to know that was just his usual morning face. "So… I don't know if you'll approve or not, but I did a bit of extra investigating that you didn't exactly ask for."

"On the skips?"

"No, on your company. Drake, Chase, Gould."

"Oh." Zachary blinked, thinking about that. He hadn't asked Heather to do anything regarding the case, had just bounced a few ideas off of her, but he didn't mind her taking the initiative. She'd obviously found something of interest, or she wouldn't be calling him. "Okay. What kind of investigating did you do? What did you find?"

"They've had a few weird stories in the media lately. This thing with Lauren wasn't the first time that something has happened to one of their employees."

"What else?"

Heather propped her phone on a stand and pulled out a file to refer to the printouts. "Okay, how about this one? A local homeless outreach program picks up a woman who claims to have amnesia. She doesn't know who she is or where she came from."

"Uh-huh…"

"And when the woman's picture runs in the news, they find out that she was an executive at Chase Gold."

"Really? What was her name? What department was she in?"

"Shelby Matters. And she was working in something called foreign futures. Don't ask me what that is. I think I'd need an entire college degree to understand what exactly it is that Chase Gold does. But apparently one thing that they do is drive their employees past the brink of sanity."

Zachary thought of Bieberstein. "Yeah. I've been a little concerned about that myself. So what happened to this Shelby woman? Did she get hit on the head? Was she drugged or sick?"

"She seemed to be in good health. The doctors said that she appeared to have been living on the street for only a few days, and nobody had reported her missing, so she couldn't have been gone for too long. No head injury. No emotional or physical trauma that anyone was aware of."

"Did they do a tox screen? Look for drugs or poisons?"

"They checked for drugs, but they said she wasn't on anything when she was brought in. No one knows why she would suddenly develop amnesia."

Zachary might have seen the reports in the news, but at the time he hadn't known anything about Drake, Chase, Gould so, while it was an interesting story, it hadn't rung any alarm bells for him. But now, thinking about Lauren hitting her head and drowning in her bathtub and Bieberstein passing out on the treadmill, he had to wonder if it was a pattern. But Shelby Matters wasn't an intern. It sounded like she worked in a completely different department. And if it was a few months back, then that had been before the current crop of interns had even started.

"Zachary…?"

He focused back on Heather's image on the phone screen. "Just thinking through the possibilities. Sorry. What else?"

"You're going to need to prepare yourself for this one," she warned.

Zachary looked at her, trying to anticipate what she meant. What had happened that she was worried was going to trigger a bad reaction for him? Another sexual assault?

"Telling me to be prepared doesn't really help me, Feathers," Zachary said, shaking his head. "What are you talking about? How is this going to bother me?"

"You told me before that you have flashbacks. And Tyrrell said that he's seen a couple of smaller ones. I just don't want to jump into this and have you panic."

Zachary took a few deep breaths. He didn't know what else to do to prepare himself. He'd gone through ideas of how to get himself grounded with his therapist and with Kenzie. Focusing on the things that he could see and hear and smell in real life to keep the flashbacks at bay. But he didn't usually know ahead of time that something was going to trigger him, and he wasn't sure how to prepare for that. His heart rate was rising just worrying about what it was Heather was going to say.

"It was a house fire."

Zachary swallowed. Yes. That was one of his triggers, alright. Anything to do with fire or candles was bad, but a house fire… that was enough to bring on the worst of his memories. He tried to keep his breathing nice and deep, but found himself gasping in between the longer breaths.

"Okay," he said, his voice strangled, "what about a house fire?"

"They had an employee, or a former employee, who had a fire. She was apparently writing some kind of tell-all book about her life in the investment banking industry in general, and Drake, Chase, Gould in particular."

"And all of her work was destroyed in the fire."

"You got it."

He nodded and breathed and waited for Heather to go on with a more casual topic, something that wasn't going to set off more flashbacks.

"She ran back into the house," Heather said, a little apologetically. "She tried to go back in to get the manuscript or her computer."

Zachary felt the burning flames. He could hardly draw in breath, because the air was superheated from the fire. Paper burned faster and hotter than anything else. She had no chance of being able to go back into the house to save her papers. And her computer… a better chance, but…

He felt himself on the floor, crawling, feeling for safety, for somewhere to hide. The flames roared all around him, sounding like a wild beast, like some living demon that had come to destroy him.

"Zachary. Zachary, it's okay. She got out. She only had very minor burns. No grafts. The firefighters were mad at her for rushing back into the house and putting the first responders who were trying to keep her safe at risk, but none of them were injured. Everyone was okay. Zachy. Zachary!"

Zachary nodded, trying to find his way out of the avalanche of sensations. He tried to do what he'd been taught. He tried to focus on Heather's voice, the smell of his coffee, anything that he could actually see or touch. The flames started to recede.

"It's okay, Zachary. You're safe. Nothing is going to hurt you."

He nodded again.

Heather started singing a silly song, her voice strained and unsure to start with. "Great, green gobs of greasy, grimy gopher guts…"

Zachary laughed. He saw her as she had been before the fire. Sunburned and freckled from many hours spent outdoors trying to keep the kids out of their parents' hair. Her blond hair bleached in the sun, tangled and stringy. Scrapes on her knees and holes in her pants. How had she managed to ruin another pair of pants? He could hear his mother's voice, reprimanding her for being so careless.

Clothes cost money, you know! You're going to have to wear clothes with holes in them to school!

Heather's elfin laugh. She continued to sing the song. The words came to Zachary's lips and he tried to sing them too. They finished together and Zachary looked at her in the small phone screen.

"Thank you."

She smiled. "You always liked that one."

"Yeah, I did. The grosser the better!"

How many times had he sung it at school or the dinner table or somewhere else it would get him in trouble? It just wormed its way into his head and he couldn't get it out, couldn't stop himself from humming or singing it.

"You okay now?"

"Sure." He took another sip of his coffee, which was starting to cool. He looked at the time, tried to get reoriented in the physical world. "Yeah. You're right. That's... a bad one for me."

"Anyway, she was an ex-employee of Drake, Chase, Gould. They said that she had signed a confidentiality agreement and wasn't allowed to reveal anything about the company to the public, but she said that was only limited to trade secrets and client confidential information, and that she could talk about the company and how they operated and the things they were doing if she wanted to. They didn't agree."

"Did they take her to court?"

"You got it. How did you know?"

"Because I know of another case where they took a whistleblower to court. How can they do that? How can they keep saying that people aren't allowed to talk about the company? Just because people are disaffected, that's not enough reason to quash them, is it? How bad is what they are doing?"

"You've been investigating them, so you're the one who probably knows best. What do you think they're trying to hide?"

"Well…" Zach considered. "I know they're hiding how many hours they are forcing the interns to work. They've got this health and wellness program that's supposed to be so wonderful… but if it is, then why are all of these things happening? Why do they have people breaking down and complaining about the way the company treated them? If they really were so perfect, they wouldn't have all of these problems, would they?"

"I don't know. Are they that much worse than any other company in the industry? Comparable in size? I have no idea if they have sued more ex-employees than any of their competitors, or if they've had more employees with mental illness concerns. I don't know if they're doing anything any differently than any other company."

"But they must. You don't hear about this kind of thing with the other companies."

"Well, I don't think that's absolutely true. I came across a few other stories when I was investigating. An intern who stepped off a building. Another who died of a cocaine overdose. There are lots of stories about how hard they work their employees in this industry."

"So maybe it's considered normal? I'm glad I'm not an investment banker."

"You and me both," Heather agreed, nodding her head and putting her papers back in the file. "You and me both."

Zachary had called Barbara to update her on where he was in his investigation, even though he hadn't come to any kind of landing on what had happened to Lauren. He didn't have anything that could definitively point to murder or to accident. He was pretty sure that the medical examiner's report was going to come back as 'accident.' He hadn't been able to find anything yet that would have convinced them otherwise, even though Dr. Wiltshire had believed Zachary in the past. He couldn't abuse that past trust, or the next time he was sure that an 'accident' needed to be reinvestigated or looked at more carefully, they wouldn't do it. It was a fine balance.

Happy that he had called, Barbara had asked if they could meet in person once again.

"I have been talking to Deidre, Lauren's sister, and she really wants to talk to you. She has been wondering how it could have happened too, and… she just wants to talk to you. Would that be okay? Could we all meet together?"

Zachary usually liked to meet with the family, so he was glad for an opening. It could be awkward approaching the family on his own if they didn't know that Barbara had opened up an investigation. It would be hard for them to understand why he was looking into it. He also didn't want them calling Detective Robinson demanding to know why Zachary was investigating it when the police weren't. He wanted to keep his relations with the police department as good as possible.

"Sure," he agreed. "I would be happy to meet with her. Can we meet at your apartment or at her place? It would be easier, I think, if it wasn't in a public setting."

He had met with Barbara in public because it was more comfortable that way. A woman by herself wouldn't want to meet at the apartment of a man that she didn't know, and even meeting at her place could be awkward if she were alone. But with there being two women, and Barbara having already met him, he didn't think Barbara would mind a private meeting so much. It was easier to express emotion without everybody in a coffee shop watching you and speculating about why you were blubbering all over the place.

"I guess… if you wanted to come to the apartment," Barbara agreed. There was hesitation in her voice, and Zachary waited for her to decide whether it was really okay with her or not. If she didn't want to talk about what she had seen that day in the setting where it had happened, she could suggest somewhere else to meet. "Yes," Barbara said eventually, in a stronger voice. "I'd be okay with that, but I'll have to check with Deidre. I don't know if she'll want to be here… where it happened, you know. I do want to get some of Lauren's things out of here, so I can see about getting another roommate. I don't really want to move, even with what happened. Though who is going to want to move into the room of someone who just died? I just don't know."

"You might not want to include that fact on Craig's List," Zachary said.

She gave a little laugh. "No, you're right. I think I might leave that part out. If I can avoid them finding out until after they are moved in, that would be better."

Zachary nodded, even though she couldn't see him. "Okay,

then, why don't you give Deidre a call and see if she's up for it, and settle on a time and place. My schedule is pretty open. I can see you today, if you like. Just give me a call back when you've worked it out."

So that was how Zachary had ended up back at Barbara's apartment, sitting on her couch and letting his eyes travel around the room, looking for the imprint that Lauren had left on the room and any stray clues he might have missed the first time he had visited the apartment. Barbara had been packing Lauren's things up for her family, but it appeared that pretty much everything in the living room had been Barbara's, since there were no obvious holes left by the removal of Lauren's items.

Barbara was watching him.

"She didn't spend a lot of time here," she told Zachary, repeating what she had said before. "Most of her things were just in her bedroom. We were roommates, equals, but she was really more like a tenant, just keeping things in her own room. I told her that we could decorate together, she could come furniture shopping with me, all of that… but she was so wrapped up with her work chasing gold that she could never find the time. So it was up to me."

"She had changed," Deidre said softly. She had similar features to Lauren's but a little softer, more blurred around the edges. She sat with her hands folded in her lap, looking calm and sedate, but exuding an aura of sadness. Her blond hair was down, just brushing the tops of her shoulders. She didn't have red-rimmed, baggy eyes, but Zachary sensed that she was in mourning just the same. Not everybody was as free with the waterworks as Barbara. "I don't understand how she could have changed so much in the time that she was with that company. It was like they had a hold over her. Not a threat, I don't mean. But a… like they had sucked her into something. Instead of being our Lauren, with all of her interests and plans, she became part of Chase Gold. A dedicated part of their machine."

"She had changed a lot?" Zachary asked, thumbing the pages

in his notebook to find a clean page. He looked over at Barbara, who hadn't suggested this when she had talked about Lauren.

"She had," Deidre said. "Before that company, she was Lauren, part of our family, with all kinds of dreams for the future, all of the ways she wanted to change the world, to make a fulfilling life. She wanted a family, a social life, volunteering to do projects overseas, that kind of thing. She was such a warm person, she wanted to make a difference in the world. But once she was there at Drake, Chase, Gould, we just lost her. She stopped seeing the family, cut herself off. She would talk about *the-company-this* and *the-company-that*. Her supervisor said this, the health and welfare program said that, the slimy owner of the company said whatever. Everything that came out of her mouth… came from *them*, instead of from inside her."

Zachary frowned, scratching down a few words to remind himself of the points he wanted to follow up on later. He looked over at Barbara again, raising his brows.

"You didn't notice any change?" he asked her.

"Well… no. Honestly. But she was already working at the company when she moved in here. I didn't know her before Chase Gold, so I wouldn't see a difference, would I? Deidre is right, she did talk a lot about what the company's philosophy was on different aspects of her life. And she didn't talk about her family or do things with them. Just like she didn't do things with me. She would say that it would be fun to go shopping for furniture together but then she didn't have time, and would say that her supervisor needed her to put in some more hours on this project or that she just needed to work a bit longer on something… her work was her life."

"And it wasn't before," Deidre said earnestly. "She was normal before. When she was in school, she was on sports teams. She went to clubs and meetups. She did things with friends. She had dinner with the family, at least on weekends. She'd find the time. She had a more balanced life."

"Did you know she was talking about having her tubes tied? To make herself more attractive to the company for the remaining permanent position?"

Deidre's jaw dropped. She caught her breath and for a minute seemed unable to control the emotions that welled up. She closed her eyes, swallowed, and breathed deeply for a minute. "No," she said unnecessarily. "I didn't know that." She shook her head, eyes welling with tears. "It surprises me and it doesn't." She took a few seconds to try to get her composure again. "That's just what she was like after she started at that company. Before she started working there, she always wanted a family. She always talked about finding the right guy and having a couple of kids. She loved babies, and she loved all of the little cousins in our family. She was always the first one to reach out to hold a new baby or comfort a crying child. Even before the mother could get there. She wanted that life, to have everything, family and friends and all kinds of different experiences. But after she started working there, she was different. She was a corporate woman. She was… I don't want to say cold, but that's how I felt around her. Like they had just frozen all of her feelings. Everything that wasn't in alignment with succeeding at her job. Like freezing off warts."

Zachary pondered the change in Lauren. To go from loving children and wanting them in her life to talking about having her tubes tied so that children would never complicate her corporate life was so very drastic. He couldn't see a person making that kind of turnaround in just a few weeks. It wasn't natural. Had she just been playing for the company? Telling them what she thought they wanted to hear in order to get the job? But what would she do once she had the job and they expected her to follow through? Would she stay that new corporate woman, willing to give herself fully to the company? Or would she try to get her old life back, to let the old Lauren personality seep back in again?

He took a deep breath, looking at the page of the notebook in front of him and addressed the next problem.

"You called the owner of the company slimy. Who did you mean?"

"The top guy. Drake. He was a piece of work. I hated him."

"Gordon Drake?" Zachary tried not to let the surprise enter into his voice. "He seemed like a nice enough guy to me."

"Nice. Yeah. He likes to give that impression, doesn't he? He's the perfect gentleman. The face of the company. He's the one who talks to the media about his wonderful organization and all of the wonderful things they are doing. He's the one that handles all of that public relations stuff and shows everyone how wonderful the company really is. It doesn't matter that people are dying at Chase Gold. It doesn't matter that they are turning workers into drones and zombies. All that matters is that the company gets to be as big internationally as all of the other investment banking firms. He believes that they can take over the world, honestly. He's got this ego that's bigger than anything you've ever seen before. Like… a god complex. He is the master of the company, and when the company is the biggest investment banking firm in the world, he will control the economy of countries. He'll control the economics of the world."

"Really. Wow. I never really got that from him."

Deidre shook her head. "The guy rubs me the wrong way. He always pretends that he cares about his employees. If you saw him on any of the news spots after Lauren died… He's mugging for the camera. He's practically crying, he cares so much. Everything he says and does is calculated to make him and his company look good."

Zachary thought about Gordon's words about the interns being the lifeblood of the company. About him reassuring Bieberstein at the hospital about how important he was and how much he meant to the company. He really did put on a good show. He *seemed* to mean the things that he said. But was Zachary just seeing what he expected to? Was he seeing Gordon in a good light because he had been kind to Zachary in the past? Because he had hired Zachary to find Bridget when she had been kidnapped, had defended him in front of the police, had admitted to the police that Bridget had been the aggressor in their dysfunctional marriage and not the other way around?

Gordon had always treated Zachary with friendliness and respect, rather than as a rival for Bridget's affections. Zachary had always assumed that it was because Gordon believed that he had Bridget for himself and she would never consider going back to Zachary. And he was right, Bridget had a relationship with Gordon that was totally different from what she'd had with Zachary. Gordon was an equal, a partner, someone that she looked up to and respected. With Zachary, it had been different. She had been half mother and half nurse. Trying to fix him and show him off to her friends. They had been besotted with each other in the beginning, but that had ended when she realized that she couldn't change him. She couldn't tell him how to behave and transform him into someone she could take with her to gala events and not have him embarrass her. She couldn't tell him to stop being depressed or having flashbacks.

And Gordon had somehow talked Bridget into getting pregnant. Her pregnancy could not have been an accident. Not when Bridget would have to use the eggs that she'd had frozen before her treatment for ovarian cancer. She had been resistant to freezing her eggs, insisting that she never wanted children. It had only been at the doctor's insistence that she had gone ahead with it. If Gordon could talk Bridget into having children with him, then how hard would it have been for him to talk Lauren out of having a family, and dedicating her life instead to Drake, Chase, Gould?

"Uh, Zachary...?"

Zachary looked at Barbara. He looked back at Deidre.

"He had me fooled," he admitted. "I'm supposed to be a good detective, but I never saw him that way."

"I bet if you looked into his background, you'd find all kinds of bodies," Deidre said. "Not literal bodies, I mean, but all of the people and companies that he stepped on to get to where he is now. He doesn't care who he hurts in his climb to the top. He's like Hitler. He doesn't believe that other people have feelings or purpose. He is bound and determined to rule the world someday, and he manipulates whatever and whoever he has to." Her mouth twisted into a bitter scowl. "He's not what he appears to be."

The thing was, Zachary *had* checked out Gordon's background. Before he'd ever started with the investigation at Drake, Chase, Gould, he had checked Gordon out, looking for dirt, looking for anything to indicate that he wasn't the person he appeared to be. He wanted to find something that he could tell Bridget, to convince her that she didn't want to stay with him. Something that he could hold up and say 'Gordon isn't better than me. Just look at what he's done in the past.'

But he hadn't found any dirt. He hadn't found any bodies. When people talked about Gordon, they smiled and spoke warmly. Past employers and coworkers, past intimate partners, everyone. They all agreed that he was what he appeared to be.

When Zachary had been called in to help find Bridget, Gordon could have thrown him under the bus. He could have told the police that Zachary had been a stalker, that he had pursued Bridget long after they had separated. He could have said that Zachary had a checkered past. That he'd grown up in foster care and institutions, and everyone knew the kind of person that bred. He could have talked about Zachary's many failings, both inside and outside of the marriage. But he hadn't. He had supported Zachary and he'd been completely genuine about it. Zachary had no doubt that he had meant what he said.

But then, it wouldn't have helped Gordon for the cops to have put Zachary in jail or arrested him for Bridget's kidnapping. Then Zachary couldn't do what Gordon wanted him to do. He wouldn't have been able to track Bridget down in time and the police would never have gotten to her until it was too late. If they had kept Zachary in custody for another day, Bridget would have been dead by the time they found her. If they found her.

So which man was Gordon? Was he the man that Zachary had seen and secretly admired, the man that he had wanted to be in his marriage to Bridget? Or was he a snake, a persona that was put on for the public, so that he could get what he wanted?

If power corrupted, then Gordon was surely corrupt.

Zachary saw Kenzie's name on his missed calls when he got out of the meeting with Barbara and Deidre. He had ignored the vibrating of his phone in his pocket, and it was probably a good thing that he had. Getting the autopsy results in the middle of a meeting with the family and client wouldn't have been a good thing. He wanted a chance to review the results and talk things over with Kenzie before he gave the results to Barbara.

Although, maybe talking the results over with Kenzie was no longer an option. It had always been part of the process before, but now that they were no longer together… were they still friends, and was that enough for him to get her ear and a little bit of her time to go through the results?

He got settled in his car and then called her back.

She answered after a minute with a brisk "Medical Examiner's office."

"It's Zachary."

"Oh, hi, Zachary. Sorry, I didn't look at the caller I.D."

"No problem. You have the results?"

"Dr. Wiltshire has made a finding of accidental death, as expected. Combination of blow to the head and drowning. Probably the lack of oxygen killed her before the intercranial bleeding."

Zachary nodded slowly. Pretty much what he had expected. "Do you have time to go over the details, or should I just come down and get the report?"

"I've got a couple of minutes."

"Anything show up in the bloodwork? Drugs, alcohol, medications?"

"Some alcohol. Not enough to have impaired her. Not considered to have contributed to her death."

"Any stimulants?"

"No."

"Any medications? Prescription, over the counter?"

"Nothing that showed up on the usual tests, but you know that we don't test for everything. Was she prescribed something specific you are looking for?"

"No. It's just that… someone else at her office had an accident this week. Passed out on the treadmill and had a seizure. Lacerations and broken bones, but he was okay."

"And you're wondering whether there was any connection between the two accidents?"

"It's an odd coincidence."

"Did the hospital find any reason for his seizure?"

"No. They said it was probably just a one-time thing, maybe he had a virus."

"And did you find anything to indicate they're wrong?"

"No, not yet," he admitted.

She was silent for a few moments. "Did you have any other questions?"

"Was there anything unusual? Any other illness or recent injuries?"

"Iron levels were low, but not drastically. Some indications of stress on the heart. Maybe she'd been sick lately, some virus. The flu."

"Like my seizure victim?"

"Well… yes. People do get the flu. Sometimes it can hit one person harder than expected. Especially if they are already run down or susceptible. And it does circulate through offices."

"What does it mean that there were indications of stress on the heart? Too much exercise? Or is that just from generic stress like being worried about something or being pressured by a deadline?"

"More like overwork. Not just one brutal exercise session or worrying about making a deadline. But a constant level of stress that put an extra strain on the heart."

"Working eighteen-hour days?"

"Well, that could do it. Yes. Was she?"

"Depends who you talk to. According to the date stamps on her emails and computer files, yes. According to her timesheet at work, no."

"Her heart would agree with the computer."

"And low iron, could that be overwork too?"

"Not directly, but if she wasn't eating properly, was drinking, had heavy bleeding, was taking a lot of Aspirin or another medication, some of those things could cause it. It is possible to die from working too hard. It's common enough in Japan that they even have a word for it. *Karoshi.*"

Zachary thought about that for a moment before going on.

"Did she have any injuries? Other than the injury to the head?"

"No. That was the only thing of note. Everybody gets scrapes and bruises from running into a coffee table or doorway or dropping something on their toes, but there wasn't anything to indicate any violence."

"Could someone have held her under the water?"

"You know from Declan's case that that would cause bruising. Unless she was drugged, which according to our tests, she was not. She hadn't had enough alcohol to knock her out."

"What if someone held her face down by the head, where she was already injured? Then you wouldn't be able to tell there was any bruising from his hand."

"But she would probably also have had bruising on the other side. On her nose or chin or some part of her face. Because he would be pressing her face down into the bottom of the bathtub while she fought back."

"What if she didn't fight back, because she was already knocked unconscious by the blow?"

Kenzie paused while she thought this through. "Possibly," she said cautiously. "Depends how bad the damage to her brain was."

"Defensive wounds?"

"Nothing that looked like defensive wounds."

"Broken hyoid?"

"You don't think I would have led with that? No, no broken hyoid or bruising on the neck."

"Do we have a more exact time of death? Anything more specific than between the time she left work and the time she was discovered?"

"That's pretty tricky, since we don't know the temperature of the water. So we don't know how warm it kept the body or how quickly it cooled it down. We can make estimates, assuming she would have run it slightly above body temperature, but not hot enough to be uncomfortable… but if she ran a cold bath to wake herself up, then we'd be completely wrong."

"Dr. Wiltshire didn't have any reservations at all? Everything pointed to an accident?"

"We didn't have your report of someone else at her company having an accident, so no. With that information, he might have thought about the possibility of foul play, but I still don't think he would have made any other finding."

"You think it's just a coincidence?"

"Sounds like it. Just one of those things. How closely did they work together?"

"Pretty close. They were both working out of the same bullpen, competing for two permanent job positions. In fact, they were the two who were thought to be the best prospects for the permanent positions."

"Huh."

Zachary thought he might sense a grudging admission of the possibility that the two accidents might be related. But she didn't jump right into it.

"It could just be that they both had the flu as it made its rounds of the office. I'll mention it to Dr. Wiltshire. Like I said, he's already made a finding and nothing is likely to change his mind… but I'll at least pass the information on. What he does is up to him."

"Okay. I'm not going to report to my client yet, not until I hear from you one way or the other."

"Fine. I'll let you know, probably by end of day."

Zachary tried calling Bieberstein. He wanted to make sure Bieberstein was okay, but didn't want to be responsible for waking him up if he'd finally gotten to sleep. Hopefully Bieberstein would at least have the sense to turn his phone ringer off if he were going to sleep.

There was no answer. The phone just kept ringing and ringing until it eventually went to voicemail after about fifty rings. Zachary called the main number at Chase Gold and had the receptionist put him through to Mandy. She answered the phone breathlessly after a couple of rings.

"Hello?"

"It's Zachary Goldman, Mandy. I was looking for Blair Bieberstein. Is he around?"

"Biebs? I don't know." There was a pause, as Zachary assumed Mandy looked over the tops of the cubicles to see if the other intern was there. "I don't see him. But I don't know. He works on other projects sometimes. He isn't always even on this floor. They farm him out wherever he is needed. Do you want me to tell him to call you? Or you could leave a message on his phone or send him a text or email."

"Could you ask whether anyone else has seen him? He was

acting kind of weird last night, and you know he got hit on the head yesterday. You wouldn't want anything to happen to him."

Mandy covered up the mike on the phone while she talked to the other interns, then eventually returned. "No, no one has seen him around since the hospital yesterday. Well, except Daniel. He says that he saw Bieberstein for a few minutes last night, before he left for the day."

"Before Daniel left or before Bieberstein left?"

"Daniel."

"Can I talk to him?"

Mandy blew an impatient sigh into her phone. "You'll have to call him on his own phone."

"Do you have his number?"

She was silent as she looked it up. Then she read it off to him. "I gotta get back to work now. Good luck."

She hung up without another word. Zachary dialed Daniel's number. Daniel of course knew who it was and answered right away.

"Hello, Mr. Goldman. Or is it Detective?"

"Zachary is fine. Mandy said you saw Bieberstein yesterday?"

"For a few minutes, yes. He was here before I left."

"Was he the only one here? When you left, I mean?"

"The only one I saw. I don't know if there was anyone else here… not in the bullpen, but a VP in his office maybe, I wouldn't know if someone was sitting with their door closed."

"How did he seem to you?"

"Weird," Daniel said. "But he always seems weird to me."

"Was he any different from usual?"

"I don't know. Honestly. Biebs is just Biebs. He's kind of nutty, but he has a brain and knows how to use it!"

"I gather the company finds him invaluable."

"Yeah, a lot of people think he's the best thing since sliced bread. Can't be replaced or improved upon."

"You don't sound like you think so," Zachary ventured, sensing a dismissiveness in Daniel's tone.

"I don't believe there is anyone who can't be replaced. It's the company that matters, not the individuals. If we work together as a company, as one smooth, efficient machine, that's what makes us great. We become something more when we contribute to the success of the company."

"Uh… yeah. That makes sense. So I guess Bieberstein wasn't there when you got in this morning?"

"No."

"Is that unusual? He must have to check in with you. Have you called around to see if he went home?"

"He's one of my interns, but he gets borrowed by other departments. Whoever needs him the most. It's sort of out of my control and I don't always know where he is."

"Have you tried calling him?"

"No."

"I'm worried about him," Zachary said, trying to convey some urgency toward Daniel, who seemed to think there was nothing to be concerned about. "When he called me last night, he was really paranoid. He hadn't slept and he thought that someone was after him, trying to harm him."

A few seconds passed before Daniel spoke. "He thought who was after him? Exactly what was he worried about?"

"He didn't specify who. Just 'them.' I told you, he was paranoid. I think he was going off the deep end and I'm worried something might have happened to him. Do you think you could spend some time and try to track him down?"

Daniel grumbled. "I don't have a lot of time to be babysitting. I'll send out an email blast to the department heads, but I'm not going to be wasting my time trying to track him down by phone. He knows where he's supposed to be. If he skips out on us, he'll get fired."

"I'm not worried about his job. I'm worried about his safety. I don't think he's skipping work. He might have had some kind of dissociative episode or another accident."

"That didn't work for Matters, and it isn't going to work for him. You either show up at work, or you're fired."

"Matters?" Zachary tried to figure out who Daniel was talking about.

"The one who pretended she had amnesia. 'Oh, no, I couldn't come into work, because I didn't know who I was. I forgot all about my job.' If you think that got her her job back, forget about it. She didn't. She could waste her time in a homeless shelter."

"That's pretty heartless."

"I don't have any empathy for someone who betrays the company. After all the time and money that they spend on us, everything they do for us, the prestige, the money, the health care and other benefits? This is an amazing place to work. If someone can't figure that out…?" He snorted. "If they can't see how much the job is worth, they can find something else somewhere else."

"I guess so," Zachary said. He sucked his cheeks in, hesitating. "So you'll send that email, make sure that Bieberstein is just working for another department, and nothing has happened to him?"

"I suppose," Daniel said grudgingly.

"If the company takes care of its employees… well, it can't do that without the employees doing their part. They can't take care of Bieberstein without your help."

"Yeah. You're right. We're all part of the machine. I'll see if I can find him."

Zachary checked his email and saw that he had one from Bev. He was surprised that it had taken her that long to come to the realization that he had Lauren's phone and computer, both of which were undoubtedly the property of Drake, Chase, Gould. He had expected her to demand their return a lot earlier.

He had the cloned drive, so he could still review any of the information that was stored on her computer. He still had the proof that she had worked the hours Barbara said she had, that she had been denied time off, that they had not even given her time when she had a signed letter from her doctor. Kenzie didn't seem to think that Lauren's illnesses and anemia had anything to do with her death—or Dr. Wiltshire didn't think so—but they still could have contributed. If she were even more exhausted because she'd had the flu and hadn't been given the time to recover from it, or if she'd fainted because she was sick or because she was weak from the anemia, then the company could be partially responsible for what had happened to her. Maybe nothing that could ever be proven in court or give her family any financial recompense, but at least they would know a little more about how she had died. Maybe it wouldn't make them feel any better, but maybe it would.

He looked one more time at her phone and computer, trying to think of whether there was anything he had missed. He didn't want to go snooping in any corporate secrets, but he did want to make sure he had looked at anything that might have affected her mentally or any sign that there was someone out there who wanted to harm her. He hadn't come across any jealous boyfriends. Jealous coworkers, maybe. People who wanted the position that she appeared to have clinched. But he couldn't find any motive for anyone outside work to have bad feelings toward her.

He brought up her social networks on his own computer, browsing through the timelines for anything weird or suspicious. There were no menacing messages before she'd died or creepy ones afterward. Any memorial messages indicated that she was a nice girl and that they would really miss her. Earlier on the timeline, before her death, he saw more messages from her family than he had noticed when looking at it before. Of course, social networks changed their algorithms all the time, depending on what you were doing and on what the overlords of the social networks wanted to emphasize. They banned or downvoted some topics and posters and upvoted or emphasized others. Something like an election or a plane crash could upend everything. Maybe it was Lauren's death itself, and an outpouring of loving messages among her family members and friends, that had changed the emphasis of certain topics and posters showing up on her timeline.

He brought the same social network up in the app on her laptop, frozen in time because it couldn't read anything else from the internet. It was handy having all of her personal accounts and social networks contained within the one program, so he could quickly switch from one tab to the other. The computer complained about not having internet access, but he could still read what had been downloaded and cached.

There was barely a word on her timeline from her family or close friends. He scrolled through both computers at the same time, trying to find a place in the timeline when the posts were synchronized, or close to it. But whatever he did, he couldn't find the posts from Lauren's family on her computer. It was like she had blocked them there. Had she been worried about having personal information on an office computer?

He looked through the various settings, trying to find some list of who she had blocked or banned. But if they were blocked on her account, they would be blocked in both places. The work laptop could be filtering certain things, but he couldn't find any user-controlled filters either.

Zachary closed his eyes, thinking about it.

"Gerry… I wonder if you could make a rush visit for me. I have a computer that I need to return to the owner, but there's something weird going on with it. I don't want to put them off for too long, so I was hoping you might have some time today…"

"Did you clone the hard drive?" Gerry demanded.

Zachary smiled. "I didn't remember right away, but yeah, I did."

"So if I can't get over there today, we can access all of the information off of the cloned drive."

"Yeah, I suppose. But do you think you might have some time today? I'd like to have some idea of whether this is important or just some rabbit trail."

"Well… yeah, I could spare an hour or two. You think that will be enough?"

"Yeah. Probably not even that long. Just a few minutes."

Gerry chuckled. "Nothing ever takes just a few minutes on a computer. Especially not anything weird."

Zachary had to admit that was probably true. "So when can I expect you? I'd like to tell the owner something, so they know it's on its way and don't sic the cops or some company thugs on me."

"Just what's going on with this computer?"

"I don't know. Maybe something, maybe nothing. But there have been a lot of accidents going on, and these guys have money, so I don't really want to take the risk of upsetting them if I don't have to."

"I'll try to be there in a couple of hours. I'll get there when I can."

"Thanks. I'll be here."

Gerry was, in many ways, the typical computer hacker/nerd. Glasses, messy hair, comfortable clothes, and a way of talking to computers that made them purr with delight. He was older than Zachary might have expected a computer nerd to be and he had a pot belly, when Zachary pictured all hackers as being skinny, underdeveloped kids. But Gerry had all of the ingredients necessary to figure out what was going on with Lauren's computer and social networks. Zachary let him sit down and showed him the difference between the information on the two computers. Gerry nodded rapidly, chewing on the top of a pencil.

"Yup. Yup. Sure. Let me look at this…"

He said more, but it was all Greek to Zachary. IP addresses and proxies and certificates. He clicked his tongue as he worked rapidly, moving from one computer to the other, settling on Lauren's computer and digging deep down into the code that was unintelligible to Zachary. Zachary sat on the couch and looked at his own email on his phone and tablet, trying not to hover or look impatient.

"This is pretty sophisticated," Gerry said eventually, turning toward Zachary.

"Yeah? What exactly are they doing?"

"The content that this computer can see is being filtered. Like you noticed, you don't see the same thing on the laptop as you see on your computer when you log into her social networks. At first,

I thought it was just the corporate program that they have set up to access the social networks and personal emails. Like, they were trying to filter out any personal stuff so that it was only being used for company work. But it's not quite that. And it's more than that."

"Meaning…?"

"The first level is within the app they're using to log into the social networks. It uses special heuristics to filter out the majority of the posts by family and friends. Not all of it, or the user might realize what's going on, but just enough to keep her… more isolated from her family and friends. You don't see your family's posts, you don't get distracted from your work, I guess. Stuff from more distant friends, and from friends at the company especially, show up. And the stuff from the corporate discussion or project groups she is in. All of that stuff is prioritized. The most important stuff—company stuff—comes to the top of the timeline."

"Do you think the employees are aware of it? That their information is being manipulated?"

"I don't know. It would be hard to spot, unless you're looking at two different computers at the same time, like you were doing. If this is your primary computer, why would you pull it up on any other computer? You've got this one with you all the time, unless they weren't allowed to take them home."

"They were allowed to take them home, and they worked long days, so they were really only home to sleep. This computer would have been the only one she used to do anything. And her phone."

"I'll look at the phone too, but if it's a company phone, I'll bet they've got filters in place there, too."

"But what if she accessed her social networks through the browser instead of the app? Wouldn't she have noticed that something was off then?"

"Only if she was looking at both at the same time. And only if the browser wasn't being filtered as well."

"Was it?"

"They've set up a bunch of private DNS hosting and corporate security certificates to control what the users can see through any program that accesses the internet. Doesn't matter what browser they install, or whether they try an incognito window or to spoof a different IP address. Whatever she did, she couldn't get any access to the internet through this computer that is not controlled."

"So… Google, email, social networks, everything?"

"Everything. As far as this computer is concerned, the internet is a much smaller place than it is on your computer. It only gets a limited window on the world."

"Wait… so…" Zachary tried to keep up with all of the ideas that flooded his brain. He stepped up behind Gerry. "Search Shelby Matters. What does it find?"

Gerry looked at him, eyebrow cocked, then turned back to Lauren's laptop and tried searching the name. He looked at the results. "Have a look."

Zachary leaned in. There were a couple of articles with quotes by Drake, Chase, Gould, and there was a page on the company's website giving details about Shelby Matter's amnesia and how the company would be looking after Matters on long-term disability, but she wouldn't be returning to work. There were links to the company's health and wellness site, how to get counseling and advice if you needed it, and so on. All very orderly and giving the impression that Drake, Chase, Gould had stepped up to help a former employee in distress, far from what Daniel had implied when he had been talking about her.

Gerry turned to Zachary's computer and, without prompting, typed in the same search. There were a lot more articles. There were social media posts and conversations about Matters and what had happened to her, speculating on what had triggered her amnesia and about Drake, Chase, Gould's reputation in the industry. The Drake, Chase, Gould results were there, but much farther down the search results. Drake, Chase, Gould was obviously throttling the information flow to their company computers.

Zachary stood there behind Gerry, trying to process it all. Not only was the company filtering social networks to keep their employees more isolated from their families and involved in their own work groups, but they were controlling their views of the world completely. Assuming that all of the employees had computers that, like Lauren's, were being filtered, the employees didn't get any news that might throw the company in a negative light. Any incidents relating to their employees or the lawsuits against or initiated by Chase Gold would be presented in whatever light the company wanted to show them in. With the company as the hero and the whistleblowers and victims as being in the wrong.

"Do you think all of the employee computers are like this? Or is it possible that Lauren's is the only one that was tampered with?"

"You'd have to get me another computer to look at. But this is a lot of trouble to go through for just one computer. It's pretty sophisticated stuff. I would speculate that it is company-wide, not just targeted at one person."

Zachary started to pace back and forth, trying to control the flow of information coming into his own CPU and to follow all of the possibilities and conclusions outward. Everything was getting clearer, but he wasn't quite there yet. Knowing that the computer was being controlled by the company and that the employees' view of the world was being manipulated was a key puzzle piece. As were the health and welfare program and the attitudes of the employees that he had talked to. The things that had surprised him throughout the investigation were coming into clearer focus, making more sense, and starting to form a picture.

"Who could do this?" he asked Gerry, who was watching him with interest.

"This isn't just someone fooling around. A project like this, with all of the servers and certificates and redirects, the sophistication of the filtering… it's not plug-and-play. It would need a pretty advanced programmer and a lot of money. This isn't just some prank."

"So the company hired someone to set it all up."

"Undoubtedly. And to maintain it. As different stories hit the news or different things become important or the company wants to emphasize certain values more or less, then they're going to need someone tweaking the filters and algorithms."

"Can they tell what sites employees go to? Where they spend their time? If they're searching for anything in particular?"

"They'll have a record of all of the traffic that goes through their servers and where it came from."

"Is this 'spyware'?"

"This in particular? No. But that doesn't mean that there isn't spyware on this computer." Gerry turned back to it and started to launch different programs and inquiries, pulling up black command prompt windows full of data and system management windows that Zachary had never seen before, moving quickly from one to another. "Yeah, it looks like they've got a few programs monitoring what employees are doing, whether they are in a browser or not. Even one that has camera access." Gerry casually picked up a pad of sticky notes from Zachary's desk, tore one sheet in half, and pasted it over the camera lens at the top of the computer screen. "Late is better than never, I suppose. If anyone is concerned about what you're doing with this computer, they might have been watching us and listening in." He rifled through some miscellany in the small toolkit he had brought with him, and pushed an adapter into the microphone jack.

"Can you…" Zachary's mind jumped ahead like a squirrel leaping from one branch to the other, skipping over the treetops. Gerry waited patiently "Can you use the information you have found to get back to the corporate server and… um…"

"Hack it?"

"Well… I don't know. I guess. Can you see what's on it? Employees must be able to access files on their server for work, right? An intern like Lauren probably wouldn't have access to everything…"

"What are you looking for?" Gerry turned back to the laptop and started typing.

Zachary looked at the computer, his stomach knotting. Gerry hadn't said that he'd killed the spyware, so Zachary could only assume that everything they typed and anything they looked at would be recorded somewhere. But he couldn't let that prevent him from investigating the situation fully. He couldn't be scared off by some electronic monitoring.

"Employee records. Whatever we can get access to. I already know they're falsifying timesheets. I'd like to see how much they have in their medical records. And if they're monitoring employee computers, I'd like to see when the computers were on and in use."

"You want to know what they were working on?"

Zachary shrugged. "Not exactly. I don't know what projects they were working on. But if I know who was busy the night or morning that Lauren died, I might be able to eliminate some suspects."

Gerry nodded. He first did what Zachary would have, navigating to the network drives and browsing through them. When he was blocked by the network security, he opened another command prompt and inserted a USB drive into the laptop. From there, Zachary was at a loss as to what Gerry was doing.

He moved back again to wait. Gerry muttered and cajoled the computer, and it was only a few minutes before he was nodding his head.

"Yup, I'm in," he confirmed. "I can get access to human resources… medical, time tracking, employee contracts… I don't see the internet access logs there, so maybe they are with… yeah, there's a security department. This is where the internet logs are stored. Webcam pics. You wanted to know who was where when your victim died?"

"Yes. If we can go through the internet access logs, then I can probably tell who was working when. And you can tell whether they were at work or at home, right? It would be able to tell what network it was connected to?"

"Or if you want to know who was here, you can check the security videos."

"They have security cameras?"

"Oh, yeah." Gerry pulled up a 3D model of the building Drake, Chase, Gould was in, the floors they occupied highlighted and marked with numerous red dots. "They've got cameras."

29

"This is crazy," Zachary said, looking at the video feeds. "They've got cameras everywhere. Wouldn't this be hugely expensive?"

"Data is getting cheaper all the time. You can store terabytes of information. Unheard of ten years ago. And security cameras—you can get them for your doorbell on your house now. Super cheap if you're buying them in bulk. These don't have to be able to move, they're just stationary cameras pointed at desks or doorways. Because there are so many of them, they don't need to be able to pan."

"Can you find a specific desk for me?"

"Sure. Do you have a name or location?"

"Blair Bieberstein."

Gerry nodded. "Is he your best suspect?"

"I'm afraid he might be another victim."

The live video feed came up on the screen. A camera pointed directly at the bullpen, showing all of the desks clearly. The interns were all there, working busily, except for Blair. "This one must be Blair's."

"Nobody there now," Gerry observed.

"No." Zachary swore under his breath. "There's no way they

can say that they didn't know what employees were working what hours. They had cameras on them all day long. They know exactly when they were at their desks and when they weren't. Unless they were away from the office."

"Don't forget the webcams," Gerry reminded him. "If they were on their computers, the company could check up on them. Unless they were away from their desks and away from their computers at a client meeting, the company could see whether they were working or not."

"And then they probably still have some way to track them," Zachary said sarcastically. "Some ankle monitor or microchip."

"It wouldn't be so hard to do. They probably keep their phones with them all the time. If not… give them a step-counter or smartwatch. Then track away."

"Sheesh." Zachary shook his head. And he knew from experience that a phone could be used to eavesdrop even when it did not appear to be active. As long as it had power, it could be getting or sending all kinds of information. "Okay, so can you move back in time to when Bieberstein was at his desk last?"

Gerry started to rewind the video. Zachary watched the other interns walking to and away from their desks backward. They interacted, looked at each other's desks and computers when they were away, put their water bottles down on their desks and walked away, leaving them unattended. Zachary watched as the cubicles cleared out in the early morning, until there were two figures on the screen, Bieberstein and someone standing next to him. Gerry released the controls and let the video play forward at regular speed. The person standing next to Bieberstein was Gordon Drake.

"Back it up a bit more and let me see what happened," Zachary said. He leaned over Gerry, knowing that he was getting too close, but intent on seeing exactly what had happened.

He should have known that Gordon had something to do with it. He had called Gordon to tell him that Bieberstein was having problems. And Gordon had gone to check it out. He hadn't called Zachary back or answered his phone, so Zachary had assumed he was tired of being harassed and didn't want to be involved in Zachary's investigation anymore. He thought about what Deidre had said about Gordon, her angry accusations. Deidre didn't know Gordon personally like Zachary did. Her accusations had been fed by the fact that her sister had died. She wanted someone to blame, and why not the owner of the company that Lauren had become so obsessed with?

Gerry backed up the video until it was only Bieberstein standing there alone, and Gordon was not yet on the scene. Zachary could see Bieberstein was talking on his phone, and wondered if that was when he was talking to Zachary. Bieberstein moved around jerkily, his head lolling out of control like he was drunk. He typed on his computer, picked up his phone, put it down, and searched through the papers on his desk for something. When Gordon walked into the view of the camera, Bieberstein jerked away in surprise. Zachary could see his mouth moving, his expression angry, but he couldn't make out what Bieberstein was saying. Maybe what was coming out didn't even make sense, since Gordon just looked at him blankly.

After a minute, Gordon touched Bieberstein on the arm, saying something to him. There were words exchanged, and Bieberstein seemed to be winding down a little, but was still jerky and unsteady.

"That guy's really impaired," Gerry observed.

"Sleep deprivation."

"Really? He's not drunk?"

"No. Probably not."

They watched as Gordon tugged Bieberstein's arm a little, trying to lead him away from his desk. Bieberstein resisted, looked around, motioned to his desk, and after a moment of discussion, went back to get his computer. He closed it and picked it up to hold it under his arm. More discussion, and then Gordon and Bieberstein walked away from the desk and the camera.

Zachary pulled out his phone and tried to call Gordon again. There was no answer on his cell phone. He tried the main reception number at Drake, Chase, Gould, only to be thwarted by the receptionist, who Zachary guessed had instructions not to let anyone through.

He needed to know that Bieberstein was okay. What if Gordon had taken him somewhere? What if he'd harmed him? Gordon would, he was sure, have some reassuring explanation, and Zachary needed to hear it. One side of his brain didn't believe that Gordon could do anything to hurt anyone, but the other side was suspicious as all hell.

Who would have thought that someone like Gordon Drake could be a dangerous criminal? Everyone would think that he was so kind, so focused on growing his company that he wouldn't have the time or inclination to do anything violent. No one believed that rich people, good society people, could do anything wrong. That was for the masses, the lower class. Poverty bred violence. Wealth didn't. Only the lack of wealth. Jealousy and greed and need.

Even though he knew better, he tried Gordon's home number. Which, of course, was Bridget's home number. He hoped that Gordon was home, that he would see the caller I.D., and that he would answer it. But it was not Gordon who answered the phone.

"Zachary?"

Bridget didn't immediately go into a tirade and recriminations, so that was good. Her tone was cautious, as if she were worried that he was bringing her bad news.

"I just wondered if Gordon was there," Zachary said apologetically. "I can't reach him at work or on his cell phone and I thought maybe he was at home."

"No, he's not here. Why would he be at this time of day?"

"I don't know his usual schedule. Or maybe he had an appointment to go to with you. Or was having something delivered to the house. Or he could have been sick."

At least the owner, if he were sick, could get time off. Zachary wondered about Chase and Gould. Did Drake have to report to them? Or did they report to him? Or neither one? Did any of them have to get the permission of the others to make big decisions for the company? Surely not for everyday things, but if the company were to start in a different direction in marketing, employee security, or a health and welfare initiative, did they have to have unanimous agreement? Two out of three? Or did they each have different assigned areas of responsibility?

"Did you hear me, Zachary? He's not here."

"Okay. Sorry to bother you. If you do hear from him… would you tell him that I was trying to get him? I don't want to be a pest, but I'm worried about one of his employees. I'd like to talk to him—"

"Don't you think you did enough last night?"

"Did enough? I just… let him know what was going on. I thought he would want to know. I didn't have the numbers of anyone else at the company."

"You had him up in the middle of the night. Which meant that he woke me up and I couldn't get back to sleep. You know I need my sleep, especially now."

How was she going to get that sleep once she had the baby? Would Gordon look after the baby at night? Were they going to hire a nanny? Bridget had to realize that the baby wasn't going to sleep all night.

"I am sorry. I didn't want to get either of you up, but I didn't know what else to do."

"Just leave him alone. Don't you think it's time to close this case? It's obvious that there isn't anything to it. The poor girl fell in her bathtub. There's no foul play involved in that. It isn't like someone murdered her. The only reason for you to be so involved in Drake, Chase, Gould is to embarrass Gordon. And it's time to back off."

"I'm sorry… it should only be a few more days. Just have Gordon call me, if you hear from him. Please."

She hung up without saying goodbye. Zachary sat looking at his phone.

"That one's a firecracker," Gerry commented.

Zachary rolled his eyes. "That she is," he admitted. Curiously, he didn't feel guilty as he usually did after talking to her. He didn't feel sad or despairing. He was calm and focused and he needed to stay that way.

Somewhere out there, Bieberstein might be in trouble.

30

"Did you want to look at any more videos?" Gerry asked. "You said you wanted to see who was working when your girl was killed, and you haven't done that."

"Uh… yeah." Zachary tried to decide how important that was. If Gordon was the one who had taken Bieberstein, then did that mean he was the one who had possibly poisoned him? And possibly had something to do with Lauren's accident? He wasn't a big, muscly guy. He was not effeminate, but he was refined and cultured. He had tailored clothing and manicured nails. So he wouldn't have likely physically attacked either of them. Poison might have been more his speed. The hospital and the medical examiner hadn't found anything. But that didn't mean there wasn't anything to find, just nothing that showed up on the usual tox screens, which was a very limited list.

If it was Gordon, then he didn't need to look at any of the other interns or anyone else in the department. It would be a waste of time.

But if he was wrong, if it wasn't anything to do with Gordon, then he was letting the real criminal walk around free and Gordon himself could be in danger. Gordon and Bieberstein could both be missing, not because Gordon had done something to Bieberstein, but because someone had done something to both of them.

Gordon had said that he would make himself available to Zachary, so why had he suddenly changed his mind? Why was he suddenly not available at any of his numbers?

"Yeah, I guess I do," Zachary decided aloud. "I'd better check them just to be sure…"

He opened his mouth to give Gerry the names that he needed to look for, but his phone vibrated in his hand and he looked over at it. He had an appointment with his therapist. But he was right in the middle of an investigation. Right at a critical juncture. Gerry grinned.

"You look like someone just took away your cookie."

"Uh… I have to call to cancel an appointment."

"Why don't you just give me the feeds you want to check, and I'll look at them while you're gone. Then you're not hanging over my shoulder waiting for them. It's going to take time to find each camera and check it for… how many hours?"

"From about ten p.m. to ten a.m."

Gerry nodded. "Checking those at a slow enough speed to see how long each person was missing from the frame, and then checking their computer logs to see if they went home and kept working or what, that's going to take a while. How many people do you need to check?"

"About… five or six."

"Write them down," Gerry motioned to a scratch pad on Zachary's desk. "Are they all in the bull pen?"

"No. Most of them should be most of the time, but they might have moved around, and their supervisor and VP wouldn't be in the bullpen. And there's Gordon… we're going to have to see where he was when Lauren died too. He wouldn't have had to be there, it doesn't exactly rule anyone out if they are alibied for the time of the accident, because she could have been given some poison ahead of time…"

"Poison?" Gerry raised his eyebrows.

Zachary thought about the video of the bullpen they had just watched.

"You'll have to watch her water bottle and coffee too, make sure there is no video of anyone putting anything into them."

Gerry nodded. "A slow review of the bullpen, and then a quicker review of any other offices that they might be in," he suggested.

Zachary nodded. "I should really stay here and do it myself. This can wait…" He indicated his phone.

"If I'm not done when you get back, we can double up and you can look on your computer and I can look on this one. But for now, you go ahead and go to your appointment. We'll pick up again afterward."

"Okay." Zachary still wasn't convinced. He looked for an argument. But Gerry was right. And Zachary had promised Dr. Boyle that he wouldn't cancel any more appointments. Even though he had just seen her, she had suggested that he needed an immediate follow-up to make sure he was managing. Zachary had told her previously that he would get there for all of them and put the time and effort into his therapy that he needed to. Just like he told Heather she needed to do. And Heather would check up on him to keep him accountable.

Zachary groaned. He wrote down the names for Gerry to look into and got ready to go.

***

Dr. Boyle sat back in her chair and looked Zachary over. "So, how are you doing today, Zachary? Feeling a little better than yesterday?"

"I'm good. Everything is going pretty well."

She didn't smile. "You seem to be pretty restless. Are you sure that's true?"

"I just… I have other things to do. I was going to cancel today. But I didn't. So… I'm just… distracted by my case."

"I see. Well, we don't want your case to derail your progress here, so you're going to need to rein it in. Can you do that?"

"I don't know." Zachary had never been very good about pulling himself away from something interesting to focus on something less pleasant. He had inappropriate focus. Inability to follow directions. He'd heard it all. "I'll try, but I'm worried about someone. About a couple of people. They could be in danger."

"What makes you think that?"

"I can't get ahold of either of them. I don't know if something happened, or if I'm just following a red herring."

"Have you told the police that you're worried about these people? They could do welfare checks, go by and see if they can make contact with them."

"I've already talked to everyone who should know where they are. They aren't at home. They aren't at work. I don't know where else to go, so I don't know where to tell the police, either."

"They could do their own investigation."

"Based on me thinking that there's something suspicious going on? No." Zachary shook his head. "I know them better than that. I can follow whatever hunches occur to me, but they have to have due cause. And they're busy with other cases that they *do* have evidence on. They don't have time to be chasing rainbows."

Dr. Boyle nodded slowly. "Well then, we'd better do whatever work we can while you're here, and then you can get back to it. Right?"

"Right."

"Have you spent some time on some inner work regarding your past?"

A knot tightened in his stomach. "Uh… I haven't done very much. I know I should have, but I've been working on this case."

"You still need to take time for yourself. You can't work all the time. That's not healthy."

"Tell me about it," Zachary agreed, thinking about Lauren and Bieberstein and the other interns.

She raised her brows. "What?"

"These people, they're working all the time. Forty-eight hours without a rest. Getting three or four hours of sleep in over four days. It's no wonder Bieberstein was getting so paranoid, when he hadn't slept in days. They say that they take care of their employees, that they care about their health and welfare, but they don't. They are abusing them, just like if they were slaves. They think that their employees' lives belong to them."

"This is your case again?"

"They're tracking them. Watching them through surveillance cameras and their computers. They're feeding them information and limiting their access to the outside world. What does that sound like to you?"

"Brainwashing? Thought conditioning?"

Zachary nodded, warming to the subject. "Exactly. It's like that syndrome. The one where people fall in love with their kidnappers, because their kidnappers hold the power of life and death over them and that's the only way that they can respond if they want to stay alive. They have to do what their captors want and feel love toward them. Not something that's faked, but real love, or they'll die."

"Stockholm Syndrome."

"Yeah. That's it. Traumatic bonding. I was thinking about it earlier in this case, and I lost track of it. But these employees really do love the company. They really believe that it's the best place for them to work and that the company goes above and beyond to pay them and give them the opportunities they do. They work together well, seem like they have good relationships. Is it all just Stockholm Syndrome? Could it be, when their captor is actually a company?"

"What difference does it make? Does a cult member get attached to the cult as well as to their leader? You bet they do. Even if they can see everything the cult is doing wrong, they still believe in it. They still believe that the cult is the best place for them, that they wouldn't survive or be happy if they were to leave."

"The *cult leader…*" Zachary mused.

"A cult normally has a dynamic, somewhat mystical leader. Someone who is very passionate, magnetic."

"Yeah. That's like Gordon. Sort of."

"You don't sound sure."

Zachary thought about Gordon. He was a nice guy, calm. He was passionate, but not in the way that Zachary thought of a cult leader. He didn't make demands, he didn't shout, he wasn't magical or mystical, he didn't claim to be talking to God. He was really just a good corporate manager. Smooth, pleasant, a good face for PR for the company.

He wondered again about Chase and Gould. Was one of them the voice behind the health and welfare program? Coming up with chants and slogans and company love? Was Gordon just an empty figurehead for the media?

"Maybe. Maybe not. I don't really know." He looked at Dr. Boyle and gave her a little chagrined smile. "I've never been in a cult."

"But you *have* felt attracted to someone who has abused you."

Zachary's stomach did a nosedive. He felt nauseated. When was the last time he'd eaten? He should have planned his meals more carefully.

"Zachary."

He darted a look at Dr. Boyle. "Maybe I should be getting back to my apartment. I don't know how long it will take Gerry to look at all of that footage. I should be there, helping him."

"Why don't we talk about how it felt to you?"

He swallowed. "What?"

"You loved your mother. Even though she was abusive. Even though she abandoned you."

"I was sad that she did that. I still wanted a family. I missed my brothers and sisters."

"And you loved your mother."

He twisted around uncomfortably. What kind of person loved an abuser? It meant he was weak. He knew people who had been in abusive families and had been happy to make a break with them. They left and they never regretted it. They didn't moon around, loving and mourning the person who had abused them. They didn't long to go back to that relationship where they had been abused.

"And you loved Bridget," Dr. Boyle said.

"Bridget wasn't abusive. She gets mad now and yells to blow off steam, but it's healthy to express your feelings. She gets frustrated over how much time we spent together, that she wasted her life with me. She gets upset when I make stupid mistakes or bother her. But that's just expressing her emotions."

"You don't think she was abusive toward you when you were together?"

"I loved her. I would do anything for her. If she wanted me to be different, that wasn't abusive. That was just telling me what she wanted."

"Even if it wasn't something that you could do? Even if what she expected from you was for you *not* to be yourself?"

"She decided that we weren't compatible," Zachary said. "People find that out sometimes. That their marriage just didn't work because they weren't actually compatible with each other."

"Just like your mother decided she didn't want children anymore. That they were too much work and caused too much trouble."

Zachary swallowed. He stared at Dr. Boyle.

"If you want to see your relationships clearly in the future, you need to be able to look at the past without those lenses. You need to be honest with yourself about what happened. Being abused doesn't make you guilty. It doesn't mean that you did something wrong to wreck the relationship. You have deep-seated feelings of guilt and blame yourself for your abandonment and for the failure of your marriage. I don't know about other relationships. Were there other times in your life when you found yourself in a relationship with someone who was abusive? But you wanted to stay with them anyway?"

Zachary was with Dr. Boyle, but not with her. His attention was fractured, split between the point that she was trying to make and being mired in his past and thinking about Lauren's death.

What if the company were the abuser and Lauren the victim? What would that look like? What if the company were the equivalent of a cult? What would have been different about the case? If the member of a cult died suddenly, under suspicious circumstances, how would the police have reacted? How would Zachary have investigated it differently?

"What if it *was* a cult?" Zachary repeated aloud. "What would have been different?"

"Zachary, you're getting distracted."

"No. This is it. That's the question. What if she was strong? What if she decided to stand up to the cult? What if she decided she'd had enough and she wanted out? She'd been abused enough. She was sick, sleep-deprived, she'd thought the company was everything she wanted it to be, but finally realized it was just a trap. That they were using her."

Dr. Boyle was silent.

"What does a cult do then?" Zachary asked. "They don't want her to leave. They don't just let her walk out, do they?"

"I'm afraid I'm not an expert in cult behavior," Dr. Boyle said dryly. "But from what I've seen and read, then no, they wouldn't just let her go. They would do what they could to stop her. Argue with her, put her through some kind of intervention or ordeal, maybe even physically prevent her from leaving them."

"Physically. A cult would try to hold on to her. Tie her up. Go after her with a gun. Threaten to hurt her family."

"Those would all be possibilities with a cult," Dr. Boyle agreed cautiously. "But when you translate that to a corporate environment, I think it would be a stretch. There's only so much that a company can do legally."

"But why would they keep it legal? If the members all believe that what they are doing is right, and that what their leader says to do is scripture, then they can take whatever action they feel they need to, and they are in the right. They can't do the wrong thing if they are protecting the company and its officers."

"But we don't see that happening. A corporate environment isn't the same as a cult."

"She's with them all day every day. She eats with them, exercises with them, wears their uniform, spouts their slogans, sleeps with them. She does whatever they tell her to. It *is* the same."

"It really isn't."

Zachary got up out of his seat, unable to sit still any longer. He paced back and forth across the room. "I think it could be. You don't know the stuff that's been going on. They burned down a house." Zachary said the words quickly to try to keep himself from dwelling on the fire and getting choked in his own memories. "You can't tell me that's typical corporate behavior. None of this is."

"Zachary… have you been taking your meds?"

"Yeah, yeah." Zachary was practically vibrating. He knew that he was right.

All along, he'd been wondering why everyone was so devoted to the company. He'd been trying to connect what happened at the office with Lauren's death without any success, because he was treating it like it was a normal murder. She wasn't murdered because of the jealousy of her co-workers. It wasn't because they were competing for the same jobs.

They had retaliated against her betrayal.

They had thought that she was the perfect corporate drone. They had been able to pull her away from her family, to convince her that the best thing for her would be to devote herself forever to corporate life and to give up her chances of conceiving just so it wouldn't inconvenience them. And then she had turned on them. She'd had an awakening and decided she was going to get out. And that was the point at which someone had—

"Zachary." Dr. Boyle interrupted his thoughts. "I think you're having a break. You're conflating Lauren's situation with your own

history. The trauma bonding. Your fear of abandonment. Your…
past traumatic experience."

"I'm not making this up. It isn't about my life and my past.
These things really did happen. Everybody who spoke out against
the company was squashed. No one was allowed to say anything
against them. The people who talked in public were sued. Or they
had bizarre accidents. It escalated. Lauren wasn't the first, she was
just one in a line of employees and ex-employees."

"Is there someone we could call who would come and get you?
I'd like you to admit yourself for observation. If you're taking your
meds like you're supposed to, you might be reacting to something.
Or you might need some other adjustment. You know occasional
adjustments are required along the way."

"I don't need a ride," Zachary said, looking at the clock on Dr.
Boyle's desk. He knew he was cutting the session short, but he
couldn't waste valuable time in finding out which employee or
employees had gone after Lauren.

Gerry might already have found something on the video
recordings. Zachary had dutifully shut his phone off when
entering the doctor's office, which meant he could have missed a
call or text.

He pressed the hardware button on the phone, waiting for it
to boot back up. "Sorry, I have to go. I have to take care of this.
We'll talk next week."

He ignored Dr. Boyle's protests and walked out of the office.

31

When his phone finished its startup routine, Zachary was already in the car. He put the phone in its holder on his dashboard and as if in response, a series of text messages popped up on the screen.

An unknown number: *If you don't back off Chase Gold, you're going to die.*

Gerry: *You'd better come back here as soon as you're done.*

Bridget: *Stay out of Gordon's business and just leave this case alone.*

Kenzie: *Call me when you get a chance.*

Talk about stirring up a hornet's nest. His thoughts were racing and for a moment he considered the possibility that they were all working in concert. It took effort to remind himself that most of them were on his side. They might be influenced by an outside source, but they weren't all working for Gordon. He tapped the message from Kenzie and the phone icon as he started the engine and pulled out.

"Medical Examiner—hi, Zachary."

"Hey. Good to hear from you. I was just thinking about the case, and I wanted to run a few things by you."

"I said that I would call you after talking to Dr. Wiltshire about the other employee's accident. While it is an interesting coincidence, he doesn't think that—"

"Given that the other employee who had an accident is now missing, he might want to reconsider that conclusion," Zachary interrupted.

"Missing?"

"He was acting paranoid last night and then he disappeared. Someone might have taken him away from there and harmed him. We might never even know what happened, if there is no body found. And there probably won't be; they've had too much reported in the media lately. They won't want this to be a suspicious death or another tragic accident. Just an employee choosing to leave the company. They'll establish a story. A logical narrative. He'd been working too hard, he had a breakdown, he decided it was time to leave. They'll have a few different employees telling the same story, saying that they've talked to him and he doesn't want to be bothered by anyone, and—"

"Whoa, Zach. Slow it down. You sound like someone changed the RPM on your turntable. You're going to be going chipmunk in a minute."

Zachary took a deep breath and tried to slow himself down. When everything started to click and he saw the whole picture, it was hard to slow himself down to everyone else's speed. He had to remind himself that Kenzie didn't know all of the details of the case. He hadn't kept her up to speed like he normally would, because they had broken up. That needed to change, but he'd have to address it later, after he'd finished tying up the case.

"Look. The blow was to the back of her head. Not the front."

"That doesn't mean anything," Kenzie said. "It's not unusual for someone who slips to fall backward and hit the back of their head."

"In the bathtub? Wouldn't she have fallen out of the tub instead of into the water?"

"You don't know that. She could easily have fallen backward and hit her head on the side of the tub and then sunk down into the water. There's nothing to indicate anyone else's presence on the scene."

"There had been other people in that bathroom. It wasn't only used by her."

"Obviously."

"So there were other fingerprints and forensic evidence in the bathroom."

"Sure."

"But that would all be ignored, because they thought it was an accident. And because she lived with a roommate. Who knows how many other people came and went? You can't match every hair and fingerprint. There will always be unknowns. People who were one-time visitors or whose hair or skin cells were on Lauren or Barbara when they came home from work."

"Exactly. Of course. The evidence of other people doesn't mean that it wasn't an accident."

"I need you to start trying to identify them. You're going to find contributions from people at her office. Some might have just clung to her, but look for larger contributions. Her roommate said that she sometimes brought men home from work with her. I want to know which men. Which ones can we actually put in the apartment because of the larger deposits of physical evidence and their fingerprints on the scene. We're going to need to do a larger analysis of the fingerprints. Identify the ones that weren't identi-fied initially."

"I don't know if forensics or fingerprints were even taken," Kenzie cautioned. "Certainly nothing was ever tested. It was evident on the face of it that this was just an accident. They wouldn't treat it like a homicide. What would be the point in investigating a non-suspicious death like a homicide? It just takes extra man-hours."

"If there's nothing to this but a tragic accident, then why are there so many stories about other past employees of the company? What happened to Bieberstein? And why am I getting death threats?"

There was a moment of silence from Kenzie. "You're getting death threats?"

"Just now. Someone sending me a text message warning me to back off the case or I'm dead. Why would they do that if it was just an accident? Think about it."

"Zachary… are you by yourself?"

"For now, but not for long. I'm headed back to my apartment. Gerry is there. I don't know what he found yet. Maybe it will be something we can use."

"I'm worried about you."

"I'm fine," Zachary assured her. At least there hadn't been a bomb in the car. Nothing had happened when he started the engine. They might be waiting and watching him, but they would have no way of knowing whether he was going to listen to their warning until they saw his resulting behavior. Then they would have to decide what kind of action to take.

"You should talk to Detective Robinson," Kenzie said. "He'll want to know about the progress you've made on the case. He can help you to decide how to deal with this death threat." He could almost hear Kenzie's doubtful thoughts. *If the death threat was real.* Like Dr. Boyle, she was worried that he was having a psychotic break and just imagining it all.

"You know what else?" he asked her. "Why would she be having a bath without taking her bath things into the room? If you were going to have a relaxing bubble bath, wouldn't you actually take it into the bathroom?"

"I don't think she had any bubbles in the bath."

"No, she didn't," Zachary agreed. "All of her bath things were in her bedroom. She had a shower caddy with everything in it."

"Maybe she was just filling the tub and was still going to go back and get it."

"You don't start the tub filling without getting your bath salts or bubble bath or whatever first," Zachary said. He remembered how Bridget had a big ritual about setting up her baths. It was different from how Zachary would jump into the shower to quickly wash away the sweat and dirt from the day. It was an event, like going to the spa.

"She could have forgotten," Kenzie maintained. "You said she was overtired. You can do a lot of stupid things when you're over-tired. Forget the order of things. Not be able to do something that you've done a hundred times before. *You* know how it is when you're not sleeping."

"But she wasn't just filling the tub, she was *in* the tub. She was already undressed and in the tub when she died. She didn't just start the tub running and then realize that she'd forgotten her things and slipped and fell into the tub. She didn't slip on the floor, she slipped in the tub."

"Yes," Kenzie agreed slowly. "But maybe she got into the tub and then realized she'd forgotten her things. She could have fallen because she got up too fast to get them."

"Or," Zachary offered, "someone hit her over the head and then put her body in the tub and filled it up with water to make it look like an accident. But he didn't know that her bathroom things were in the bedroom. He wasn't familiar enough with her to know that."

Zachary's thoughts raced on. It wasn't someone that she took home with her regularly. They would know that her bath things were in her bedroom. She would shower or bathe before going to work in the morning, and he would know that she had to take her caddy from the bedroom to the bathroom first. Unless the guy was totally clueless, he would know her routine.

"I've got to go," he told Kenzie. "I'll try to get you more details when I know them, but in the meantime, if you can get them started on identifying the hair and fibers and fingerprints, that would be really helpful. Even if it's just preliminary stuff, putting them into groups like hair color and curl. That will make it faster to match once I have a name for you."

"Zachary—"

"Don't worry about me. I'll call you back when I've got something."

Gerry was the next sender who Zachary knew was on his side. Zachary's apartment wasn't far from Dr. Boyle's office, so he was nearly there by the time he finished the call with Kenzie. He parked quickly and took the elevator up to his apartment, impatient with how slowly it rose to his floor. He practically ran into his apartment.

Gerry jumped and looked around at him, face white. "What the heck, Zachary? You scared the crap out of me."

"Sorry. I just wanted to get here as quickly as I could and make sure that you were okay."

"Why wouldn't I be okay?"

Zachary didn't tell him. Gerry didn't need to know about the death threat. About the accidents and the house fire and the employee with amnesia. The killer could easily have made it to Zachary's apartment before he was able to get there. And he'd obligingly left the door unlocked, not thinking there was any need for any special care.

"You said that you needed me to come back. What's going on?"

Gerry gestured at Lauren's computer screen. "They discovered what I was doing and blocked me," he said regretfully. "I'm sorry. We knew they were surveilling this laptop, but I thought I could get through the video feeds before they figured out what I was doing and how to stop me."

"Did you find anything out before they did?"

Gerry handed Zachary the scratch pad from the desk, where Zachary had written down the names of the people they needed surveillance footage for. Zachary scanned the list.

As the witnesses had told him, most of them left around the same time as Lauren had. It was bad for someone to leave first and be identified as less devout than anyone else. They left as a group to keep anyone from being singled out as lazy.

Except Bieberstein. He seemed to be able to come and to go as he pleased, working for different departments on whatever projects they needed him on.

And he wasn't the one. It was clear from Gerry's notes that Bieberstein had been at the office from the time that Lauren had left. It had been an all-nighter for him, even though everyone else had gone home.

"If one of these people went home with Lauren, which one was it?" he asked Gerry.

Gerry looked baffled. "What?"

"If you had to guess which one was going home with her, which one would it be?"

"None of them left with her, exactly."

"It might have been covert. They might have been trying to keep it from the others."

"Hmm." Gerry looked over the list and the notes he had made. "Gordon Drake, Daniel Service... the interns all left around the same time, but they looked pretty wiped out. Honestly, I can't see any of them having the energy to pursue any hanky-panky."

Zachary laughed.

Gerry shrugged, his face turning a little pink. "Really," he insisted.

"I believe you. What were Gordon and Daniel doing there that late?"

Of course, the senior staff could be there whenever they wanted to, but Zachary had gotten the feeling that they didn't stay late like the peons.

"They were together, meeting in Gordon's office."

"I'm surprised they were there so late. And either of them could have joined Lauren after they left?"

"Yeah, they left a few minutes after she did."

Zachary sighed, rubbing the center of his forehead. One name kept coming up over and over again. The one name that he didn't want to associate with Lauren's death.

"Okay. Thanks. If they've blocked you from accessing anything else, then I guess we're done."

"I could try again. I might be able to break in again. They might have changed the password, but won't have had time to put any new security measures in place. They'll be watching, though, waiting for me to show up again."

"It isn't like we're going to get video that proves conclusively which one of them killed her. We can't absolutely eliminate any of them."

Gerry eyed Zachary, brows down.

"What?"

"Before you left, you were saying it was an accident. Now you're saying one of them killed her."

Zachary brought up the text messages on his phone and tapped the threatening one. He turned it face out so that Gerry could read it. His mouth pressed into a straight line.

"And why would they threaten to kill you if it was just an accident?" he summarized.

"Exactly. And some other things came up while I was gone."

"You be careful, man. I wouldn't want to lose a paying customer."

"I will. Send me your invoice. I guess that's all I'm going to need today."

"Well, you know who to call if you need anything else."

Zachary paced after Gerry left. He didn't have anything to take to the police. No proof of any foul play. No evidence that it was anything other than an accident, like Kenzie had said. Lauren could have just slipped, hit her head, and drowned, just as the medical examiner had determined.

But Zachary must have been getting close, or he wouldn't have upset someone enough to be getting death threats.

He could show the threat to the police, and they could track down the phone that had sent it, but that still wasn't proof that Lauren was intentionally killed or even that the threats were serious. Zachary got threats from cheating spouses and insurance scammers all the time.

There was a knock on the door. Zachary glanced over at the computer desk to see whether Gerry had left something behind by accident. He didn't see anything, but went to the door and opened it to let Gerry in.

But it wasn't Gerry.

Gordon smiled pleasantly at Zachary.

Zachary stood frozen, not sure what to do. He knew better than to open the door without checking to see who it was first. But what would he have done if he had looked? Would he still have opened the door for Gordon, or would he have hidden and pretended that he wasn't at home? What good would that do? Sooner or later, he would have to face Gordon.

"You've been trying to reach me?" Gordon suggested. He put his foot into the doorway, preventing the door from being closed again. "Can I come in?"

Zachary allowed him in. Gordon walked through the kitchen into the living room and looked around. He saw the computers on Zachary's desk.

"Is this one of ours?" He pointed at Lauren's laptop. "If you're done with it, I really should take it back. We don't like to have them floating around when they might have confidential information on them."

"Yes. You can take it. And the phone was Lauren's too. It's company issue."

"Ah, very good." Gordon pocketed the phone. He folded down the lid of the laptop, moved it over to deal with the electrical cord, and picked it up. He took it with him as he sat down on Zachary's couch, putting it down at his feet. "How else can I help you, Zachary?"

Zachary looked around. He could run. There was nothing between him and the door, and it wasn't like Gordon was holding a gun on him. He wasn't making any threat at all.

"I was worried about Bieberstein," he ventured. "Especially since he wasn't at work this morning... those interns never miss a day."

"Bieberstein is fine." Gordon's voice was perfectly calm, with no hint of stress. There was nothing in his face that hinted at a lie. His eyes were steady, looking at Zachary but without too much aggression or intensity. He didn't look anything like the egomaniac that Deidre made him out to be. He didn't look like a crazy cult leader who thought he was the Messiah. Zachary saw just what he had always seen. A wealthy businessman, pleasant and cultured, easy to talk to. All of the things that Zachary wasn't. But not a maniac who was going around trying to get rid of any employees who disagreed with him or didn't fit into his corporate culture.

"He's fine? You know where he is?"

Gordon nodded. "You were right to call me last night. It wasn't easy to get him settled down and in a reasonable state of mind. He's going to take a few days off to get the sleep he needs. Paid, of course, and with no impact on his chances at the permanent positions."

"Do you think..." Zachary hesitated.

Gordon raised his eyebrows and waited. His state of calm was almost hypnotic. Zachary could feel his heart slowing and had an intense desire to tell Gordon all of his concerns and theories.

But he still had to consider Gordon a suspect. He'd been around when Lauren had left work that final day. He was on the same floor as the interns, walking by the bullpen half a dozen times a day. He was the owner of the company and could get around and do whatever he desired without anybody questioning it. The company was his baby and, while Zachary couldn't envision him doing anything violent, people often did terrible things to get what they wanted.

Had Gordon risen to where he was without stepping on anyone else?

"Do you think that Bieberstein was right, that he was in danger?" Zachary asked finally, pushing the words out all at once so that he wouldn't get stuck.

Gordon scratched his jaw, thinking about it. "I don't like there being two accidents so close together. I know that Bieberstein only fell on the treadmill at a walking pace, but it could conceivably have been much worse. Whether it was because someone wanted to hurt him or because he's been working too hard or he picked up a bug… I felt like he needed a rest. Somewhere safe."

"Where?"

Gordon just raised his brows and didn't answer. Zachary got it. If no one knew where Bieberstein was, no one could hurt him. And even if Zachary had been the one to ring the alarm bells, *no one* meant *no one.*

"So was there anything else?" Gordon asked. "Anything at all?"

Zachary wanted to ask him about the health and welfare program, the fraudulent computer records, employee monitoring, information control, and everything else. How much of it did Gordon know and how much of it had been implemented by someone else, right under his nose? Did he really think that he had a company full of happy, dedicated employees, or did he know that they were being manipulated?

Zachary just swallowed and shook his head.

Gordon's phone rang. He looked at the face and tapped to answer it. "Hello, my dear."

Bridget, of course. Zachary couldn't help taking a quick look around his apartment to assess it, as if she might show up at any minute and would be making a list of deficiencies. Everything was reasonably tidy. There were papers out on his desk, his coffee mug that he hadn't washed after his morning cup. It could probably use a good dusting and vacuuming, something Zachary didn't get around to very often. And by the smell of the kitchen, it was time to take the garbage out.

"Yes, I'm there now," Gordon said. He gave Zachary a conspiratorial wink. "I'm sorry I was off the grid for a few hours. Phones had to be turned off."

He listened some more. Zachary imagined Bridget had a long list of grievances to air if he had turned his phone off when she wanted to reach him. Especially since Zachary had called looking for Gordon.

"Yes. Of course, dear. Alright."

After a few more comforting noises, he said his goodbyes and hung up. He slid his phone into his pocket.

"There is a woman who does not like to be ignored."

"No," Zachary agreed with a laugh. "She gets kind of testy if she thinks she's not getting the attention she deserves."

"Well, I do have work to get back to. They'll be calling me too. Actually, they already have, but things will keep until I get back. You're sure that's everything you need?" He smiled once more, and Zachary was again struck by how friendly and trustworthy he made himself appear. He made Zachary feel as if he could trust him absolutely.

And yet, he didn't.

33

After Gordon left, Zachary locked the door and reminded himself sternly that he needed to check who was there before he answered it. He had to pay attention and not just open it the moment someone knocked.

He went back to his desk and leafed through his handwritten notes, puzzling through the more cryptic or unreadable ones, trying to remind himself of every step along the way. He should know what had happened. He had all of the details. He'd seen where it happened. He knew the medical examiner's results. He'd talked to all of the players.

He was sure that it hadn't just been an accident. Lauren wouldn't have gone to the bathroom to have a bath without her shower caddy full of toiletries. That meant that someone else had been there and had tried to cover it up. And since there was water in her lungs, it wasn't just a case of her accidentally hitting her head and dying. She had still been alive when he had put her into the water.

It wasn't Mandy. She was too small. Bieberstein was also too small and he had an alibi. He'd been at work that whole night. It could have been one of the other interns. Or Gordon. Or Daniel.

If it were one of the other interns, then it was someone who wanted the position that she apparently had locked up. They were all pretty desperate to sign on permanently. No one wanted to be left out in the cold, the guy who had interned at Chase Gold but didn't make the cut. As the time was getting closer, they were getting more desperate.

Or it was someone in higher authority than the interns, who had reason to stop her. Had her comments about being prepared to have her tubes tied to lock in her position with the company been true? Or had she been bluffing? Or had that just been a story that Aaron had made up to distract Zachary from the truth?

Her family said she wanted children. Had she finally reached the breaking point and decided that was where she drew the line? She wouldn't give up all of her other dreams to get a permanent position with Drake, Chase, Gould?

The firm had had to deal with too many defectors in the previous few months. Too many employees or ex-employees who made the company look bad. If Drake, Chase, Gould were going to be properly positioned to spread internationally and gain a position in the world economy, they had to be clean. They couldn't abide a situation where potential investors looked at the company and saw a problem.

Zachary busied himself with cleaning up while he thought. If he had all of that restless energy, he might as well do something with it. His phone started to vibrate, so he put his coffee mug in the sink and put down his dust rag and answer it. It was Daniel.

"Just wondering if I could come by there to get Lauren's computer, Zachary," he said. "Bev said that she asked you for it but hasn't gotten it back yet. I know you don't want her on your back, so I figured since I was in the area…"

"Gordon Drake was by just a little while ago. He picked it up. And her phone."

"Gordon was by?" Daniel repeated, his tone something of a cross between curious and irritated.

"Yeah. So you can ask him about it, if Bev says she hasn't got it back yet. He could have just put it in his briefcase and forgotten about it. But that's where it is, if you want it."

"Great. That's all I need, then."

After Zachary hung up, he walked back into his living room and looked at his computer. A slide show played as his screen saver, waiting for him to come and wake it up again. The connection came to him suddenly. It had started to form when he'd been at Dr. Boyle's office, and then his attention had been scattered by talking to everyone who had been trying to reach him.

He sat down at his desk, touching the mouse to wake the computer up, picking up his phone to make a call.

"Hey, man, I thought we were done," Gerry complained, as soon as he answered his phone. "If you changed your mind, you're going to have to wait until tomorrow. I have other jobs I need to get finished today."

"I had to give back Lauren's computer, but I cloned Lauren's hard drive, so I can still use that to see everything on her computer, right?"

"You don't touch the cloned drive. That's your failsafe. I created a VM of the cloned drive on your computer, and you need to boot off of that to be mostly safe."

"Mostly?"

"There are still some risks, but it's the safest way we've got for you to access Lauren's data."

"And what's a… VM?"

"Virtual machine. It's like having a second computer system running in a separate window."

"Okay. That sounds like it is going to be complicated… what do I do?"

"It's not that bad, Zachary," Gerry promised. "I'll walk you through it."

He didn't sound angry and impatient with Zachary for taking more of his time. Whatever else he had to finish, he didn't seem to need to get to it immediately.

Zachary put his phone in speaker mode and set it down on the desk so that he could use both hands. Gerry walked him through starting the VM. It wasn't as bad as Zachary had anticipated.

"Now what are you looking for?" Gerry asked. "Do you know how to find it?"

"You said that there was a spyware program accessing her camera."

"Yeah. So you might want to cover yours up now, if you don't want them snooping on you through your own computer this time."

Goosebumps rose on Zachary's arms. He did as Gerry had done and covered the camera lens with a sticky note.

"Okay. Yeah. So what did the program do? Was it on all the time?"

"It was on when the computer was in use. So theoretically, it would stop recording while the computer was idle, and no one had to worry about having their picture taken while walking around the house naked, or steamy bedroom scenes ending up on the company's server. And they weren't videos, but stills taken every twenty seconds. Takes up a lot less space, but still gives them the information they need on what the employee was up to. If they weren't connected to the internet, it would just keep taking pictures and would upload them the next time they connected. Then the company knows what they are doing whether they are online or off. Combine that with keystroke loggers and records of any internet address they visit, and you've got a pretty complete picture of everything your employee is doing while on the company computer."

"So if Lauren had the computer on when she went home that night, it might have recorded something important, without her even knowing it."

Gerry whistled. "Pretty smart, Zachary, pretty smart."

"So how do I access the pictures that it took? I assume it doesn't just put them into the 'pictures' folder."

"No. Do you want me to come tomorrow and take a look? It could be kind of tricky to give you instructions over the phone."

Thinking about Gordon picking up Lauren's laptop and about Daniel's call, Zachary was too uneasy to wait another day. One of them might have figured out there was something incriminating on Lauren's computer, and if they thought he had found it… they might not be willing to wait until he made a move to reveal it.

"I know it's a pain," he told Gerry apologetically, "but if you could just tell me where to look, I'll do the heavy lifting. If there was a picture of Lauren's killer on her drive, I want to find it and get it to the police tonight."

Gerry sighed, but didn't protest. "Okay, you're going to have to tell me what you see as we go through these different folders, because I don't remember exactly where they were stored and it might not be simple to open them to view them. They're only meant to be temporarily stored on the laptop, and are probably compressed and encrypted for transfer."

"I'll do my best."

Zachary reported on each screen Gerry led him through and, although it took longer than he had hoped, he did manage to find the folder of pictures and get them into a viewer where he could page through them as he looked for the ones that were taken on Lauren's last night on earth.

"It looks like these must be the ones that were taken after she got home," Zachary said. "She must have gone online even though she was tired."

"People like to check their social networks," Gerry said. "Touch base with what their family and friends are doing, maybe watch some videos to unwind before bed. Play a game of Solitaire or Sudoku."

Zachary paged through the photos quickly. One person's last hours, divided into twenty-second segments. She was tired. Her eyes were red and she had rubbed off the make-up around them. It made her look strangely childlike. A couple of times, the camera caught her looking over her shoulder, back behind her. But he couldn't see anything going on in the background that should have caught her attention.

He was going through the photos too fast to stop himself when he saw something he wanted to take a closer look at. He backed up through the last couple of photos of an empty room, back to the last pictures of Lauren before her death.

Zachary swore.

"What is it?" Gerry asked.

Zachary swore again.

"Thank you. This is it, Gerry. This is what we needed."

Gerry's answer was drowned out by a knock on the door. Zachary looked toward the door warily.

No one should be coming to his door. Gerry was gone, and Zachary was on the phone with him. Kenzie wasn't coming by anymore. Bridget knew that Gordon had been there, but she wouldn't have come looking for him. If she came to yell at Zachary to back off, he'd have the proof to show her. He could prove that it wasn't just his client's imagination and his own paranoia. He had the proof now.

No one else was likely to come by his apartment without calling first. Not when he could have been off doing surveillance or some other job and the chances of finding him at home were too remote. Not Tyrrell. Heather and Mr. Peterson were too far away. Mario would call first and Detective Robinson was too busy to talk to him and would be closing his file now that they had the medical examiner's ruling.

Zachary stood up halfway, clumsily banging into his desk and making everything on it jump and rattle. Way to be covert and make his visitor think that no one was at home.

He reached out to stop his pen jar from rattling. He steadied the computer, the most valuable thing on the desk, even though its wide base kept it from moving. His sleeve caught on the sticky note he'd used to cover the camera lens. Papers avalanched over his phone. Zachary moved more carefully, quiet as a mouse, tiptoeing over to the door to look into the hallway at the caller.

He never got that far.

He was considering whether he dared go right up to the peep-hole, or whether looking out the peephole would block the light from inside the room and the visitor would instantly know that he was home. He needed to get a video cam in the hallway, so he could see a clear picture of who was out there without giving his presence away.

Hovering there, just inside the kitchen, considering his next move, he was distracted by the smell of the kitchen garbage. But he'd taken the garbage out, so what was the smell? He frowned at the sink and the microwave, trying to remember what he'd been working on when Daniel had called and interrupted his house-keeping duties.

There was the sound of a key in his door. The building manager coming to check on something? Maybe there was a sewer problem, and that was what he was smelling. He let out his breath, relieved.

There was another sound from the doorknob, like a light hammer tap, and then the handle turned and the door swung open to reveal the building manager.

Only it wasn't.

3 4

He had on a baseball cap to obscure his face and a loose black hoodie disguised his build, but Zachary knew instantly it was Daniel, even before he closed the door, tilted his hat back, and grinned a self-satisfied smile at Zachary.

"No," Zachary said, backing up a few steps. "Get out of here. You can't break into my apartment. Get out!"

His words might not make much sense, but that was what fell out of his mouth. On TV, the PIs were always great at thinking on their feet, working out what to say to the bad guys to convince them to do something that would let the PI escape and get away scot-free, to return on the next week's episode well and safe.

Zachary's brain was running in overdrive, trying to work out his next move, but his mouth was miles behind.

He backed up a couple more steps and looked over to the desk for his phone. Daniel followed Zachary's eyes and saw the computer.

He looked at the picture on the screen: Lauren looking back over her shoulder, her mouth opening in a scream as Daniel walked into the bedroom behind her. She had clearly not been expecting him, and the next picture in the series was even more wrenching, his hand over her mouth while she struggled to escape his grasp.

"I knew it," Daniel said, his mouth tight and his words clipped and precise. "You little weasel. I knew that you wouldn't give back her computer without finding something first."

"That's you, Daniel," Zachary said, his voice sounding too loud in his own ears. "That's a picture of you breaking into Lauren's apartment and attacking her the night of her 'accident.' Caught right on the company's own spyware. Or was it your spyware? Did you install the spyware to keep an eye on her, just like you broke into her apartment, and broke into mine?"

Daniel chuckled. It was a sound that made Zachary's skin crawl. All of the hairs on his neck stood up as if electrified.

"She thought she had everyone fooled. She thought she had said and done all of the right things and that everyone believed that she would do whatever it took to get that job and hold on to it. She had them thinking that she would give up her family and her future to give herself to that job. But I knew better. I knew she was a liar. I knew they were just words."

Zachary took another step away from Daniel. He couldn't see any weapons on Daniel. Nothing other than the small mallet he had used on the bump key to get in through Zachary's locked door. That mallet wasn't enough to kill him. He must have used something else on Lauren. The skull-crushing blow that she'd received had been from something larger, like the edge of the tub, not from a little hammer. If he got hit with the mallet, it would hurt, but Zachary didn't think it would be enough to disable him.

"How did you know what she was really thinking?" he prompted, side-stepping to prevent Daniel from getting closer to him. "Did she tell you? Or someone else?"

"One thing about being a good liar is you get really good at spotting the signs in someone else. Someone like me or Gordon, we can say anything we want and never give ourselves away. But people like Lauren have tells."

"You and Gordon?"

"Psychopaths. People who don't feel guilt or other inconvenient emotions like the rest of you. You go through your whole lives a slave to your emotions instead of just going all out and getting what you want. You're so worried about everyone's feelings and how your actions affect them, that you don't put yourself first. In this world, if you want to get ahead, you have to put yourself first."

"Gordon? Were the two of you working together?"

"Gordon is a visionary. He knew what he wanted and he was building it. Since I'm not at his level yet, all I could do was help and admire him from afar. I knew that the more I was able to accomplish, the closer I would get to him and the more he would notice me. Until the two of us are equals and can talk openly about our goals and plans for the company, and how we can use it to accomplish our desires."

"The night you killed Lauren, you had a late-night meeting with Gordon."

"You *have* been busy, haven't you?"

Daniel advanced. Zachary again retreated. His escape was cut off. He didn't want to have to fight Daniel hand-to-hand. He'd had enough fights as a teenager to know that he wasn't that skilled. He'd learned a few dirty tricks, but he was no martial arts expert. He was too light to be a wrestler. Too small to be much danger to anyone. But he'd fight if he had to. If he was lucky, he might manage to hold Daniel off or get past him and out the door. He was under no illusions about being able to school Daniel. His best hope was escape.

"Yes, Gordon and I had a wonderful meeting. I told him how much I admired the company he had set up and how I believed we could accomplish great things together. He told me how pleased he was with how I was managing the interns, and that he trusted me to make the decisions that were best for the company, even though they were often difficult." He smiled proudly. "He trusted and admired me."

"He recognized how much you have contributed to the

company," Zachary said, hoping that Daniel would hold off on any violence as long as he was being praised. Zachary's stomach turned at the thought of Gordon telling Daniel he trusted him to make the hard decisions. Had he intentionally aimed Daniel at Lauren, or was he unaware of how Daniel would take his words?

"That's right," Daniel agreed. He took a deliberate step toward Zachary. He had told Zachary he could tell when people were lying. Since Zachary was not a psychopath, he assumed Daniel could see that Zachary didn't really admire him.

Zachary swallowed and tried to inch toward the door, but Daniel watched him like a cat watching a mouse, keeping his body in position so that Zachary wouldn't be able to slip past him.

"When did you decide you needed to get rid of Lauren?" Zachary asked.

"I could see she'd made a decision. She wasn't going to stay on and take the job. She was going to make trouble for the company. I knew the instant she decided, and I knew I would have to take action. Drastic action." He took a deep breath and let it out. "Something that I had never done before."

Still, Zachary doubted him. He hadn't been involved in any of the other violence toward the other ex-employees? It might have been the first time he had killed, but Zachary didn't think it was the first time he had ventured into those waters.

"And it was so easy," Daniel said, shaking his head and blinking at Zachary to express his surprise. "I had her address. It was easy to get into her apartment. There was no one else there. So I could just take care of business and get back out again, with no one the wiser."

"No one suspected you," Zachary agreed. He strained his ears for the sound of anyone nearby that he could call out to for help. But it was a quiet evening, he couldn't hear anyone in the hall or the hum of the elevator as it made its way to the floor.

"No one even thought it was murder. Except you. Why?"

"It wasn't me, it was her roommate. She just didn't think it felt right, but she didn't know why."

Daniel shrugged broadly. "That's it? Just instinct? It was easy enough to do, I don't know why anyone wouldn't believe it."

"You did make one mistake, but she didn't catch it. Not consciously."

"What?"

"Lauren had a shower caddy with all of her soap and shampoo and accessories in her bedroom. She wouldn't have left it there, gotten undressed, and gotten into the tub without them."

Daniel made a noise of disgust and shook his head. "How could I have known that?"

"You would have had to have looked around her room and seen it. But you were running on adrenaline. You couldn't be expected to notice."

"That still doesn't prove anything. Even if you took that to the police, that wouldn't convince them it was murder and it wouldn't lead them to me."

"No." Zachary agreed.

Not like the webcam picture.

He could hear the elevator. It was more of a feeling that came up through his feet that an actual sound. He'd noticed it before, standing in the kitchen near his door. He was farther away now, but his body was sensitized by the danger, alert to every change in his environment. He sensed booted feet too. Not in the elevator, but maybe in the hallway. Someone going out to the bar or to visit a friend? Was it someone who could help him if he called out? He didn't want to put anyone else in danger.

He opened his mouth to speak to Daniel, hesitating for a fraction of a second while his brain processed the noises and unusual movement outside his apartment.

There was a crash and, unlike with Daniel's quiet breach of Zachary's apartment, the door slammed open and uniformed officers ran into the apartment, their booted feet pounding. They shouted, guns raised to point at both Zachary and Daniel. Zachary held his hands up high, wide-open palms facing them so that they could see he was unarmed. A couple of them threw him to the floor, shouting instructions that he couldn't make out in the cacophony of sound. He put his hands on the back of his head and interlaced his fingers, hoping that would be close enough to their instructions for them to see that he was being compliant and not hurt him.

Daniel, on the other hand, was shouting and struggling and trying to convince them to let him alone.

Good luck with that.

Hands frisked Zachary, and he endured the violation, letting them feel for any hidden weapons. In a few minutes, they had Daniel subdued and the chaos quieted.

One of the cops helped Zachary to his feet and made a show of dusting him off. "Sorry about that, sir. It's not possible for us to tell in a split-second who might be dangerous and who is not. Are you alright?"

"Yeah, I'm fine. Thank you. Can I…" He motioned toward his desk, asking permission to move across the room and to touch things.

"Go ahead."

Zachary went back to his desk, shuffled the papers to find his buried phone, and looked at the name still displayed on the screen in bright letters. The call was still active. He raised it to his ear.

"Gerry."

Gerry swore. "Man, Zachary. I was scared as hell. I thought he was going to kill you before the police could get there."

"They arrived pretty quickly. It just *felt* like an eternity."

Gerry's chuckle was warm and comforting to Zachary. "Did it ever." He swore again and let his breath out in a whistle. "Good to hear your voice, man."

"So when we booted off this hard drive, it was like we were on Lauren's computer, right?"

"Uh… yeah. Exactly like it."

"And when I was looking at the surveillance pictures that the spyware took, did it stop taking more pictures until I shut down that viewer?"

"I'm not there, so I can't tell you for sure, but I doubt it. It would have kept taking pictures and trying to send them back to the server."

"So it was taking pictures of Daniel here, in my apartment?"

"And still taking pictures of you and the cops now. Yeah."

"Good. And could you hear him? Everything he was saying?" Zachary had been worried that Gerry would hang up in order to call the police. But he had apparently stayed on the line.

"Yeah. I tried out 'text to 9-1-1.' Didn't know if they even had text service here, but I guess they do!"

That had been pretty smart. "So you heard him say that he killed Lauren."

"I heard everything."

Zachary exhaled, relieved. It was one thing for him to tell the police that Daniel had confessed. They didn't have his voice recorded—unless the spyware did that too—and they didn't have any physical evidence. Not yet. Maybe there were some of Daniel's hair or skin cells at the scene. The picture of him grabbing Lauren from in front of her computer was convincing, but it didn't actually show the murder. He could say that he was an invited guest and they were just role playing. That she had been alive when he left.

But Gerry had heard the confession too. He could testify as to what had happened at Zachary's apartment. It would all wrap up nicely into a neat package that would ensure Daniel was put away for a long time.

One of the policemen was looking at the picture on Zachary's laptop.

"Is that the woman who was in the papers? The one they said slipped and fell?"

"Yes."

He swore, eyes open wide in disbelief. He looked in the direction of Zachary's door, where they had just escorted Daniel out. "Holy crap! I guess he's going away for a long time."

"Yeah. I hope so," Zachary agreed.

He looked at the door swinging on its hinges. They had broken it through the frame, which meant he wasn't going to be able to sleep there until it was fixed. He pondered who he should call.

It was a while before Detective Robinson made it to the scene. Maybe he was out to supper with his wife or was at a kid's school play. Something big and important. Things were quiet when he got to Zachary's apartment. There wasn't much for the police to take pictures of, no evidence to gather other than the burglary tools Daniel had on him. What had Daniel been planning to do to him? Choke him? Slam his head on the bathtub? Use some tool or poison that he found on hand?

They wanted Zachary's computer, but he pointed out that everything was on the hard drive, not his computer, so they could take that for evidence. He emailed himself the pictures first, both the pictures of Daniel with Lauren and of Daniel in Zachary's apartment. He wanted to make sure they were preserved, no matter what happened to the hard drive.

Detective Robinson walked into Zachary's apartment through the open door and looked around. His wrinkled dress shirt clung to his thin body and he gazed over the contents of Zachary's front room through his thick eyeglasses, looking a little like a baffled owl.

"Somebody want to explain to me what happened here?" he asked of the air.

Zachary waited to see if anyone else was going to answer him, but the police who were left were just low-level officers there to make sure everything was cleaned up and taken care of. They looked at him, looked at each other, and shrugged.

"Didn't anyone brief you?" Zachary asked.

Detective Robinson looked at him, giving him a look that Zachary was sure was meant to intimidate him. But Zachary had already been intimidated; a grumpy detective didn't frighten him.

Zachary looked at his watch. "I'm going to have to clear out of here if I'm going to find someone to stay with tonight. I can't exactly stay here, when the door won't shut and lock properly."

"Didn't I tell you to just stay away from this case?"

"Didn't you tell me it was an accidental slip-and-fall?" Zachary countered glibly, irritated by Detective Robinson acting like Daniel being a murderer was somehow Zachary's fault, rather than apologizing for being wrong.

"It would appear… that we were mistaken."

"Yeah, it would appear."

"That doesn't change the fact that you put yourself in danger."

"I didn't provoke him. I was just investigating the case. Looking a little deeper than the police department did."

He didn't make any accusations, but figured his point was

obvious. If they had looked at it harder, Zachary would not have been in any danger. They would have figured out that it was Daniel, and no one else would have been put in danger. Not Zachary. Not Bieberstein. Not anybody.

Where was Bieberstein? Could he really believe Gordon's story that he was somewhere safe? Zachary still couldn't decide whether Gordon and Daniel had been in on it together, or whether it was just Daniel, and Gordon was clueless that he had been praising and encouraging a dangerous man.

"How did Daniel Service know where to find you?"

"I imagine he asked around. I've tried not to list it publicly anywhere, I've been using a post office box since… well, since somebody else found me. But Daniel works with… my ex-wife's current partner. So…"

"Bridget's?"

He should have known that Detective Robinson would know Bridget. Everybody in the police department knew Bridget.

"Yeah. Bridget's partner. Gordon Drake."

"The investment banker. Where Lauren worked."

Zachary nodded. It all went in a full circle.

"Was it Gordon Drake who hired you to investigate Lauren's death, then?"

"No. I told you, it was her roommate. I didn't know at the time that I accepted it that she had worked for Gordon's company. I never really clued into… *Drake*… you know."

Detective Robinson looked at him through the thick lenses, his eyes looking slightly warped. Zachary wondered if he were legally blind.

"I would expect a smart private investigator to figure that out."

His expression was so blank, Zachary thought fleetingly of Daniel's brag that he was a psychopath. That he felt nothing toward his victims.

"You would, wouldn't you?" he agreed.

Detective Robinson cracked a smile. "It is the nature of man to make mistakes."

Zachary figured that was as close as he was going to get to an apology.

"So what did you discover in the course of your investigation?" Robinson asked. "I assume there was more, or Service wouldn't have been worried about you discovering him."

Zachary considered this. He motioned to the couch. Detective Robinson followed the motion, then looked back at Zachary.

"Let's sit down," Zachary suggested. "I'll go though the other stuff."

Robinson considered for a moment, then sat down. Zachary picked up his notebook and started filling him in on the details.

Zachary decided to try Kenzie. He knew he could use Mario Bowman as a fallback if she refused, but it was worth his while to try Kenzie. If she said yes, it might be the beginning of a path back into her life.

He ran several scripts through his head before dialing her number. He knew the conversation would come out nothing like he planned, but he tried anyway to anticipate what she might say and to come up with counterarguments to her objections. In the end, if she really didn't want him there, he wouldn't impose on her.

He tapped her number and waited for it to ring through.

"Zachary?" Kenzie answered it almost immediately. "What took you so long?"

Zachary pulled the phone away from his ear to look at the screen to see if he had any missed calls or messages from her. Nothing. He put it back to his ear as she called to him.

"Zachary? Are you there? Is everything okay?"

"I'm here. What do you mean what took me so long? You didn't call, did you?"

"No. But I thought I'd hear back from you a lot earlier."

"Oh. I told you I'd get you the names of the suspects to check against the forensics."

"Well, yeah, and I kind of heard that you didn't need to guess who the perp was anymore, since he showed up at your door."

Even though she wasn't there, Zachary felt the warmth of the blush that traveled over his face. She had already heard the details from someone in the police department. Maybe Robinson himself.

"Oh, that. Yeah. He did."

"So does that mean you don't need the forensics now?"

"You'll still need to test it to see if he did leave behind any physical evidence. Even though we have his picture and his confession, we need to tie it up as tightly as we can, with every detail we can get."

"I'm teasing you."

Zachary cleared his throat. "Okay. Yeah, you already know what I need."

"Mmm-hm. Started on it today, but I'll have more time for it tomorrow. Detective Robinson wants to push it through as fast as he can. As you say, tie it up as tightly as we can."

"Thanks. I'm sure Lauren's family and friends will appreciate it."

"Have you talked to them yet?"

"No... just sent Barbara a message. I'll have to follow up with her on the details."

"Face-to-face is always better for that kind of thing."

"Exactly," Zachary agreed.

Kenzie was quiet. Zachary decided it was his opening and he'd better take it while he had the chance.

"Did Detective Robinson tell you that they broke down my door?"

"Seems to me he might have mentioned something about that."

"So... I can't stay in my apartment until the building guy gets it fixed for me. It wouldn't be safe."

"So you'll be at a hotel?"

Zachary supposed that the hotel was an option. He was surprised that it was one he hadn't seriously considered. He had immediately thought of staying with a friend. Especially Kenzie. When his apartment had burned down, he hadn't even had a wallet or credit card to book a room at the hotel. He'd been forced to rely on the kindness of his friends. Mario had stepped up then, agreeing to have Zachary stay with him for a few days, which had ended up being a few months before he told Zachary that it was time for him to be getting out on his own again.

"Are you still there?" Kenzie asked.

"Yeah. I was just wondering… I mean, I *could* get a hotel room…"

"Or…?"

"I wondered if you had a spare room where I could crash for a day or two."

"No. No spare room."

"Ah. I guess I'd probably be in your way on the couch."

"Yes. I don't like people sleeping in my living room."

"Okay. I might call Mario. Or maybe I'll just book a hotel room."

"Why don't you come over? I might not have a spare room or a couch you can use, but I might be able to find *somewhere else.*"

A warm, tingly feeling washed from Zachary's head to his toes. He was glad she couldn't see him. She always laughed when he got red. Such a tough guy, turning to mush whenever a girl teased him.

"Yeah…?"

"Sure. You've never seen my house. After all of the times you've entertained me, I should probably return the favor."

Zachary smiled. He'd never asked her why she didn't invite him to her place. He figured that a woman just needed a safe, secure place to go. If she didn't feel comfortable with him being there, then he could respect that. Maybe Kenzie had realized that he hadn't been the only one holding something back in the relationship.

"Do you want the address?" Kenzie asked.

"I've got it."

"Private detective. I should have known. How long will it take you to get here? You need to pack a bag?"

Zachary cleared his throat, giving a little laugh. "I'm already here."

He waited, holding himself tense. Stalker behavior. Looking up her address and sitting in his car outside her house when he called her. He hadn't meant it to be creepy, but sitting there waiting for her response, he knew it could be interpreted that way.

"Well then, come on in."

Zachary had set up a meeting with Barbara before breakfast the next morning. Or maybe it was breakfast. They had coffee, and he never really had much else for breakfast, but he didn't know if it was breakfast for her.

"So does this mean… you have something to tell me, or that you've gone as far as you can and you're telling me that you're done?"

"It means I have something to tell you. Are you ready for that?"

She looked at him, head cocked slightly. "I guess it depends what you have to tell me. You mean that you have a suspect? Is it like Deidre said? Is it Gordon Drake?"

Zachary hesitated and shook his head. "No. And it's more than a suspect. I got a confession."

She blinked. "A confession?"

"Her supervisor, Daniel Service. He followed her home. Broke into her apartment."

"Why? Was it some sex thing? She rejected him?"

"No. He was afraid she was going to do or say something that was damaging to the company. He felt like it was his job to make sure that she didn't."

Barbara stared at Zachary for a disconcertingly long time. She shook her head. "This was… to protect the company from slander? From a bad reputation? I don't get that."

"You know how devoted she was to them… but I guess she had made the decision to make a break with them. It was affecting her health, so maybe she decided that she'd had enough and she'd better stop before it did any long-term damage. Maybe she knew that it would kill her if she kept going like she was without taking care of her body. But once Daniel thought that she was going to betray the company… I'm sorry."

"So it really wasn't an accident. He hurt her on purpose? It wasn't… in the middle of an argument?"

"No. It looks like it was planned and premeditated."

"Because… she had decided not to stay with the company?"

Zachary shrugged. "It's hard to understand why other people do the things they do. Other people's motives don't always make sense to us. But yes… he felt very protective of Drake, Chase, Gould, and he wanted to make sure that she couldn't do anything to harm it. He was set on it becoming a world leader. He wanted to rise to the top of the industry and to be a part of its success."

"Unbelievable. And for that, he would kill someone like Lauren. Just for a job."

"For him, it wasn't just a job."

"It never was for her, either. It was so important to her. It was everything."

"Until she decided that it couldn't be. For what it's worth, I think she made the right choice."

"Even though it got her killed?"

"That wasn't her fault. She couldn't have foreseen the consequences. Her decision was to have a life that wasn't just focused on money and success."

"And that was right."

Zachary nodded. "Exactly."

He wasn't sure what to do about Blair Bieberstein and Gordon. He had fudged his answers as much as he dared with Detective Robinson, explaining that he didn't know where Gordon was or if he had been involved. Leave that to Daniel to explain, because Zachary didn't have the answers. He just didn't know what Gordon had known or understood about Daniel. If Daniel could read other people as well as he claimed, did that mean that Gordon could too?

Could he tell when he looked at Zachary or Daniel or Detective Robinson what they were thinking? Or maybe not Daniel, since Daniel claimed not to have any tells.

The case was finished, his invoice to Barbara submitted and collected on, but Zachary decided to keep an eye on Drake, Chase, Gould, just to ensure that everything had settled down and that no one else had been in on the coverup. Had Gordon known? Had Bev? Was there someone who was supposed to review the security pictures? Did he know what had happened and just didn't tell? Or had he been asleep on the job and not noticed those last few pictures?

Or had he told Gordon or whoever his boss was, and Gordon had told them to keep it quiet?

Zachary just wanted to watch the employees as they came and went and to be sure that they were alright. And hopefully to catch a glimpse of Blair Bieberstein returning to work. And Gordon? Did he want to see Gordon?

He didn't want to see Daniel. If they released him on bail and he returned to Drake, Chase, Gould, Zachary didn't want to know about it.

He sat in his car, watching people coming and going. There was one security checkpoint on the way into the building, which made it easy for Zachary, since everyone had to arrive through that one set of doors.

On his second day of surveillance, Zachary saw a familiar little man, not quite as squirrely looking, walking up to the entrance.

Zachary jumped out of his car and jogged over to see him. Bieberstein drew back, startled, then took in who it was.

"Oh. Zachary Goldman. I'm glad to see you."

"I just wanted to make sure that you were okay."

Bieberstein's head bobbed up and down. He glanced around to make sure no one was listening to them. "Sure. I'm fine. Just… had to take a couple of days to rest after the accident." He indicated his cast and the bandage on his head. "You know."

"Sure. You just disappeared so suddenly… I was worried about you. I wasn't sure if something had happened."

"Whether they got me?" Bieberstein gave a nervous laugh. "I guess I was talking a little crazy. Just lack of sleep or the side effects of the painkillers."

"I don't think it was crazy. Did you hear about Daniel?"

Bieberstein shrugged uncomfortably. "I don't know what happened with Daniel… I don't get it."

"I don't know if any of us do. He thought he was doing something to protect the company. But…"

Bieberstein looked around, his eyes fastening on something behind Zachary. Zachary turned, but he had a pretty good idea who he was going to see before he did.

Gordon.

"Zachary," Gordon greeted with his trademark friendly smile, and a hand reached out to shake Zachary's. "You came through for us again. You certainly have a knack for digging down and finding out the truth. This company owes you a debt of gratitude."

Zachary hoped that was what Gordon really felt, and not what a disappointment it was to lose his avenging angel. He shook hands with Gordon as expected, pulling back when he felt like Gordon had held on for long enough.

"I just wanted to make sure that Bieberstein was okay," he explained, motioning to the other man.

"I told you he was. I told you I just hid him away somewhere he could get a little sleep, and be away from any other threats.

Since you unveiled the threat… he should be safe now. Shouldn't he?"

"As long as you get control of these overtime hours."

Gordon raised his brows. "I beg your pardon?"

"You need to get rid of all of these overtime hours and make sure that employees are getting the medical care that they need. Days off when they are sick. Not working so many hours that they are going to work themselves to death. Lauren's death could just as easily have been karoshi. Her heart showed signs of stress. It was being damaged."

Gordon took this in, frowning. He nodded slowly and patted Zachary on the arm as if comforting him. "You're right. I'll look into it. That shouldn't be happening."

Zachary breathed out. "Good. These people are very devoted to your company. You need to take care of them."

"So many people to take care of," Gordon said ruefully. "Bridget and the babies, and now… several hundred people who work for me. I thought that the structure we had set up would reduce my need to be quite so hands-on with everyone. But it would appear that I need to rethink that decision. I'll consider what I need to do."

He put his arm around Bieberstein and pulled him close, like a father with a teenage son, and talked to him in a paternal tone. "We need to take care of our families, don't we, Mr. Bieberstein?"

Zachary watched them walk into the building, Gordon's words echoing in his head.

Did you enjoy this book? Reviews and recommendations are vital to making a book successful.

Please leave a review at your favorite book store or review site and share it with your friends.

Don't miss the following bonus material:
Sign up for mailing list to get a free ebook
Read a sneak preview chapter
Other books by P.D. Workman
Learn more about the author

Sign up for my mailing list at pdworkman.com and get Gluten-Free Murder for free!

PREVIEW OF SHE TOLD A LIE

CHAPTER 1

Zachary tried to stay in the zone he was in, just on the border between sleeping and waking, for as long as he could. He felt warm and safe and at peace, and it was such a good feeling he wanted to remain there as long as he could before the anxieties of consciousness started pouring in.

The warm body alongside his shifted and Zachary snuggled in, trying not to leave the cozy pocket of blankets he was in.

Kenzie murmured something that ended in 'some space' and wriggled away from him again. Zachary let her go. She needed her sleep, and if he smothered her, she wouldn't be quick to invite him back.

Kenzie. He was back together with Kenzie and he had stayed the night at her house. It was the first time he'd gone there instead of her joining him in his apartment, which was currently not safe for them to sleep at because the police had busted the door in. It would have to be fixed before he could sleep there.

Kenzie lived in a little house that was a hundred times better than Zachary's apartment, which wasn't difficult since he had started from scratch after the fire that burned down his last apartment. While he was earning more as a private investigator than he ever had before, thanks to a few high profile murder cases, he wasn't going to sink a lot of money into the apartment until he had built up a strong enough reserve to get him through several months of low income.

Zachary had been surprised by some of the high-priced items he had seen around Kenzie's home the night before. He supposed he shouldn't have been surprised, given the cherry-red convertible she drove, but he'd always assumed she was saddled with significant debts from medical school and that she would not be able to afford luxuries.

Maybe that was the reason that she had never invited him into her territory before. She didn't want him to see the huge gap in their financial statuses.

Once Zachary's brain started working, reviewing the night before and considering Kenzie's circumstances as compared to his, he couldn't shut it back off and return to that comfortable, happy place he had been just before waking. His brain was grinding away, assessing how worried he should be. Did any of it change their relationship? Did it mean that Kenzie looked down on him? Considered him inferior? She had never treated him that way, but did she think it, deep down inside?

Once he left her house, would he ever be invited back? He had only been there under exceptional circumstances, and while he hoped that it was a sign that Kenzie was willing to reconcile and work on their relationship again—as long as he was—he was afraid that it might just have been one moment of weakness. One that she would regret when she woke up and had a chance to reconsider.

With his brain cranking away at the problem and finding new things to worry about, Zachary couldn't stay in bed. He shifted around a few times, trying to find a position that was comfortable enough that he would just drift back to sleep, he knew that it was impossible. His body was restless and would not return to sleep again so easily.

He slid out of the bed and squinted, trying to remember the layout of the room and any obstacles. The sky was just starting to lighten, forcing a little gray light around the edges of Kenzie's blinds and curtains. Enough to see dark shapes around him, but not enough to be confident he wouldn't trip over something. Zachary felt for the remainder of his clothes and clutched them to him as he cautiously made his way to the bedroom door and out into the hallway.

He shut the door silently behind him so that he wouldn't wake Kenzie up. There was an orange glow emanating from the bathroom, so he found his way there without knocking over any priceless decor. He shut the door and turned on the main light. It was blinding after the night-light. Zachary squeezed his eyes shut and waited for them to adjust to the light that penetrated his eyelids, and then gradually opened them to look around.

Everything was clean and tidy and smelled fresh. Definitely a woman's domain rather than a bachelor pad like Zachary's. He needed to upgrade if he expected her to spend any time at his apartment. He'd used her ensuite the night before rather than the main bath, and even though it was more cluttered with her makeup and hair and bath products, it was also cleaner and brighter than Zachary's apartment bathroom.

He spent a couple of minutes with his morning routine, splashing water on his face and running a comb over his dark buzz-cut before making his way to the living room, where he'd left his overnight bag when he and Kenzie had adjourned for the night. He pulled out his laptop and set it on the couch while it booted up, wandering into the kitchen and sorting out her single-cup coffee dispenser to make himself breakfast.

CHAPTER 2

I t was a few hours before he heard Kenzie stirring in the bedroom, and eventually, she made her way out to the living room. She had an oriental-style dressing gown wrapped around her. She rubbed her eyes, hair mussed from sleep.

Kenzie yawned. "Good morning."

"Hi." Zachary gave her a smile that he hoped expressed the warmth and gratitude he felt toward her for letting him back into her life, even if it was only for one night. "How was your sleep?"

"Good." Kenzie covered another yawn. "How about you? Did you actually get any sleep?"

"I slept great." Zachary wasn't lying. He didn't usually sleep well away from home. For that matter, he didn't sleep that well at home either. But after facing off with Lauren's killer and dealing with the police, he had been exhausted, and the comfort he had found in Kenzie's arms and the luxurious sheets in her bed had quickly lulled him to sleep. There was a slight dip in the middle of her mattress, testifying to the fact that she normally slept alone, and that had made it natural for them to gravitate toward each other during the night. It had been reassuring to have someone else in bed with him after what seemed like an eon of lonely nights.

It was the best night's sleep he'd had in a long time.

"You couldn't have slept for more than three or four hours," Kenzie countered.

"Yes… but it was still a really good sleep."

"Well, good." She bent down to kiss him on the forehead.

Zachary felt a rush of warmth and goosebumps at the same time. She didn't appear to regret having allowed him to stay over. "Do you want coffee? I figured out the machine."

"Turn it on when you hear me get out of the shower. That should be about right."

"Do you want anything else? Bread in the toaster?"

"The full breakfast treatment? I could get used to this. Yes, a couple of slices of toast would be nice."

Zachary nodded. "Coffee and toast it is," he agreed.

He saw her speculative look, wondering whether he would actually remember or whether he would be distracted by something else.

"I'll do my best," Zachary promised. "But it better be a short shower, because if it's one of those two-hour-long ones, I might forget."

"I have to get to work today, so it had better be a quick one."

He did manage to remember to start both the coffee and the toast when she got out of the shower, and even heard the toast pop and remembered to butter it while it was hot. He had it on the table for Kenzie when she walked in, buttoning up her blouse.

"Nice!" Kenzie approved.

"Do you want jam?"

"There's some marmalade in the fridge."

Zachary retrieved the jar and made a mental note that he should get marmalade the next time he was shopping for groceries. If that was her preferred condiment, then he should make an effort to have it for her when she came to his apartment. He tried to always get things for her when he was shopping, because as Bridget put it, he ate like a Neanderthal. Not one of those fad caveman diets, but like someone who had never learned how to cook even the simplest foods. Most of his food was either ready to eat or just needed to be microwaved for a couple of minutes.

Or he could order in. He could use a phone even if he couldn't use a stove.

"So, your big case is solved," Kenzie said, "what are your plans for the day?"

"I still need to report to the client and issue my bill. Then I've got a bunch of smaller projects I should catch up on, now that I'll have some more time. And I need to get my door fixed. I wouldn't want to impose on you for too long."

Kenzie spread her marmalade carefully to the edge of the toast. "It was nice last night. I'm glad you called."

Zachary's face got warm. All they had done was to talk and cuddle, but he had needed that so badly. He had been concerned that she would be disappointed things had gone no further, so he was reassured that she had enjoyed the quiet time together too. Their relationship had been badly derailed by the abuse Zachary had suffered at Archuro's hands, which had also brought up a lot of buried memories of his time in foster care. However much he wanted to be with Kenzie, he couldn't help his own visceral reaction when things got too intimate.

"Hey," Kenzie said softly, breaking into his thoughts. "Don't do that. Come back."

Zachary tried to refocus his attention on her, to keep himself anchored to the present and not the attack.

"Five things?" Kenzie suggested, prompting Zachary to use one of the exercises his therapist had given him to help him with dissociation.

Zachary took a slow breath. "I smell… the coffee. The toast." He breathed. "Your shampoo. The marmalade. I… don't know what else."

His own sweat. He should have showered and dressed before

Kenzie got up. Greeted her smelling freshly-scrubbed instead of assaulting her with the rank odor of a homeless person.

Kenzie smiled. "Better?" She studied his face for any tells.

Zachary nodded. "Yeah. Sorry."

"It's okay. It's not your fault."

He still felt completely inadequate. He should be able to have a pleasant morning conversation with his girlfriend without dissociating or getting mired in flashbacks. It shouldn't be that hard.

"Are you going to have something to eat? There's enough bread for you to have toast too," Kenzie teased.

"No, not ready yet."

"Well, don't forget. You still need to get your weight back up."

Zachary nodded. "I'll have something in a while."

He still hadn't eaten when he left Kenzie's. She was on her way into work, and he didn't want her to feel like she had to let him stay there in her domain while she was gone, so by the time she was ready for work, he had repacked his overnight bag and was ready to leave as well. She didn't make any comment or offer him the house while she was gone.

"Well, good luck with your report to Lauren's sister today. I know that part of the job is never fun."

Zachary nodded. "Yeah. And then collecting on the bill. Sorry your sister was murdered, but could you please pay me now?" He rolled his eyes.

Kenzie shook her head. "At least I don't have to ask for payment when I give people autopsy results."

They paused outside the door. Zachary didn't know what to say to Kenzie or how to tell her goodbye.

"Call me later," Kenzie advised. "Let me know whether you got your door fixed or not."

Zachary exhaled, relieved. She wasn't regretting having invited him in. She would put up with him for another night if he needed her.

"Thanks, I will."

Kenzie armed the burglar alarm on the keypad next to the door and shut it. Zachary heard the bolt automatically slide into place.

"See you," Kenzie said breezily. She pulled him closer by his coat lapel and gave him a brief peck on the lips. "Have a good day."

Zachary nodded, his face flushing and a lump in his throat preventing him from saying anything. Kenzie opened the garage door. Zachary turned and walked down the sidewalk to his car. He tried hard not to be needy, not to turn around and watch as she backed the car out onto the street, checking to see whether she was still watching him and would give him one more wave before she left. But he couldn't help himself.

She waved in his direction and pulled onto the street.

Late in the afternoon, Zachary headed back to his apartment, hoping to find when he got there that the door had been repaired and he could feel safe there once more. Of course, if the door had been fixed, he would need another reason to go back to Kenzie's. Or he could invite her to join him and they could go back to their usual routines. Just because she had allowed him over to her house once, that didn't mean she would be comfortable with him being there all the time.

But he could see the splintered doorframe as he walked down the hall approaching his apartment. The building manager had promised to make it a priority, but it looked like whatever subcontractor he had called hadn't yet made it there. Zachary pushed the door open and looked around.

Nothing appeared to have been rifled or taken in his absence. Of course, he didn't have much of value. He'd taken all of his electronics with him and didn't exactly have jewelry or wads of cash lying around. Anyone desperate enough to rifle his drawers and steal his shirts probably needed them worse than he did.

Though he hadn't thought about the meds in the cabinet. There were a few things in there that might have some street value.

Zachary started to walk toward the bedroom, but stopped when he heard a noise. He froze and listened, trying to zero in on it. It was probably just a neighbor moving around. Or a pigeon landing on the ledge outside his window. They spooked him sometimes with the loud flapping of their wings when they took off.

He waited, ears pricked, for the sound to be repeated.

Could it have been a person? There in his apartment?

The last time he'd thought that someone was rifling his apartment and had called the police, it had been Bridget. She'd still had a key to the old apartment. She'd checked in on him at Christmas, knowing that it was a bad time for him, and had cleaned out his medicine cabinet to ensure that he didn't overdose.

It wouldn't be Bridget this time.

She didn't have a key to the new apartment, though he would have been happy to give her one if she had wanted it. Bridget was no longer part of his life and he needed to keep his distance from her, both to avoid getting slapped with a restraining order and because he was with Kenzie, and he needed to be fair to her. There was no going back to his ex-wife. She had a new partner and was pregnant. She didn't want anything to do with him.

There was another rustle. He was pretty sure it was someone in his bedroom. But it didn't sound like they were doing anything. Just moving quietly around.

Waiting for him?

He hated to call the police and have it be a false alarm. But he also didn't want to end up with a bullet in his chest because he walked in on a burglary in progress.

Unlike private investigators on TV, Zachary didn't carry a gun. He didn't even own one. With his history of depression and self-harm, it had always been too big a risk.

Zachary eased his phone out of his pocket, moving very slowly, trying to be completely silent. He wasn't sure what he was going to do when he got it out. If he called emergency, he would have to talk to them to let them know what was going on. They wouldn't be able to triangulate his signal to a single apartment.

Just as he looked down at the screen and moved his thumb over the unlock button, it gave a loud squeal and an alert popped up on the screen. Zachary jumped so badly that it flew out of his hand, and he scrambled to catch it before it hit the floor. He wasn't well-coordinated, and he just ended up hitting it in the air and shooting it farther away from him, to smack into the wall and then land on the floor.

***

She Told a Lie, Book #8 of the *Zachary Goldman Mysteries* series by P.D. Workman can be ordered at pdworkman.com

ABOUT THE AUTHOR

Award-winning and USA Today bestselling author P.D. (Pamela) Workman writes riveting mystery/suspense and young adult books dealing with mental illness, addiction, abuse, and other real-life issues. For as long as she can remember, the blank page has held an incredible allure and from a very young age she was trying to write her own books.

Workman wrote her first complete novel at the age of twelve and continued to write as a hobby for many years. She started publishing in 2013. She has won several literary awards from Library Services for Youth in Custody for her young adult fiction. She currently has over 50 published titles and can be found at pdworkman.com.

Born and raised in Alberta, Workman has been married for over 25 years and has one son.

Please visit P.D. Workman at pdworkman.com to see what else she is working on, to join her mailing list, and to link to her social networks.

If you enjoyed this book, please take the time to recommend it to other purchasers with a review or star rating and share it with your friends!

facebook.com/pdworkmanauthor

twitter.com/pdworkmanauthor

instagram.com/pdworkmanauthor

amazon.com/author/pdworkman

bookbub.com/authors/p-d-workman

goodreads.com/pdworkman

linkedin.com/in/pdworkman

pinterest.com/pdworkmanauthor

youtube.com/pdworkman

www.ingramcontent.com/pod-product-compliance
Lightning Source LLC
Chambersburg PA
CBHW071228210726
48293CB00002B/625